BODYGUARD DADDY

Lisa Childs

HARLEQUIN® ROMANTIC SUSPENSE

Recycling programs
for this product may
not exist in your area.

ISBN-13: 978-0-373-27977-7

Bodyguard Daddy

Copyright © 2016 by Lisa Childs

All rights reserved. Except for use in any review, the reproduction or
utilization of this work in whole or in part in any form by any electronic,
mechanical or other means, now known or hereinafter invented, including
xerography, photocopying and recording, or in any information storage
or retrieval system, is forbidden without the written permission of the
publisher, Harlequin Enterprises Limited, 225 Duncan Mill Road,
Don Mills, Ontario M3B 3K9, Canada.

This is a work of fiction. Names, characters, places and incidents are
either the product of the author's imagination or are used fictitiously,
and any resemblance to actual persons, living or dead, business
establishments, events or locales is entirely coincidental.

This edition published by arrangement with Harlequin Books S.A.

For questions and comments about the quality of this book,
please contact us at CustomerService@Harlequin.com.

® and TM are trademarks of Harlequin Enterprises Limited or its
corporate affiliates. Trademarks indicated with ® are registered in the
United States Patent and Trademark Office, the Canadian Intellectual
Property Office and in other countries.

Printed in U.S.A.

"You told me she's alive.

"You need to tell me where she is," Milek said, and his voice cracked before he could add, "Where *they* are..."

FBI special agent Nicholas Rus's wide shoulders slumped with guilt, his black-haired head bowed. "I shouldn't have told you."

"No. You shouldn't have told me *now*," Milek explained. "You should have told me a year ago."

"I didn't know you a year ago... I didn't know if I could trust you."

"Obviously you know now, or you wouldn't have told me that she—that *they*—are alive."

Rus cursed. "And that was a mistake."

"Why?" Milek asked.

"Because now you want to know where she is."

He didn't just *want* to know. He *had* to know. He had to see her—had to see for himself that she was really alive. And so was their son...

He'd broken up with her nearly five years before her death, and he hadn't gotten over her in all that time. It didn't matter that he knew she was alive; he was still mourning her.

"I need to see her."

* * *

Don't miss the next book in Lisa Childs's Bachelor Bodyguards series, coming spring 2016.

If you're on Twitter, tell us what you think of Harlequin Romantic Suspense! #harlequinromsuspense

Dear Reader,

The Payne Protection Agency has another assignment—and like their previous assignments in the Shotgun Wedding series and in the Bachelor Bodyguards series, it's personal. Bodyguard Milek Kozminski thought he'd lost his ex-fiancée and their child in a horrific car accident a year ago. But while helping his brother Garek survive *His Christmas Assignment*, the first story in the Bachelor Bodyguards series, Milek learned assistant DA Amber Talsma and their son, Michael, are alive. He's not the only one who's discovered the truth. The person who wanted Amber dead is even more determined to kill her.

Milek has his hands full protecting her and his heart full of feelings for her. But the reason he broke their engagement all those years ago hasn't changed—because he isn't sure that he's changed from the outlaw he once was. He thinks Amber deserves a better man.

Amber has only ever wanted Milek. But while she trusts him to protect her life, she isn't willing to trust him with her heart again. He broke it once, and she worries that he'll break it again if she survives the attempts on her life. Milek will do anything to protect his family—even give up his life for theirs.

I hope you enjoy this second book in the Bachelor Bodyguards series.

Happy reading!

Lisa Childs

Ever since **Lisa Childs** read her first romance novel (a Harlequin story, of course) at age eleven, all she ever wanted was to be a romance writer. With over forty novels published with Harlequin, Lisa is living her dream. She is an award-winning, bestselling romance author. Lisa loves to hear from readers, who can contact her on Facebook, through her website, lisachilds.com, or her snail-mail address, PO Box 139, Marne, MI 49435.

Books by Lisa Childs

Harlequin Romantic Suspense

Bachelor Bodyguards

His Christmas Assignment
Bodyguard Daddy

Harlequin Intrigue

Special Agents at the Altar

The Pregnant Witness
Agent Undercover
The Agent's Redemption

Shotgun Weddings

Groom Under Fire
Explosive Engagement
Bridegroom Bodyguard

Harlequin Nocturne

Taming the Shifter
Mistress of the Underworld

Witch Hunt

Haunted
Persecuted
Damned
Cursed

Visit the Author Profile page at Harlequin.com for more titles.

With great appreciation for my awesome family!
You're the reason I enjoy writing about families—
like the Payne family—like our family.

Prologue

Flames leaped from the wreckage of the mangled vehicle, rising from the blackened metal into the night sky. The scene drew Milek Kozminski's attention from the drink sitting before him on the bar to the television screen above it. Country music emanated from the speakers of the jukebox, so he couldn't hear what the reporter was saying about the crash. He could hear only the twang of the singer as he crooned about drinking.

Milek could relate.

To the singer.

Not to the crash.

"Milek..." A soft voice, cracking with emotion, called to him. He twirled his bar stool to find not only his sister, Stacy, standing behind him but her husband, who was also his boss at the Payne Protection Agency. Hell, most of Payne Protection had come with them—Logan's twin,

Parker, and their younger brother, Cooper, and younger sister, Nikki. And Mrs. Payne, her warm brown eyes full of sympathy and something else, stared at him the way the others did—with concern.

"What the hell is this?" he wondered aloud. "An intervention?"

He had been drinking more lately than he should have but never enough that he lost control. He couldn't afford to lose control—as he once had, so long ago. That time had sent him to a juvenile detention center and his brother, Garek, to prison. But Garek hadn't actually done anything wrong.

The others said nothing, just continued to stare at him. And his heart began to beat quickly and heavily. Tears streaked down his sister Stacy's face while her thin frame—but for the slight swell of her newly pregnant belly—trembled with sobs. Was something wrong with her baby?

He turned to Garek now—as he and Stacy always had since they were little kids. Their parents had never been there for them, but Garek had.

Garek's face was flushed with emotion, and he strode over to the jukebox and jerked the cord from the wall. The music died, leaving the bar eerily silent but for the television anchor's voice.

"Assistant district attorney Amber Talsma lost control of her vehicle on slick roads, causing it to roll down a steep ravine, where it burst into flames. She and her young son are confirmed dead in the crash."

His heart stopped beating.

No, not Amber...

He twirled back toward the television. In a corner of the screen there was a picture of Amber with her bright green eyes and vibrant red hair. There was also a photo of her son—with his blond hair and pale gray eyes.

A big hand grasped his shoulder, offering support and turning him back toward the others who all stared at him with so much concern and pity.

"He was yours," Garek said.

With his hair and eye color, the little boy looked like both Milek and Garek.

"She never told you." Garek looked at their sister. Usually her tears would have affected him—would have had him fussing over her, especially now. Amber had been her best friend. But Garek stared at their sister as if he'd never seen her before. "Stacy knew. But I didn't know, Milek. I swear I didn't know. I'm so sorry." He dragged Milek from the stool then and into his arms. "I'm so damn sorry…"

He had known. Even though another man had claimed the boy as his, Milek had known the truth. But he'd thought then that the kid would be better off without him as a father—just as he'd believed Amber would be better off without him as a husband, which was why he'd broken their engagement.

Even though it had nearly killed him, he had forced himself to give them up—because he'd loved them and wanted better for them. Now they had nothing. And neither did he.

They were gone.

Chapter 1

Amber Talsma had been dead for a year. But no one had gotten any closer to finding out who had killed her. Or tried to. Amber hadn't lost control of her car and driven into a ravine. She had actually been shot at—just weeks after her boss had been gunned down outside his home. Someone had wanted her dead, too.

So she had died—to keep herself and her son safe. The accident had been staged; empty caskets buried in their graves. Then she and Michael had disappeared. They were Heather and Mason Ames now.

But when she glanced in the rearview mirror—as she did now as she drove to Mason's school—she still saw Amber. Her long red hair had been cut and dyed brown. Brown contact lenses covered her green irises. But her features were the same. Was that how someone had recognized her?

The letter had arrived just an hour ago—delivered to the mailbox of Heather Ames. She hadn't recognized the handwriting, but she'd opened it. Photos had fallen onto the floor. Several of them of her and Michael—at the park. At his school. At the grocery store. And through the front window of the very house in which they lived now. She'd turned over the back of one of those photos to find a note, an implicit threat, scrawled across the back: *I know who you really are...*

And obviously where she was, as well.

But how?

Only one person knew she was alive: the FBI agent who had helped fake Amber's and Michael's deaths. Special Agent Nicholas Rus had been the one she had called about the shots being fired at her—into her home.

She shuddered as she remembered how close the bullets had come to hitting her son—to taking his life. If she'd lost him...

It wasn't a risk she'd been willing to take. Sure, she could have hired bodyguards. Agent Rus had even suggested that—while he tried to find her boss's killer, who was probably also the person who'd shot at her—she should hire the Payne Protection Agency.

But she had been too proud to reach out to Milek again. He would have cared she was in danger, but would he have believed she was? He hadn't believed her when she'd told him she was pregnant with his son. He'd accused her of using her pregnancy to get him back—to trap him.

Even now, over five years later, the heat of embarrassment rushed to her face. That was why she had never admitted to her best friend she'd actually told Milek about his son. But it hadn't been just embarrassment. Her best friend was also his sister, and she hadn't wanted to cause problems between Stacy and her brother.

Growing up as they had, the Kozminski siblings were close. They'd had to stick together because they'd had no one else. When Milek had been in juvenile detention and Garek in prison, Stacy had grown close to Amber, too—so close that they were like sisters. Her husband, Logan Payne, the CEO of Payne Protection, would have protected Amber and Michael. Or he would have tried.

But a year had passed without the DA's killer being apprehended. Could anyone have kept Amber and Michael safe for a year if the killer had known they were alive?

It had been safest for her and her son to play dead. She had convinced the FBI agent of that, and he'd agreed to help her. Then.

But he'd also promised to find whoever was after her—whoever had killed her boss. The FBI agent had been assigned to the River City Police Department to clean up the corruption within. The DA could have been killed to cover up some of that corruption, so it had definitely been Rus's case. But it was one he had failed in his promise to solve.

She had trusted him, not just because he was an FBI agent but also because he was the half brother of Stacy's husband. But he wasn't a Payne. And the corruption in the police department and perhaps in the DA's office, as well, proved that nobody was incorruptible.

Had Agent Rus sold out to whoever wanted her dead? Had he told them where she was?

"You told me she's alive. You need to tell me where she is," Milek said, and his voice cracked before he could add, *Where* they *are*...

FBI Special Agent Nicholas Rus's wide shoulders slumped with guilt, his black-haired head bowed. "I shouldn't have told you."

"No," Milek agreed.

His blue eyes wide with surprise, Rus glanced up from his desk in his office at River City PD. His assignment was lasting so long he'd been given an office that had once belonged to one of the captains he'd arrested for corruption. It had windows looking out onto the busy precinct. But his attention was focused only on Milek.

"You shouldn't have told me *now*," Milek explained. "You should have told me a year ago."

"I didn't know you a year ago."

Milek snorted. "We met at least a year ago."

"We met," Rus said. "But we didn't know each other yet. I didn't know then if I could really trust you."

"Obviously you know now that you can, or you wouldn't have told me she—*they*—are alive."

Rus cursed. "And that was a mistake."

"Why?" Milek asked.

"Because now you want to know where she is."

He didn't just want to know. He *had* to know. He had to see her—had to see for himself that she was really alive. And so was their son…

"That's not all I want to know," he said.

Rus groaned.

"I want to know *why*." For a year she had haunted him—so many images of her had played through his mind. Amber smiling, her beautiful face aglow with love. Her face flushed with passion, her lips swollen from his kisses. Amber crying, her green eyes drenched with tears. But the one that had haunted him most had been the horrific footage of that crash. He'd imagined those flames consuming her and their son—taking them away from him forever.

But they had never really been his.

He shook off his regrets and asked, "Why would she go to such lengths to fake her death?"

And the death of their son…

"Was it because her boss was murdered and she was afraid she might be next?" She had worked more closely with the DA than any other assistant had. It was possible that whoever murdered him might have wanted to kill her, too.

Rus sighed again and leaned back in his chair. "There was no *might* about it. She and her son were nearly killed the night before the crash."

Milek shuddered. He hadn't lost them, but he'd come close. "What happened?"

"Shots were fired into her house."

"I didn't see it on the news." Not the way he had seen the footage of the vehicle crash. And if the shooting had been reported, it would have been brought up during the coverage of the accident. The media would have speculated that the crash hadn't been an accident. But nobody had questioned it. There had been an ice storm the night of the crash; it hadn't just seemed possible but probable that she'd lost control.

But Amber had never really lost control of anything. Not the way he had…

Because he'd known her so well, he should have questioned the wreck—especially after her boss's murder. And because he'd once been so connected to her, he should have *known* she wasn't really dead. But he had lost her years before she "died."

"She didn't report it to the police or the media," Nicholas Rus replied. "She reported it to me."

She had called the FBI agent. Why hadn't she called *him*? Probably because she hadn't trusted he would come. Or that he would care...

When he'd broken their engagement, he had worked hard to make her believe he hadn't cared about her anymore. He had succeeded—too well.

"And you kept it quiet."

Rus nodded.

Milek cursed him.

"I didn't know who I could trust," Rus reminded him. "I came to River City to investigate corruption. I didn't know who all might be involved in that corruption."

"Me?"

Rus nodded. "You and your family have quite the notorious reputation."

And that was why Milek had ended their engagement. For her...

His reputation hadn't been the only reason, though.

"Now I know that reputation is undeserved," Rus added.

It was undeserved for Garek and Stacy. Milek couldn't claim the same. He sighed. "You were right," he grudgingly admitted. "You were right to keep the shooting quiet. You were right to trust no one."

If not, Amber and Michael might really be dead.

"I didn't think it would take this long," Rus murmured.

Milek glanced out the windows of the corner office. Even though the detectives and some uniformed officers appeared busy, they spared glances at Rus's office—at Rus. Some of those glances seemed uneasy. "To clean up the corruption?"

He nodded. "That, too. But I meant I didn't think it would take this long to find her boss's killer. I didn't think she would have to stay dead as long as this."

"Was that why you told me?"

"You weren't getting over her."

Milek had broken up with her nearly five years before her death, and he hadn't gotten over her in all that time. It didn't matter that he knew she was alive; he was still mourning her—still mourning what they'd once had, such passion. His pulse quickened just thinking about her—about how badly he'd *wanted* her—*needed* her.

But if it had only been passion, he wouldn't have broken their engagement. He'd loved her too much to risk ruining her future. "I need to see her."

To talk to her. To apologize.

"I can't risk it," Rus said. "Until now, I was the only one who knew the truth."

"I'm not going to tell anyone," Milek said. He wouldn't compromise her safety, or their son's.

"We can't take the chance of either of us going to see her. We can't risk someone following one of us."

"But why would they?" Milek asked. "Nobody but us knows she's alive. So they're not looking for her any longer." But somebody needed to be looking for him— for the shooter who had nearly killed her and Michael.

He believed Rus was still working the case. But it wasn't his only case. He'd just taken down a major crime boss. "Does Chekov have any ideas?" Milek asked. "He's been talking to you pretty freely."

Because he had cut a deal to keep his daughter from going to a maximum security prison for murder. She was going to a locked psychiatric facility instead. Milek doubted she would ever leave it.

Rus shook his head. "Chekov claims he doesn't know anything."

"Do you?" Milek asked. "Where are you at with this case?" He needed to be apprised of the investigation, so he could help. Payne Protection bodyguards protected their clients by physically guarding them, but also by eliminating the threats to their safety.

Rus admitted, "I know who killed the DA."

Milek gasped. "Really? If you think that's the same person who went after Amber, why the hell is she still gone?"

Had she decided she liked her new life better than the one she'd left behind?

"I know who pulled the trigger," Rus said. "But I haven't apprehended him. And until I do, I won't know who hired him."

"The shooter was a hired killer?"

Rus nodded. "Ballistics matched up to other hits. A fingerprint recovered from a shell confirmed the shooter is Frank Campanelli."

"You know who it is but you can't find him?" Milek was appalled. Rus needed help. He needed Payne Protection. Nikki Payne could track down anyone.

"They call Frank Campanelli 'The Ghost,'" Rus shared. "So I don't know when or if I'll be able to find him. Nobody has ever been able to arrest him."

"The same was true of Chekov," Milek reminded him, "until Garek and Candace and I helped you." And Milek had even more motivation now. Anger heated his blood, making it pump fast and hard through his veins. When Milek found the man who'd tried to kill Amber and his son, he might make *him* a ghost.

Rus shrugged. "Even if we catch Campanelli, I doubt

he would talk. Hired assassins rarely give up their clients. So I'm focusing on finding the real killer—whoever hired him. I'm checking into all the cases DA Schievink and Amber Talsma were both working at the time Schievink died, and even the cases they'd worked together before his death."

Milek nodded. "Someone could have gunned down the DA out of vengeance."

Rus narrowed his gaze and studied Milek.

Milek couldn't deny he had a motive to want to kill Gregory Schievink. The guy had done his damnedest to break up him and Amber. When she'd become pregnant, Schievink had sought out Milek and insisted the baby was his—not Milek's. His hands curled into fists as they had that day. But that day he hadn't kept them clenched at his sides; he'd swung. He'd hit the slimy bastard, and in doing so, Milek had confirmed his worst fears to himself.

"Schievink was an amoral son of a bitch. But I wasn't the only one with a grudge against him. You have to have a long list of criminals." Not to mention the man's wife— Schievink had been married.

Rus nodded. But his intent stare didn't leave Milek's face. Of course, he probably ranked Milek among those criminals, if not at the top of the list.

"I would never hurt Amber and Michael." Not intentionally. Not physically. In fact, he'd done everything in his power so he wouldn't hurt them.

"Was it a mistake to trust you, Kozminski?" the agent asked.

Milek shook his head.

But he could tell the FBI agent wasn't convinced. The man opened his mouth, but before he could ask whatever question he'd wanted, an alarm beeped from his computer.

Rus glanced at his computer monitor, then turned his full attention to it. As he read whatever was on the screen, a muscle twitched along his tightly clenched jaw.

This obviously wasn't good news for the agent.

"What is it?" Milek asked. Hadn't the city been through enough over the past year or so?

"I flagged my computer to alert me whenever a report came through with a certain name on it," Rus said.

He knew. Instinctively Milek knew what that name was. But he moved around Rus's desk to stand behind his chair. He needed to see it for himself.

"Amber Talsma…" It was highlighted within a police report. He glanced up at the corner of the screen to read the incident number. This wasn't an old report—from a year ago. This was a recent one. From just days ago.

"Why did it take your computer so long to alert you?" he asked.

"The incident happened days ago," Rus confirmed. "But the report just got completed and uploaded to the system."

"What took so long?"

"It wasn't a priority," Rus said.

Anything involving Amber was a priority.

"Why not?" He leaned closer, trying to read more of the report over Rus's shoulder.

As he read, Rus surmised, "It was assumed to be just vandalism, malicious destruction of property…"

"What does any of that have to do with Amber?" Milek asked. "Her house was sold nearly a year ago." He doubted she had any other property in River City.

"This incident didn't happen at her house," Rus replied. "It happened at a cemetery."

Milek's heart began to hammer hard and fast—with dread. He already had a sick suspicion, but just as he needed to see Amber and Michael to believe they were really alive, he needed Rus to confirm his suspicion. "What happened?"

"Two graves were desecrated," Rus said. And he pointed to that highlighted name. There was another one after it. Michael Talsma.

It should have been Michael Kozminski. Milek should have claimed his son while he'd had the chance. Because he wasn't certain he would have the chance again…

Another curse slipped through Rus's lips. "You know what this means…"

Yeah, he knew what it meant.

"That someone went to the time and the trouble to dig up two empty graves."

They were no longer the only ones who knew Amber and Michael Talsma weren't really dead. And the only person who would have gone to the trouble of confirming they were alive was the person who wanted them dead.

Chapter 2

Her hand trembled slightly as Stacy Kozminski-Payne attached the last jewel to the plush body of the stuffed bear. The jewels were made of shiny material and felt, and attached so well to the bear that they couldn't be torn off and eaten. She wouldn't expose the children for whom she made the bears to choking hazards. A jewelry designer by trade, Stacy only made the bears for family.

For her children.

And for her nephews and nieces. It was hard to make the bears now without thinking of the first one she'd made—for her first nephew. Michael was gone now. Maybe he'd been clutching the bear in those final moments—before the flames had consumed him. Maybe it had given him some comfort.

Strong arms slid around her, offering her comfort. "I don't know why you keep putting yourself through this," a deep voice murmured. Warm breath caressed the side of her face before lips skimmed over it.

She trembled again—for another reason entirely. Her husband's touch never failed to excite her. "I always make them for the babies."

"Yes, you've already made them for all the babies who've been born," Logan said. "You don't need to make another one."

"Garek—"

His deep laugh interrupted her. "Garek and Candace have just gotten married. And those two aren't likely to ever have children."

"Why not?" she asked. "Nobody thought they were likely to ever get married, either." But they had. On Christmas. Tears stung her eyes as she remembered how beautiful the wedding had been. At least one of her brothers was happy now.

"Hey," he said as he caught the hint of tears she fought. "I'm sure you're right. You're always right. I never noticed how those two felt about each other. But you knew."

She had known how Garek and Candace felt about each other. How had she not known how Milek had felt about Amber? She'd believed her friend—believed that Milek had broken their engagement because he hadn't really loved her. When Amber died, Stacy had realized how wrong she'd been—when she'd seen how devastated Milek had been. That devastation had lasted the whole past year. But he was getting better now.

Or maybe that was just what she wanted to see. He didn't seem as depressed or angry. He just seemed edgy; something was still bothering him. But she dared not push him. He'd only just begun to talk to her again.

"What's wrong?" Logan asked. And he turned her in his arms, holding her closely. "Tell me what's wrong."

She wanted to say nothing. She wanted to be completely happy. But that happiness brought her guilt—that she could be happy when Milek was still miserable—when her best friend was dead. But she was happy. She wrapped her arms around his neck. "I'm not making this bear for Garek and Candace."

She wouldn't dare presume. She and Candace had only recently forged a friendship and Stacy didn't want to risk losing another friend.

Logan arched a dark brow over one of his sparkling blue eyes. "Then who…?"

She let the happiness out then with a smile. "We are."

Logan let out a whoop. Lifting her in his arms, he swung her around the workshop he'd converted from a spare bedroom in their house. With another baby on the way, they might need to convert it back or buy a bigger house.

She wouldn't worry about that yet. She didn't even have to worry about coming up with a name. They had already agreed what the name would be for their next child. It had been too soon when their little Penny was born, her grief too fresh. But Stacy was ready now.

If they had another girl, they would name her Amber. And if the baby was a boy, Michael…

"Mommy, I'm not sick," Mason protested from the backseat of the minivan that belonged to Heather Ames.

Stopped at a light, she turned back toward him with a weak smile as she drummed her fingers on the steering wheel. The light needed to turn green. Now. "I know, honey."

"Then why did you get me from school so early?"

He had been in class only a couple of hours when she came for him.

"Because we need to leave…" she murmured as she turned back to study the long red light.

"School?"

The light changed—finally—so she pressed hard on the accelerator. What if someone had followed her from the house to the school? What if someone was following her now?

The photos proved she'd been under surveillance. Someone had been watching her—them. She doubted he'd stopped now. So she kept glancing into the rearview mirror.

But she didn't know how to detect and lose a tail—like FBI Agent Rus—like Milek and Garek. Their father was a jewel thief; he'd taught his sons not only how to steal but how to elude arrest. Eventually he'd been caught, though, and imprisoned. Milek and Garek had done time, as well.

She almost understood now what they'd gone through and what she had put many criminals through. For the past year she had felt imprisoned—trapped in a life and even in a body where she hadn't wanted to be.

"We're leaving town," she told her son.

He clapped his hands together. "We're going home!"

"No…" That was the last place they could go.

"But I wanna go home." She glanced back and confirmed his bottom lip was jutted out in a pout. "I wanna see Aunt Stacy…"

So did Amber. She had never needed her best friend more. But Stacy was related to Agent Rus now. Would she believe he had betrayed her? Would she forgive Amber for not coming to her a year ago?

She couldn't risk going back to River City. That was where the attempt had been made on their lives—where Gregory had been murdered. She and Michael would be in more danger there. Not that they weren't in danger now.

I know who you really are...

And all those photos. Somebody had been watching them—for weeks. She glanced in the rearview mirror again. Was he watching her right this minute?

She shuddered.

"We can't go see Aunt Stacy yet," she said.

"You always say that..." The disappointment and irritation in his little voice broke her heart.

She had turned his world upside down a year ago. And now she had to do it again.

"We have to leave now," she said. "I packed up all our stuff." At least, everything she'd thought they would need and had been able to pack in less than an hour.

"Where are we going?" he asked.

She had no idea.

He turned in his seat and peered into the cargo area behind him. "Where's Jewel?"

Stacy had lovingly made the bear for her nephew. She probably thought it had burned up in the crash with them—since Amber hadn't been able to leave it behind in their house.

She was sure she'd packed it; it had been on top of the last box she'd brought out to the van. "It's back there—in the open box."

She'd been in such a hurry she hadn't had time to tape any of them shut. But the last one she hadn't even bothered to fold in the flaps.

Michael leaned around his seat to face the back. She heard a sob slip out. "Jewel's not here!"

She had been juggling that last box as she tried to pull the door shut behind her. But the wind had caught the door and pulled it from her grasp, and she'd nearly dropped the box, as well. She might have lost the bear then.

Michael had already given up so much. His family. His friends. She couldn't ask him to give up his favorite toy—his one connection to his past.

When she pulled over to check inside and around all the boxes in the back, she didn't find the bear. With Michael sobbing brokenheartedly now, she had no choice. She had to return to the house where those pictures had been sent. Where one of them had been taken…

Where the killer might be waiting for them…

"This is a mistake," Agent Rus remarked, holding tightly to the armrest as Milek steered around a sharp curve. "We could be leading the shooter right to her."

Milek glanced in the rearview mirror and shook his head. "Nobody's following me." Nobody could. Garek had trained him too well in how to tail someone—so well that he hadn't even noticed Milek tailing him a few times. But he'd taught him even better in how to lose a tail.

Drive it like you stole it…

He would have smiled, as he always did when he heard his brother's advice inside his head. But his head was already pounding—with his madly beating pulse. "Or we could be too late…"

His greatest fear was that the shooter had already beaten them to her. She wasn't very far away—just a few hours north of River City near the Lake Michigan shore.

"Nobody but me knows where she is," Rus maintained. "Until now…"

He'd told Milek. But someone else must have figured it out. Or why else would their graves have been dug up?

"You should have stashed her farther away," Milek said. "Maybe someone recognized her." And then dug up the caskets to confirm they were empty.

"I wanted her to be close enough," Rus said, "in case she needed me."

Milek understood the FBI agent's logic, and now that he was nearly to the town where Rus had moved her, he could even appreciate her not being any farther away. Rus had made wise choices. But Milek wished *he* was the man she had turned to—as she once had. Her passion had equaled his; she'd wanted him as badly and as often as he'd wanted her. Her kisses, her touch had driven him crazy—had tested his already tenuous control. She had once wanted him, but she hadn't trusted him when she'd needed help.

He understood why she hadn't. He hadn't been there for her when she had needed him before—when she'd learned she was pregnant with his son. If only he could have explained…

But he knew Amber. She wouldn't have accepted the truth. It had been easier to lie to her and to pretend he hadn't cared.

Rus lifted his cell phone. "She hasn't called," he said. "She doesn't need me."

Or she couldn't call. Milek's heart slammed into his ribs at the horrific thought. And he pressed harder on the accelerator.

"Stop!" Rus shouted. The man shouldn't have been afraid. Milek was sure he had participated in more than his share of high-speed chases. "You missed the street."

Milek steered the SUV into a sharp U-turn, tires squealing, as he drove onto the road Rus indicated. It was a suburban block—little bungalows sitting side by side on the tree-lined street.

Amber had had a bigger home in River City. As a lawyer, she had been able to take care of herself and their son. Financially.

"What does she do here?" he asked. She wouldn't have been able to practice law without a license.

"Paralegal," Rus replied, "at an estate law firm."

It would have been a big demotion for her. In responsibility and pay. She had given up a lot. But he knew why she had. For their son…

She'd wanted to keep him safe. That was the same reason Milek had stayed away from her and him. To keep them safe…

But then he hadn't realized there were dangers beyond the ones he'd posed.

"Which house?" he asked as he slowed the vehicle.

Rus pointed toward a nondescript white one. Even its door was white as was the trim and foundation. It was so bland that it was nearly invisible. But that had probably been the point. Amber had wanted to be invisible. But someone must have noticed her.

The tires squealed as he braked at the curb. He didn't bother shutting off the ignition, just threw the transmission into Park and jumped out the driver's door. While he ran to the front porch, Rus moved more slowly and called out behind him, "Wait…"

Heedless of the warning, Milek vaulted up the steps. But then he paused, and not because of the hand that suddenly clamped down on his shoulder.

"Wait," Rus said again. "You don't want to startle her or the boy."

But Milek pointed toward the front door. It wasn't just unlocked; it was standing wide-open. Fighting the paralysis of fear, he reached for his holster and drew his weapon. Then he walked through the open door. His stomach knotted with dread over what he might find inside the nondescript home.

Rus had drawn his weapon, too, and he followed closely behind Milek—protecting his back. Milek didn't care about his own safety. He cared only about hers.

While the house was bland on the outside, inside the walls had been painted bright colors. Vibrant reds and blues and greens. It looked as if it had once been loved and lived in—except it was empty of people and left in a mess.

All the doors had been left open—from the closets in every room to the cupboards in the kitchen. Drawers had been pulled out, too.

"Do you think someone broke in to toss the place?" Rus asked as he gazed around at the chaos.

Milek moved back toward the front door. The jamb wasn't broken, and there were no gouges in the lock. Unless he or Garek had picked it, there would have been some indication that it had been forced.

He shook his head. "No."

"Then it looks like someone just left in a hurry," Rus remarked.

"But why?" Milek asked. Had Rus warned her that Milek knew she was alive? Had she not wanted to see him?

They'd lived in the same city for almost five years after they'd broken up and hadn't seen each other, though. She probably wouldn't think he cared that she was alive—not enough to seek her out. "Could she have heard about the graves being dug up?"

"How?" Rus asked. "I didn't know myself until just an hour ago."

But maybe Rus wasn't the only person with whom Amber had stayed in contact. Maybe she'd kept another link to her past—to River City.

The door bumped against something as he pushed it open again, so he pulled it forward and looked behind it. A small stuffed bear lay on the foyer floor next to a table littered with junk mail.

He leaned down to pick up the bear. He recognized the detail. The jewels weren't real, but he knew who had made it. Stacy.

Was that who Amber had stayed in contact with? She and Stacy had always been so close—like sisters.

That was another reason Milek never should have gotten involved with Amber. And, really, he'd tried to just be friends with her, too.

But she was so damn beautiful, and the attraction between them had been so intense. Even knowing she was his sister's best friend, he hadn't been able to resist her. He hadn't been able to resist her until he'd fallen completely for her. Only then had he been strong enough to do the right thing.

As he leaned down to pick up the stuffed animal, he noticed something else: a photograph lay beneath the bear. He scraped up the picture from the hardwood floor. A woman and child cuddled together on a couch—the very one in the room behind him. Her head bent close to his, the two looked at a book together. His breath caught, burning in his lungs, as he recognized them—the woman and the child he'd never thought he would see again. They didn't look the same. Her hair was different—brown instead of shiny red, and it wasn't as long and wavy. Her eyes looked dark, too.

Even the boy's hair looked darker. But his eyes were still the same pale gray as Milek's. He was too young for contacts, so his disguise wasn't as complete as hers.

Was that what had happened?

Had someone recognized them?

That photo had been taken through her front window. He flipped it over and read the message scrawled across the back: *I know who you really are...*

He passed the picture over to Agent Rus. "This is why she left in such a hurry."

Rus cursed. "How the hell did someone find her?"

Milek had begun to consider the FBI agent a friend—especially since he'd admitted the truth to him, since he'd reassured Milek that the woman he had always loved and his son had not died. But now he regarded the man with suspicion.

Could he trust him?

Should Amber have trusted him?

Frank Campanelli shook his head as he followed the minivan back toward the neighborhood he'd thought Amber Talsma had left for good. Earlier he had watched her load the back of the van with boxes and suitcases before she'd gone to the elementary school to pick up her son.

"Why the hell are you coming back here?" he asked aloud.

He'd sent the photographs to give her a chance to escape him. Just as he'd fired those warning shots into her house last time.

He was a professional and had no guilt over killing for money. But it was different with women and kids. Their deaths haunted him.

That was why he'd been glad when Amber Talsma had heeded his last warning and staged her death. He'd claimed responsibility for that and had still collected his payment from his client.

He would have left her "dead"—if not for that damn FBI agent cleaning up River City. Frank had lost another client when Viktor Chekov had gone to prison—to join so many other clients of Frank's.

He needed money. So he would set aside his guilt and finish the job he should have completed a year ago. It had taken the photos and digging up those damn graves in order to convince his client to pay him again.

So this time he would have to produce bodies. He would have to prove he had actually completed the job. That Amber Talsma was really dead.

He slowed as he turned onto the street behind her. With one hand on the steering wheel, he leaned across the passenger's seat and popped open the glove compartment with his other hand.

Then he reached inside and pulled out the gun he kept there. The Glock had a silencer on the barrel, just like the one he'd fired at Amber Talsma's house a year ago. That was why no one had reported hearing gunfire. Despite the suburban neighborhood and all the little houses sitting closely on small lots, nobody would hear anything this time, either.

The only thing that would be different this time was that he would not miss. He would make sure every bullet fired struck its target: Amber Talsma.

Chapter 3

"Where the hell is he?" Garek Kozminski asked as he pushed open the door to FBI Special Agent Nicholas Rus's office at the River City Police Department. His hands were already curled into fists—ready to swing. He was angry. Not as angry as he'd been when someone had been trying to kill the woman who was now his wife, but he was beyond irritated. And the damn agent wasn't even in his office...

A hand touched his arm, long fingers wrapping around it. Even through his coat and sweater, his skin tingled at her touch. He turned back toward her, and as always, his breath caught at her beauty. With her black hair, silky skin and thickly lashed blue eyes, she was stunning.

She looked at him with concern and love. "You don't know for sure Milek is working for him."

He knew. "Milek has been refusing to take any body-guard assignments," he said. "He's preoccupied. Rus roped him into something."

"Are you sure that's a bad thing?" Candace asked.

Garek lost his breath again—for another reason than his wife's beauty. "What?"

"He seems to be doing better than he's been since..."

Since he'd lost the woman he loved and his child. Garek didn't know how Milek had survived the loss—the grief. If Garek ever lost Candace...

He shuddered at the horrific thought.

Candace continued, "He's less despondent."

That was a good thing. For the past year Garek had lost his brother to his grief—to the point that Milek had had him move out of the condo they'd shared. But working for Rus was not a good thing. Garek worried he might lose his brother to more than grief—to death.

"I've done a special assignment for Rus," Garek said, although he didn't need to remind her. "And all of us—you and I and Milek—nearly got killed."

She squeezed his arm in reassurance. "Nearly," she said. "We all survived."

Maybe Milek wasn't happy he had. Maybe working for Rus again was some kind of death wish for him—a wish to join the woman and the child he'd lost.

"Hey, Candace!" A man stopped in the doorway to Rus's office. He was a big, barrel-chested man with a scruffy beard and long, stringy hair.

Although his wife needed no protection, Garek pulled her against his side and wrapped his arm around her shoulders.

"Bruce," Candace greeted the guy with a smile. So

Garek doubted the man was a criminal. She hadn't always had the most affection for them—until she'd fallen for him.

"You're looking great," Bruce said with an appreciative grin as he checked out her lean, sexy body. "We could really use you back in Vice."

She laughed, but not with her usual self-deprecating humor. She wasn't refusing the man's compliment—the way she used to Garek's. Now she saw herself as he saw her—as the true beauty she was.

Garek glared at the interloper, but the guy paid him no attention.

"Is that why you're here?" Bruce asked. "Giving up the bodyguard business?"

She laughed again. "Not at all. My husband and I are looking for Agent Rus."

Bruce glanced at him then. "You look like the guy who was with him right before they tore out of here."

"Why'd they tear out of here?" Garek asked.

"Did something come through Dispatch?" Candace asked.

"Something always comes through Dispatch," Bruce said. "But Rus usually doesn't go out on calls."

Unless it involved something he was already working on—like when he'd been trying to take down Chekov with Garek's help.

"Was anything patched through to him?" Candace clarified her question.

Bruce shrugged. "I don't know. If he was called out because of some kind of incident, he didn't ask for backup. It was just the two of them. Before they ran out of here, they were at Rus's computer."

"Thanks," Candace told the man. And he must have picked up from her tone that she was dismissing him.

The moment he turned away, she closed the office door. Then she slipped from Garek's grasp and moved around Rus's desk. She tapped on his keyboard.

"Isn't it password protected?" he asked. He could break into any building or safe, but computers were beyond his area of expertise.

"It was," she said as she continued tapping on the keys.

"You broke in?" he asked and whistled in appreciation and pride.

She nodded. "Nikki's been teaching me about computers," she said. "And I've been teaching her about self-defense and weapons."

Candace was a good teacher. Logan Payne would soon have no more excuses to keep denying his sister field-work.

A soft gasp slipped through Candace's red lips.

"What is it?"

"I don't know..." she murmured. But her blue eyes were wide as she stared at the monitor.

Garek moved around the desk to lean over his wife's shoulder. "What the hell..."

"Why would someone have dug up Amber's and Michael's graves?" Candace asked.

Garek could think of a reason, but it was too far-fetched to contemplate. Or was it?

He grasped his wife's hand and tugged her toward the door. "Let's find out."

Maybe that was where Rus and Milek had raced off to, but he suspected they'd gone someplace else entirely. Amber and Michael were already dead, so desecrating their graves wouldn't have harmed them.

Unless...

* * *

This is a mistake.

Amber knew it the moment she turned onto the street. She shouldn't have come back here. "Sweetheart," she murmured. "Maybe we'll have to get Jewel another time." Like never. Maybe it was good to have no reminders of the life they'd had to give up, because she had a feeling they would never be safe to return to it.

"No, Mommy!" Michael burst out. "I want Jewel!" Then sobs broke up his little voice.

And broke her heart.

He was too young to understand. And she couldn't explain. She couldn't tell a child that someone wanted them dead. It was too much for him to handle.

It was too much for her to handle alone. But she had no choice now. She could trust no one. Apparently she shouldn't have trusted Agent Rus.

"Okay, okay, we'll get Jewel," she assured him. It was broad daylight. Surely no one would try to kill her now— with so many possible witnesses.

An older couple walked hand in hand along the sidewalk. A garbage truck picked up bins from the ends of driveways. A mailman cut across yards as he made his deliveries.

And in front of her house, a black SUV idled at the curb—a thin stream of exhaust emanating from its tailpipe. Her blood chilled. Someone was here. The SUV belonged to no one she knew now—not that she'd made many friends in their new town. She hadn't wanted to get close to anyone and risk their discovering her secret.

I know who you really are...

Despite all of her precautions, someone had learned

the truth. Someone knew who and where she was. She shouldn't have come back.

"Mommy!" Michael exclaimed. "That man has Jewel."

She saw him then—standing on her front porch—with the small bear clutched in his big hand. Sunlight reflected off his blond hair. And his eyes...

He stared right at her—as if he recognized her despite the dyed hair, despite the contacts. But then she didn't look different enough. If Rus hadn't betrayed her, then that must have been how someone had found her—by recognizing her.

And now so had Milek Kozminski. Or was he the one who'd sent the photos? Was he the one who'd warned her?

Another man stepped out of the house and joined him on the porch. Special Agent Rus. Of course he was who had led Milek to her. Was Milek the only one he'd told about her? Or had he told the man who'd fired the shots that night?

Despite her legs shaking as she trembled with fear, she pressed hard on the accelerator, and the minivan jumped forward.

"Mommy!" Michael cried out in protest. "I want Jewel!"

It wouldn't matter whether or not he had the bear if they didn't survive. She couldn't trust Agent Rus—couldn't trust he didn't pose a threat to her. She knew Milek was dangerous; he'd already hurt her more than anyone else ever could have.

"We have to leave," she told her son. "Now!"

His tears broke her heart, but she was too scared to cave—too scared to do anything but run. She pressed harder on the accelerator and sped away.

* * *

Milek watched her drive off, and once again he was paralyzed. Not with fear this time. But with shock. "She's alive…"

The back windows of her vehicle were tinted, so he hadn't been able to peer through the dark glass to clearly see his son. But there had been a shadow back there. Michael had to be with her.

They were both alive—just as Rus had claimed. But Milek hadn't allowed himself to believe him—to hope. He'd needed to see for himself.

"Son of a bitch!" Nicholas Rus cursed and gestured at the vehicle following the minivan down the street. "That's the Ghost."

"Ghost?" Amber wasn't dead; Milek had just seen her.

"Campanelli!"

"No!" The paralysis ended as he ran toward the running SUV. He pulled open the driver's door and slid behind the wheel. He was already steering away from the curb when Rus jumped into the passenger's side.

"Damn it!" the FBI agent cursed.

Milek didn't know and didn't care if he was cursing him. He had to catch up to Amber before Campanelli did. "How the hell did he find her?"

Rus cursed again. "I don't know. I don't know…"

At the moment it didn't matter how, though—it only mattered that he had.

Milek sped up to close the distance between his SUV and the rental sedan ahead of them. "Is this it?"

The car's windows weren't tinted. He could see clearly inside—could see a big man was in the driver's seat. But he must have had only one hand on the wheel, because he lifted a gun with his other hand and pointed it toward the minivan in front of him.

"That's him!" Rus shouted. He lifted his gun as Campanelli had. But then he shook his head. "I can't shoot—I can't risk it. The bullet could go through the car and into the van."

Milek didn't need a gun; he had the SUV. He stomped on the accelerator, propelling the vehicle forward so its front bumper rammed the rear bumper of the sedan.

Metal crunched and tires squealed.

Was there a shot?

Had the man fired the gun?

Milek peered through the car to the van ahead of it. The rear window was shattered, glass raining down from it onto the street and into the back of the van. His heart constricted; fear squeezing it.

He cursed. "The son of a bitch…"

Campanelli had fired the gun. Had a bullet struck Amber or the little boy? Milek was certain his son had been in the backseat.

Anger joined his fear. He pressed harder on the accelerator and struck the sedan again. But as he struck it, the car catapulted forward and hit the van. Maybe that was why the minivan swerved—or maybe it was because Amber had been shot.

A cry burned Milek's throat, but his jaw was clenched too tightly to utter it. A curse slipped through Rus's lips and resonated inside the SUV.

Tires squealing, the van scraped along a row of parked cars. Metal crunched, sparks flying from the contact. Then the van swerved again across the street. The turn was so sharp, the van tipped and rolled onto the driver's side. The car swerved, just missing the van as it squeezed between it and those parked cars.

Milek drove forward and stopped beside the undercarriage of the van. He didn't care that the Ghost was getting away. He cared only about Amber and Michael, and making sure they were all right. But as he reached for the driver's door, Nicholas Rus grabbed his arm to stop him.

"He's coming back."

Apparently the car had turned around on the other side of the van and was heading right toward them. But it wasn't the vehicle they needed to worry about—it was the gun held out the window, the barrel pointed directly at them.

Bullets pinged off the metal of the SUV and shattered the glass. As it had rained into the van, it rained onto them. He and Rus raised their weapons and returned fire.

Pain throbbed in Amber's head, pounding as fast and frantically as her heart. She blinked, trying to clear her blurred vision. But it wasn't her vision that was blurred—or it wasn't just her vision. The windshield had cracked like a spiderweb and ballooned inside—toward her face.

She blinked again as something trickled down her forehead and into her eye. She lifted her hand and brushed it away, and blood, bright red and sticky, smeared her fingers.

She didn't care about herself, though. Her fear was all for someone else. Her baby...

Pinned beneath the steering wheel, she struggled to twist around—to peer into the backseat. Fear choking her, she could only hoarsely whisper, "Are you okay?"

Big tears rolled down his flushed face. He was terrified. Too scared to even utter the sobs that should have gone with his tears.

She couldn't cry, either. She could barely breathe as her heart continued to hammer frantically in her chest. It sounded like a war zone outside the crumpled van. Gunfire erupted in angry bursts, probably as the men reloaded. She flinched with each shot.

Had it been a bullet that had shattered her rear window? Unlike the front window, which had only spider-webbed, the glass had fallen completely out of the back window—some of it had fallen inside. Shards were strewn about the vehicle—like the other articles that had flown from the moving boxes when the van rolled.

She didn't care about possessions, though. She shouldn't have taken the time to pack them. And she shouldn't have risked returning—even for Jewel. She had put her son in danger.

Had that bullet struck anything besides the glass? She reached out for Michael. Strapped into his booster chair in the middle of the backseat, he was up higher than she was, which put him in danger if any of those shots flew through that broken rear window.

The van lay on the driver's side, the metal crumpled beneath her. Pieces of that metal and the plastic interior shell of the door protruded into her seat, poking her arm and her hip. She struggled with her seat belt, pushing the button to free the clasp. But it held tightly. Her fingers trembling, she pushed hard on the button and tugged on the strap.

And finally it snapped back. She settled heavily against that crumpled door, wincing as the metal dug through her clothes and into her skin. But that was only a minor discomfort in relation to her overwhelming fear for her son.

She reached up again—for the seat belt holding Michael's booster chair against the backseat.

"Are you hurt?" she asked him. "Do you feel any pain?"

His eyes wide, he shook his head.

But she couldn't trust he wasn't like her—in shock, with so much adrenaline coursing through her that she might not have realized if she'd been shot.

What about Milek? Was he shooting or getting shot?

What the hell was going on outside her van?

Then suddenly the gunfire ended—leaving an eerie silence behind but for the squeal of tires against asphalt. Someone was driving away.

Who? Which shooter?

Did it matter? She could trust no one.

She had to get away. "I'm going to undo your seat belt," she warned Michael. "And you're going to fall. Fall toward me, and I will catch you."

Tears still streaming down his little face, he nodded agreement.

But before she could reach the clasp, the door slid open on the passenger's side of the van. And big hands reached through the opening, reaching for her son.

Terror overwhelmed her and she screamed. "No! Don't take my son! Leave him alone!"

Chapter 4

"Where the hell are they?" Garek asked the question already echoing inside Logan Payne's head as he stared down at the empty caskets.

Dirt slipped from beneath his feet as he stood on the mounds built up around those open and empty caskets. The graves were in a remote area of the River City Peaceful Acres cemetery—far from the street. So nobody had heard or seen anything—until the caretaker had stumbled across those piles of dirt. At least that was what the investigating police officer had shared with Logan.

The young officer was talking to Candace now, his head bobbing as he answered her questions. The kid didn't know any more than he'd already told them, though. So Candace left him quickly to return to her husband's side. Logan suspected there was only one man who could answer their questions.

Standing on another mound next to him, Garek clicked off his cell phone and shoved it into his pocket; his hand was shaking. Candace took it in hers. "Milek's phone keeps going to voice mail."

Logan also had his phone to his ear, listening to his half brother's recorded voice. *Special Agent Nicholas Rus. I am not available at the moment. Leave me a message, and I will return your call.*

"Bullshit," he cursed as he jerked the phone away. Rus hadn't returned the message he'd already left him. "Nick's is going straight to voice mail, too."

Garek repeated, "Where the hell are they?"

With her free hand, Candace gestured toward the empty caskets and suggested, "A better question might be where the hell are *they*?"

The inside of both caskets was pristine. There had been no bodies decaying within them for a year. Logan doubted there'd ever been a body in either.

"Nick knows," he said, and anger surged through him. He'd just begun to forge a relationship with the half brother who'd turned his family upside down when he'd shown up in River City. But it wasn't Nick's fault that their father had had an affair with Nick's mother.

It was Nick's fault for letting Stacy and Milek suffer, thinking that Amber Talsma and her son had died in a horrific crash.

"The son of a bitch must have staged the whole *accident*," Garek said, his anger and disgust apparent. "How could he put everyone through that?"

Candace squeezed her husband's hand, offering her love and reassurance. "He must have had his reasons."

The comment gave Logan comfort, as well. No matter

what Nick had done since he'd come to town, he'd had a reason for every action.

"What are you thinking?" Logan asked. "Witness protection?"

"She must have seen something," Candace replied. "Maybe she witnessed her boss's murder."

DA Gregory Schievink had been gunned down outside his house. But if the rumors were true about the deceased DA and his assistant, Amber could have been with him—especially since his wife had been out of town at the time.

"But she's been gone a year," Garek said. His voice hoarse with anger, he added, "Milek has mourned her for a whole freaking year. Until..."

Nick must have told him that she was alive. He had probably revealed the secret while Milek had been helping the special agent keep Garek and Candace alive. Since then, everyone had noticed the younger Kozminski brother had been doing better.

"Some cases take a year or more to go to trial," Logan said. Even after he'd left the River City PD to start the Payne Protection Agency, he'd had to testify in cases he'd investigated while he'd been a detective.

"What case?" Garek asked. "There have been no arrests in the DA's murder. If Amber witnessed the shooting and was alive, there would have been an arrest."

While Garek hadn't always been on the right side of the law, he understood how it worked.

"That's true," Logan acknowledged. "There must be some other reason..."

But what? Why the hell would an FBI agent have helped the assistant DA fake her death and that of her son?

Logan punched in Nick's number on his cell again. But just like before, it went straight to his voice mail.

Where the hell are they?

* * *

He had her son. He had taken him away before she could reach for him—before she could rescue him. Then the front passenger's door opened and big hands reached inside for her.

Instinct had her shrinking back against the crumpled driver's door. But then stronger instincts kicked in—of a mother protecting her child. And she struggled from beneath the steering wheel.

"Wait," a deep voice advised. "Don't move. You might be injured."

She recognized the voice and the hands. Those same hands had lifted her son from the backseat. Those hands had once touched her, caressed her…

Held her.

"Where's Michael?" she asked. "Where'd you put him?"

"He's out here," Milek replied, even as he leaned inside the van. "He's safe. For the moment…" His silver eyes darkened to gray—with concern, with fear. He was worried that whoever had been shooting at them might return. "We need to get you out—if you're not hurt, if you can move."

She was moving. But as she moved the van rocked, threatening to roll over again. Her breath caught, trapped in her lungs, as fear overwhelmed her. Then those hands slipped beneath her arms and easily lifted her, as if she weighed no more than their child.

Once she cleared the passenger's door, he didn't put her down, though. He held her, his arms tightly clasping her against his madly pounding heart.

"Are you all right?" he asked.

"Are you?" she asked. "I heard the gunshots." So many gunshots...

She shuddered at the memory. At least there had been no sound the night those bullets had been fired into her home. At first she hadn't understood why the windows had shattered, why the pictures had fallen off the walls. She'd figured it might have been an earthquake; there had been a couple of small ones in the area around that time. But then she'd heard the car drive away, tires squealing, and when she'd stepped outside, she'd seen the shells on the ground.

"We're fine," Milek said. And he must have accepted that she was, too, because he set her on her feet. She hadn't realized how badly her legs were shaking until they nearly buckled beneath her.

He caught her, wrapping his arm around her to hold her up. His other hand touched her face, his fingers skimming from her temple over her cheek. Just as it always had, her skin tingled from his touch. "You're bleeding."

He turned away from her and spoke to someone else. "Rus, we better take her to the emergency room."

Special Agent Nicholas Rus stepped forward, her son in one arm while the other was against his side, his gun grasped tightly in his hand.

Fear slammed her heart against her ribs. But Michael was blissfully unafraid. Because he recognized the man who had helped them hide, he trusted him.

Amber couldn't do that anymore. She pulled away from Milek and reached for her son. "Give him to me," she said, her tone sharp. "Let go of my son!"

Michael's silvery-gray eyes widened with shock. He looked so much like his father. Did he see it? Did he see how much he looked like the man who'd originally lifted him from the van? Why had Milek handed him over to the FBI agent?

To help her from the van? Or because he still didn't want their son?

But before she could take the boy from Rus's arms, Milek reached for him. He easily clasped their son against his chest. "He's fine," he assured her.

Michael didn't look fine, though. His little brow was furrowed as he stared up at his father. Maybe he saw it now—the similarities between them. "You look like somebody," Michael said and confirmed her suspicion.

"Aunt Stacy," Amber quickly answered. "Milek is Aunt Stacy's brother."

Their little boy's eyes narrowed as he continued to study his father's handsome face. Was it possible Milek had gotten even better looking the past year? His already chiseled features were even more defined—his cheekbones sharper, his jaw squarer—harder. But his lips looked soft, kissable...

She had kissed them so many times, but that had been years ago. Would he kiss the same now? Would his kiss—his touch—affect her the way it once had?

Maybe she'd hit her head when the van had rolled. Why else would she be having such inane thoughts? Such desires? She didn't want Milek Kozminski anymore.

She wanted only her son.

"Does that make you my uncle?" her little boy asked.

Milek coughed. "No. I'm not your uncle. I'm your—"

Whatever he'd been about to say was lost—swallowed by the sound of sirens. Had he been about to admit he was their son's father?

"We need to get out of here," Rus said. "Now!"

Milek pointed toward her forehead. "She needs to go

to the hospital," he said, "and have someone check her out and make sure she doesn't have a concussion. And she's going to need stitches."

She lifted her trembling fingers to her head. The blood was just trickling now. "No…"

"Mommy," Michael exclaimed, his bottom lip beginning to quiver. "You're bleeding."

"I'm fine," Amber assured her son and his father. Despite her ridiculous thoughts about Milek, she didn't think she had a concussion. She had never lost consciousness, and she had no pain. "I didn't hit my head. It's just a scratch." Which could have been caused by broken glass or crumpled metal or maybe even one of those flying bullets…

"We need to get out of here," Rus said, "before anyone else sees you and knows you're alive."

Amber pointed toward the wreckage that had once been her minivan. "Obviously someone already knows."

And didn't want her to stay alive. Rus hadn't put away his gun yet; it was still clasped tightly in his hand. For protection? Or as a threat?

Instead of being intimidated, she was angry. Her life, and more important her son's, had already been threatened. She narrowed her eyes and glared at Agent Rus. "How do they know? Who did *you* tell?"

"Me," Milek said. "He told *me*."

Had telling Milek put her and Michael in danger?

Her breath feathered across his ear as Amber leaned close to him and whispered, "He could have told someone else."

Despite the warmth of her breath, he shivered slightly. It was cold outside—where they'd gone onto the hotel balcony to talk. Through the partially open sliding door, they could see their son—sleeping in one of the twin beds in the hotel. He'd seen her suspicion of the FBI agent. If Rus hadn't left the room, she probably wouldn't have left their son's side. Milek hadn't wanted to leave it, either. And they'd left the door open, so they could hear if he cried out or if someone tried to come through the door to the hall.

"He didn't need to tell anyone else."

"But he must've," she insisted. "For the whole past year, nobody bothered Michael and me...until those photos showed up today."

She looked at him then—with that same narrow-eyed stare she'd given Rus—as though she was interrogating him on a witness stand. She must have missed that—the cross-examination; she wouldn't have had much chance of doing it over the past year.

"I have no reason to want you dead," he said. And every reason to want her alive.

She kept that stare on him, unblinking. She looked so different—with the dark hair and contacts. But yet she was so familiar, too. "You haven't asked me why..."

"Rus told me," he said, "about the shooting." About her and their son nearly being killed in their own home.

"You haven't asked me why I didn't go to you after the shooting happened."

He shook his head. "I didn't need to ask you why. I knew..." He had already let her down.

But she told him anyway. "I didn't think you'd care..."

He flinched. But she wasn't trying to hurt him. She was only stating what he'd made her believe. That he didn't care about her or their son.

"So why did you come here with Agent Rus?" she asked.

They were just on the outskirts of the little town where Nick Rus had helped her hide. Rus had gone back into town to talk to the authorities, who were no doubt trying to figure out just what the hell had happened on her block. A traffic accident or a drive-by shooting.

Both.

Things like that happened all the time in River City. He suspected that wasn't the case in this scenic little town. Why had it happened here? Why did someone want Amber dead?

"He told me you and Michael were alive."

"So?" she asked. "You didn't want to see me all the years before I *died*. Why did you want to see me now?"

He wanted to tell her how her death had affected him—how it had devastated him. How he'd realized when he'd lost her and their son that he had lost his reason for living. But after how he'd treated her, how he'd rejected her and Michael, he had no right to those feelings.

He peered through the slider, making certain their son slept soundly, so he wouldn't overhear their conversation—even with the door only partially open. He didn't want to traumatize him any more than that afternoon probably had. "Someone dug up your graves."

She shuddered.

"He opened the caskets," he said.

She expelled a shaky breath. "He knows they're empty, then."

"I suspect he already knew," he said. "He just had to confirm." And once the hired killer had confirmed it, he'd come after her—after them.

She uttered a very unladylike curse.

Milek drew out his cell phone and held up the screen showing the call log. "He's not the only one who knows." He hadn't had to play his messages to confirm that. He knew his family well.

Ever since Amber's accident a year ago, they'd been watching him closely. They had noticed the difference in him after Rus had shared the truth with him. Garek had made his suspicions clear that he thought Milek was working for the FBI agent. With his new wife's help, he would have kept digging. But it wasn't just Garek and Candace who'd been calling him. The entire Payne family had called.

"They all know…"

She let out a soft gasp. "Stacy?"

He glanced at the call log again and nodded. She'd called too many times to just be checking on him. She knew.

"She's going to hate me."

"She's going to be happy you're alive."

"For how long?" Amber asked. "The shooter knows I'm alive. And he wants me dead."

"I'm not going to let that happen," Milek assured her.

She shook her head. "You won't be able to stop him."

"I stopped him today." He wasn't sure if it had been his shots or Rus's that had come close enough to either injure or scare off the killer.

"You can't be with me every minute," she said. "I need to wake up Michael and get out of here." She reached for the handle of the slider.

He covered her hand with his and stopped her from opening the door. Her skin was cold and silky to his touch. He tightened his grasp. "You can't hide."

He couldn't lose them again.

"I can," she said. "I just won't make the mistake of trusting Agent Rus again."

"Rus didn't betray you," he said. "If someone hadn't dug up your graves, I'm not sure he would have ever told me where you were."

"Then why did he tell you that Michael and I were alive?"

Because he had been suffering. But he doubted she would believe him. Since she was already having trouble trusting, he wasn't going to push his luck. Not when he had another proposal to make.

"It doesn't matter why," Milek said. "But now that he told me, now that I know you're both alive and in danger, I intend to keep you and Michael safe."

She stared up at him and asked, "And how do you intend to do that?"

"By bringing you home."

She shuddered. "To River City?"

"To my place," he clarified. "I want you and Michael to move in with me." Of course, doing that might actually put her in more danger—from *him*.

He hunched down in the driver's seat and stared up at the hotel room where, moments ago, two people had stood on the balcony.

They hadn't seen him following them from the crime scene. But then, he was the Ghost. Nobody ever saw him—until it was too late. Until today…

Frank lifted his fingers to his forehead and flinched. A bullet had grazed him. He hadn't had a call that close in a long while. It had shaken him.

He didn't want to actually become a ghost. But he had

to make some more. He glanced down at the screen of his phone where a news broadcast played. It was out now.

Their graves found empty, Amber Talsma was believed to have faked the deaths of herself and her young son. There was speculation about all the reasons why.

Only Frank knew the truth—the whole truth. He was a professional, though, so nobody else would ever know. And because he was a professional it was time he finished the job. He could have tried when they'd been on the balcony, but he hadn't had a clear shot. So he would wait. He was a patient man.

But he didn't have to wait long before his targets walked out. The man had the boy clasped in one arm and his other arm wrapped protectively around the woman. But he wasn't actually offering them much protection. He wouldn't be able to draw his weapon this time. He wouldn't be able to return fire when Frank started shooting.

Chapter 5

She was the one with a new name. New hair. New eye color. New career. Home. Life.

But Milek was the one who had changed. He wasn't the man she remembered—the one she had loved. She had fallen for his sweet sensitivity. She saw none of that in the man who had pulled her from the wreckage of her van.

So why had she agreed to go home with him? She didn't even know him. She'd already been scared to return to River City—since that was where it had all begun, where Gregory had been murdered, where she'd nearly been gunned down, as well. And living with Milek? Being with him all the time? That terrified her.

But he'd been insistent that they needed to leave the hotel. Now. Because she'd wanted to be gone before Agent Rus returned, she'd readily agreed.

Now, as she walked with him across the hotel parking lot, she wasn't certain she'd made the right decision. Milek had proved over five years ago she couldn't trust him with her heart.

But could she trust him with her life and Michael's?

He had changed. He was no longer the sensitive artist he'd once been. He was a bodyguard, all steely-eyed and focused.

Even now, as he walked her and Michael from the hotel with an arm around each of them, he wasn't focused on them. He was focused on everything around them. The parking lot was dark, the light from the hotel faint. She could see nothing.

But she felt the moment he did. His body tensed, and his grip on the gun he held against her side tightened.

"We're going to play a game," he whispered to their son. "We're going to play hide-and-seek. You and your mother are going to hide. You're going to hear bangs again but you're not to come out until *I* tell you to."

There was that sensitivity—just a glimmer of it—when he tried to convince their son that the danger they were in was just a game.

After that brief explanation, he acted fast, though. He passed their son to her and stepped in front of them. "Run back into the hotel," he told her.

Before she could say anything, shots rang out. She didn't know who was shooting—Milek or whoever he had seen in the darkness. She couldn't ask. She couldn't move. Fear paralyzed her.

"Run!" he yelled.

And finally her legs moved. Michael clasped closely to her chest, she ran straight for the hotel lobby. But the glass doors stopped her, drawing her up short. Was she locked out?

Slowly they began to part. So the automatic opener was just slow. Too slow. She ducked as more shots rang out. Something whizzed past her head. She hoped she imagined it, but then the glass of those slowly parting doors shattered.

She shrieked.

And Michael echoed her scream, his body trembling against hers. She swung him out of her arms and through the narrow opening. As Milek had told her, she told their son, "Run!"

He was smaller—a smaller target. The shooter was after her. Not Milek. Not Michael. But he was putting those she loved in danger. Anger coursed through her—along with the fear. And she thought fleetingly of running back—of trying to negotiate with a killer. Her life for the lives of her son and Milek. But her little boy paused in the middle of the lobby, staring back at her, his eyes wide with fear. He needed her; he needed his mommy.

She squeezed through the metal frames of those shattered doors and caught up with him, swinging him back up into her arms. But she didn't know where to go. Outside the gunfire continued. And inside all she could hear was screaming. And crying.

But she and Michael had gone silent—probably with shock. The screaming and crying emanated from behind the check-in and concierge desks. She could have carried Michael back there. But the night clerk's fear would terrify Michael even more.

She needed to take him somewhere safer. She had the key to the room Special Agent Rus had booked for them. But how had the shooter found them? Had Rus told him where they were? Or was it Rus out in the parking lot—shooting at Milek?

She shouldn't have trusted the FBI agent. She hadn't been certain she could trust Milek when he'd told her that they needed to leave right away, that he would take them home with him where he would be able to protect her and Michael.

He was protecting her now, putting his own life in danger to save her and their son. Maybe he was the one man she could trust. And she might be losing him...

Panic pressed on her heart, painfully squeezing it. The gunfire grew louder—the shots even closer now. Windows splintered next to the already shattered doors. And vases and pictures broke, exploding into sharp fragments.

Clasping Michael more tightly in her arms, she ran again—through the lobby to the bank of elevators and the stairwell. She couldn't go back to the room Agent Rus had booked for them. He could be the one shooting at Milek and the hotel, and he had a key to that room. She had to go somewhere, though, somewhere safe from the person so determined to kill her that he didn't care who got hurt or worse along with her.

Was Milek okay? Would he survive?

Or would he die her hero?

Glass raining down around him, Milek ducked down between two rows of cars and cursed. He'd thought the hired assassin was called the Ghost because he had eluded the authorities for so long. But maybe he was called the Ghost because he was impossible to stop. No one could kill the already dead.

No one could see them, either. Milek hadn't sent Amber back to the hotel with their son because he'd seen the assassin or the gun. The darkness complete, there had been no glimpse of the man or glint of his weapon.

Milek had *felt* his presence. When he and Amber and Michael had stepped into the parking lot, Milek had instinctively known they weren't alone. Maybe it was the year of being a bodyguard that had honed those instincts—instincts instilled in him since childhood when his father had groomed him and his brother to be thieves. Those instincts had also told him it wasn't another hotel patron hanging out in the lot. It was someone waiting for them.

Waiting to kill them.

He'd barely passed Michael to Amber and sent them into the hotel before the gunfire had opened up. He'd heard the glass break—in the cars around them and in the hotel lobby windows. Had they been hit?

He had heard only one scream. But then Amber wasn't a screamer. She was too controlled for that—too strong. And she must have passed that strength onto their child, because no screams could be heard from Michael now, either.

Unless…

His heart pounded frantically with fear, but he couldn't consider such a horrific possibility. They hadn't been hit. But the shooter was getting closer to the hotel—firing more shots through those windows.

A shriek rang out.

It wasn't Amber's. Her voice wasn't as high-pitched. It wasn't a child's cry, either.

Had someone else been hurt? Caught in the cross fire?

Milek cursed again. But he hadn't fired toward the hotel. He was firing in the direction from which the shots seemed to be coming. There had to be a silencer on the assassin's gun, because Milek heard only a faint whoosh of air when a bullet left the barrel. But he still couldn't see the shooter.

So Milek was just wasting ammo now. He reached into his coat pocket and pulled out his last magazine. He needed to make these shots count. He needed to hit the Ghost this time or he risked becoming one himself.

Because a hired assassin wasn't about to run out of ammo. The man would have enough bullets left to kill Milek and Amber and Michael if he found them.

He prayed she had listened to him—that she would hide herself and their son where the killer wouldn't be able to find them. Because he wasn't sure how much longer he would be able to protect them.

As evidenced by the shriek, there were other people in the hotel, though. The night clerk and the concierge. Maybe a bellhop. And several other hotel guests. Someone would have called 911 by now.

Help had to be on its way. The Ghost wouldn't stick around; he wouldn't risk getting caught. Unless Milek could distract him until the police arrived...

"Frank!" he called out. "Frank Campanelli!"

Movement ceased. There were no more whooshes of air, no more breaking glass. He'd stopped shooting; he was listening.

"Yeah, Frank," Milek continued. "The police know it's you who killed the district attorney. They know it's you who fired the shots into Ms. Talsma's home. And the FBI agent saw you today." Apparently Nick Rus could see ghosts. Milek had been so totally focused on Amber and his son that he hadn't gotten a good look at him. "You're a wanted man, Frank. You're not going to get away with this."

A chuckle came from out in the darkness.

Of course the assassin had no fear of getting caught. No one had come close to apprehending him during his long and infamous career.

"The special agent who's after you—it's Nicholas Rus," he said. As Milek talked, he moved closer to where that chuckle had come from. "He's the agent who brought down Viktor Chekov. Rus is River City's version of Eliot Ness."

Hunched low, Milek slipped between the rows of cars. One of his father's lessons on how to be a thief had been about moving silently. Like everything they'd been taught, Garek had picked it up more easily—was better at it, even now. But Milek was good.

If he'd been driving to the hotel, he knew Frank wouldn't have been able to follow them the way he must have followed Nicholas Rus. Rus was a good agent, but he wasn't a bodyguard. He didn't know all the ways and means of protecting an endangered client.

But Milek had wanted to sit in the backseat—close to his son. He hadn't been able to stop staring at the little boy and it hadn't been just to make certain Michael was okay. While he'd had his reasons, Milek regretted never seeing his son, and for the past year he'd thought he had missed the opportunity of ever getting to know his child.

But maybe that car ride to the hotel was all the time he would have—because another rule of being a bodyguard was giving up your own life to protect your subject. And Milek had never been as willing to do that as he was now.

That was why he spoke again. Frank would know where he was, that he was getting closer. But it was a risk Milek had to take, so he could pinpoint the hit man's exact location and make his remaining bullets count.

"Rus didn't bring down Chekov alone," Milek continued. "He had help."

Frank snorted; Milek was close enough now that he clearly heard it. "Feds never act alone," Frank said. "A whole bunch of Feds have tried to take me down, and they haven't succeeded yet."

"It wasn't other Feds who helped Rus take down Chekov," Milek said. "It was me and my brother."

Frank laughed again but cocked his gun.

Milek heard the telltale click of the bullet sliding into the barrel. He was close.

And Frank knew it, too.

Close enough that neither of them would be able to miss now.

"Not that I care," Frank said. "But who the hell are you?"

Garek was the cocky one—the one who enjoyed annoying other people. Milek had never understood his brother's enjoyment of that until now—until he wanted to infuriate the man who had tried and was trying to kill the only woman Milek had ever loved and the child they'd created together.

"I guess you should know the name of the man who's finally going to bring you down," he agreed. "I'm Milek Kozminski."

There was no snort now. No laughter. Frank Campanelli knew who he was. For the first time, Milek found an advantage to being as infamous as he and his family were.

Frank said, "You worked for Chekov."

Garek had. But Milek would let the man believe whatever he wanted.

"Your family…"

"Is basically a bunch of criminals," Milek finished for him. "Maybe that's what it takes to catch one…"

The saying was actually it took a thief to catch a thief. But maybe it was also true that it took a killer to catch a killer.

Milek had killed before. And in order to protect Amber and Michael, he would willingly kill again.

Frank laughed, but the chuckle was gruff and shaky with nerves. He must have realized he wasn't dealing with a Fed or a regular bodyguard.

He probably thought he was dealing with a man like himself—one with no scruples or morals or conscience. Unfortunately, Milek had a conscience. But he doubted it would bother him if he took out a hired assassin—a man who'd killed again and again for money.

Milek cocked his gun.

This was it. His last magazine. His last chance to take out the Ghost—even though he risked becoming one himself. He didn't care, though. He didn't care about anything but Amber and Michael. To save their lives, he would gladly give up his own. So even knowing he would draw Frank's gunfire, he straightened up from where he'd been hunched over between the cars. He would rather have Frank fire at him than into the hotel any longer.

And now Milek was close enough to the Ghost that the hit man might not miss him when he fired back. As Milek squeezed the trigger, gunfire erupted again.

They were gone. Nicholas Rus had searched the entire hotel. But he found no trace of them. Maybe that wasn't such a bad thing—since he had found no bodies. Of course, that didn't mean they weren't dead.

It would be more of a surprise if they had survived.

The hotel looked like a war zone. Shattered glass. Broken vases. And the parking lot was even worse.

Cars had been destroyed, their windows broken, the metal dented with bullets. Could anyone have survived such an onslaught of gunfire? Even Milek Kozminski...

Nick shone the beam of his flashlight on the asphalt. The fragments of glass sparkled in its glow—except for those fragments spattered with blood. The blood, thick and dark, pooled around the fragments, too.

Someone had been hit. Maybe badly.

He hoped like hell it had been Frank Campanelli. But if the Ghost was dead, where was his body? Where were Milek and Amber and the boy—if they hadn't been hurt?

His cell rang; he felt it vibrating inside his pocket. But he hesitated to reach for it. He knew who it would be and what they would want to know.

He had already answered enough questions for the night—when he'd had to explain the accident scene to the local authorities. He hadn't admitted to them who'd been driving the van, though. He hadn't wanted any more people to know Amber Talsma wasn't really dead. That was why he'd convinced her and Milek to leave the scene— why he'd driven them to this hotel—thinking they would be safe here.

He had been a fool—a fool to let someone follow him and a fool to think that anyone, even Milek, could have protected Amber from as highly skilled an assassin as Frank, The Ghost, Campanelli.

He'd been a fool to think he could keep it from getting out that she was alive. On the way back to the hotel, he'd heard the report on the radio—the news of their empty graves and the speculation that she must have faked her death. Everybody knew she was alive now.

His phone stopped vibrating before he ever reached for it. But that was fine. Whichever one of them who'd called would leave a voice mail—like all the voice mails they'd left before demanding information from him.

But Nick had no answers for the Payne/Kozminski family. He didn't know where Milek and Amber and the child were—let alone if they were all right.

Had Frank taken them—taken their bodies? Maybe after he'd let his targets get away last time, he had needed the evidence of their deaths in order to get paid.

"Son of a bitch..." he murmured into the darkness.

An officer glanced over at him. The local authorities had been called here. Nick had heard the calls come in to Dispatch while he'd been talking to a detective.

Shots fired at the Harbor Hotel.

"Why do you want to go to that call?" the detective had asked when Nick said he needed to leave.

He'd said nothing.

"Who are you protecting?" the detective had asked.

But that was just the thing. Rus hadn't protected anyone. He'd left them behind—with the killer, who must have followed him to the hotel. They hadn't even had a vehicle in which to escape. He'd taken the shot-up SUV to the police department. So where were they?

Maybe Milek had utilized the skills his father had taught him and stolen a car. Nick found himself actually hoping the guy had committed a crime. But nothing had been reported stolen. The only report had been of those shots fired.

Shell casings gleamed in the darkness, illuminated when crime scene techs took flash pictures of the casings beside which they had already placed evidence tags. So many shots had been fired.

And the blood…

He should have been here. He shouldn't have left them alone—not with a notorious killer after them. He cursed again, but silently—the words echoing inside his mind.

His phone began to ring once more—vibrating madly inside his pocket. He didn't need to answer it; he could feel the anger and frustration of his family.

They probably didn't think of him that way. But he had begun to think it—that they were his family. He had never had a real family before. Until she had died a year ago, it had been just his mom and him, and she'd been no Penny Payne. There had been nothing maternal about her.

Nick had gotten more love and attention from the neighbors. Of course, as an adolescent he'd been annoyed to have the younger kids tagging along; Gage had even followed Nick into the marines and then into the Bureau. Recently he'd quit the Bureau, though, and reenlisted in the marines.

And Annalise…

Nick's heart contracted in his chest. He couldn't think about Annalise anymore—not the way he used to think about her. He had destroyed that relationship just as he'd probably destroyed the one he'd been building with the Paynes. He stared down at the puddle of blood and felt as if his own was draining away.

Nick hadn't just lost the woman and child he'd been trying to protect for the past year. He had lost his family, too.

Chapter 6

Her heart pounded hard and fast with nerves as she clasped her arms around her son and held him tightly—protectively—while they cowered inside the janitor's closet she'd found unlocked. She had locked it from the inside, after pulling Michael into the closet with her. It wasn't dark. A bare bulb hung over their heads, illuminating the small space.

She would have fumbled for the switch. But Michael was afraid of the dark. If she shut it off, he might begin to cry.

"Mommy, this is a good hiding place," he whispered.

"Shh," she said, her voice shaking with fear. "We have to be very quiet." So the killer did not hear them. Was he out there? The gunfire had stopped. But that wasn't necessarily a good thing. What if Milek had been wounded, or worse?

Now fear clenched her heart. What if he hadn't survived? What if she'd lost him again?

Not that she'd ever really had him. If she had, he wouldn't have broken their engagement and her heart. But she didn't care about the pain he'd caused her. She didn't want him in any pain—especially because of her. And she wanted him alive—even if he was never with her again.

Please, be alive...

The door rattled as someone tried the knob, and her breath caught. Michael let out a soft cry of surprise, then slapped his hand over his mouth. Tears welled in his eyes.

She had locked the door. Surely that would keep out whoever was out there. But the knob continued to rattle. Then it turned. He had unlocked it.

Maybe it was the janitor. But she doubted it. All the staff had been hunkered down behind the front desk. It was someone else. Someone who meant her and Michael harm.

So as the knob turned, she screamed.

And jerked awake from the nightmare she'd lived just hours ago. She'd only been dreaming about what had happened back at the hotel. She wasn't dreaming now. A hand covered her mouth. It wasn't hers. It was big and strong and slightly calloused.

Disoriented from sleep and the dream, she had no idea where she was or where Michael was or who held a hand over her face. Panic overwhelmed her, and she struggled, grasping the hand to pull it away as she tried to rise.

But a big body covered hers, pushing her down into the mattress on which she lay. "Shh..." a deep voice advised.

Or warned?

But then she recognized the voice and stilled.

"Shh," he said again. "You'll wake Michael."

The thought of her son, and wanting to hold him, had her struggling again. But Milek had carried their sleeping child into another room of the warehouse he'd converted into a condo years ago. Then he'd brought her in here—the master bedroom. He'd left her alone, though. She had no idea how long ago. Had she been asleep for hours or minutes?

"You're safe now," Milek assured her—just as he had when he'd opened the door to that closet back at the hotel.

Just like then, she wanted to believe him but she couldn't bring herself to trust. She couldn't trust him or the situation—not completely. She shouldn't have agreed to come back to River City with him. And she really shouldn't have agreed to come back to his condo.

But would it matter where they were? The killer had found them and was more determined than ever to kill her.

She shook her head.

He moved his hand, finally, but just from her lips. That big palm cupped her cheek. And he continued to lie partially on top of her, one heavy thigh covering both her legs, his muscled chest pushing against her breasts.

She didn't remember him being so big. He'd always been tall, but he was broader—with bulging muscles. He was a bodyguard now. The man she'd known and loved had been an artist—sensitive and moody. She wasn't sure who this man was. Yet her body didn't react as if he was a stranger. Despite his new muscular build, despite the years they'd been apart, her body recognized his. Her skin flushed with heat, and she began to tremble with desire.

He must have mistaken her trembling for fear, because he assured her again, "You're safe…"

She didn't feel safe. She felt betrayed—even by her own body. How could she want a man who had hurt her so badly? But she couldn't deny the desire building inside her. She wanted to kiss him, to touch him…

Her hands were trapped, though—beneath him. She couldn't move them. But she could feel his heat—his strength. He was strong, but he wasn't invincible.

"How can you say we're safe?" she asked. "You were nearly killed."

"I'm fine."

"You were hit."

He touched his fingertips to the cut on his chin. "It was just flying glass."

"It could have been a bullet." So many of them had been fired. She shuddered now as she thought of it, thought of how close she'd come to losing Milek. "You could have been killed…"

He shook his head. "I'm fine."

He didn't look fine. Dark circles rimmed his eyes. Stubble darkened his jaw. And that cut marred his chin. He must have seen the doubt in her eyes, because he chuckled. "Maybe I look like death," he said, "but I'm alive."

Those silver eyes darkened with emotion and his fingers stroked along her cheek. "And so are you…" His breath shuddered out on a ragged sigh of relief. "You're alive."

"Because of you," she said. And finally she was able to wriggle her hands around, so she slid them up his chest. "You risked your life for ours."

He shrugged those broad shoulders. "That's what bodyguards do."

She tensed beneath him. Of course it hadn't been personal. She was only another assignment to him. He would have risked his life for any other client. While she had been hiding the past year, he'd been willingly putting his life on the line for others.

"I can't believe you're a bodyguard," she mused.

"A lot of people can't," he said, his voice gruff with bitterness.

"Why not?" she asked. "You saved me and Michael from two attempts on our lives."

"A lot of people suspect a Kozminski to make attempts—not stop them."

She snorted. "A lot of people are idiots." And Stacy and Garek had never cared what those people thought. Milek had cared, though, and apparently he still did. Too much…

He laughed, though. Maybe in agreement, maybe just in amusement. "You're not an idiot," he said.

She wasn't always so sure about that.

"So why can't you believe I'm a bodyguard?" he asked.

"You never expressed any interest in it," she said. "Not like your art…"

Now he tensed and pulled away, rolling onto his back beside her. "My art never saved a life."

She wasn't so sure about that, either. She had seen his work and, while she was no expert, art critics had agreed the work was powerful. But he hadn't had a show for years—not since he'd broken their engagement. Maybe he didn't paint anymore.

"Thank you," she said. She couldn't remember if she had said that when he'd pulled open the door to the janitor's closet. He'd explained he had picked the lock because he hadn't been sure if it was she and Michael hiding inside or the killer. So while he'd assured her she was safe then—with him—he'd rushed her and Michael from the shot-up hotel. There hadn't been time to thank him then.

And during the drive in the vehicle he'd bought from the room service waiter, he'd been so focused on the road behind him—on making certain no one had followed them—she hadn't dared to speak. He probably wouldn't have been able to hear her anyway, since the rusted old truck had lacked a muffler. He'd bought it before looking at it, before he'd started walking her and Michael across the parking lot. He had been that desperate to get them away from the hotel and from that town. But the killer had already found them.

If Milek hadn't acted as quickly as he had...

She trembled as she thought of what would have happened to them all. The least she owed him was her gratitude. So she said it again now, "Thank you for protecting our son and me."

But *words* of gratitude didn't seem enough for his saving their lives, so she pushed herself up on her elbow and leaned over where he lay on his back next to her. And, giving in to the desire she could no longer deny, she pressed her mouth to his.

The minute their lips met she realized the mistake she'd made. While she'd wanted to kiss him, to touch him—he obviously didn't feel the same way. But then he never had or he wouldn't have broken their engagement.

His big body tensed even more than it had when she'd mentioned his art. He froze beside her...until she tried to pull away.

Then his fingers tangled in her hair as he held her head close to his. And he kissed her back. He kissed her thoroughly and passionately, his lips pressing tightly against hers before parting them. Then he slid his tongue into her mouth—tasting her, teasing her.

Desire overwhelmed her, and she moaned. She had missed him and not just the year she'd been dead. She had missed him all the years they'd been apart. But he wasn't back with her. He was only protecting her. He was only doing his job.

She needed to find her pride and pull away from him. But she'd missed him too much—because once she had loved him too much. And when he had broken their engagement, he'd nearly destroyed her. She had survived the attempts on her life and creating a new life more easily than she had survived losing Milek. Her heart began to pound, but not just with passion. She felt a fear nearly as intense as when those shots had been fired at her and Michael.

Because if she kept kissing Milek, it wasn't just her life that would be in danger; her heart would be, too.

His face flushed with anger and pain, Frank Campanelli stared into the mirror over the double sink in the spacious bathroom. He looked like hell and had nearly wound up there. During the first shoot-out, a bullet had grazed him. But the second one in the hotel parking lot hadn't. It had hit him. The son of a bitch had shot him.

Milek Kozminski.

Frank knew the name. Anyone who'd ever lived in or had passed through River City knew the name. The kid's old man and uncle were renowned jewel thieves. The old man had gunned down a cop and spent the rest of his life in prison. If Frank remembered right, the kids were killers, too. They'd just been too young at the time they had killed to do hard time. They'd also claimed they had only killed in self-defense.

Frank snorted. He doubted that. Milek Kozminski had taunted him in the parking lot. Then he'd shot him. He pressed his hand to the bandage on his shoulder. Blood was already seeping through the white gauze, and the flesh beneath it throbbed painfully.

"Don't touch it," the doctor advised. He straightened up from mopping Frank's blood off the marble tiles of the opulent bathroom.

They weren't in a hospital. Or even a clinic. The doctor had let him into his house—into his damn mansion—and patched him up in one of the bathrooms. Dr. Gunz wouldn't have had that mansion if Frank hadn't helped him out—hadn't taken care of a couple of witnesses in a potential career-ending lawsuit. So he owed Frank—like so many other people did.

That was why the doctor had taken care of Frank—because Frank had taken care of him. Now Frank had to take care of Milek Kozminski. He had made it a rule to only kill if he was getting paid for the hit. It was never personal for him. He never killed out of anger or passion.

Until now…

He wanted Milek Kozminski dead and not just so he could get to the little redheaded assistant district attorney. He wanted him dead because Kozminski had shot him. Despite his dangerous job, Frank had never been shot before. The only real danger he had faced was getting caught. But no one had ever come close—until Milek Kozminski in the hotel parking lot.

"You're lucky," the doctor said. "A few more inches and that bullet would have struck your heart. You're lucky to be alive."

Frank was lucky.

But Milek Kozminski wasn't. Frank wouldn't miss the next time he shot at the younger man. He would make sure he put a bullet right through Kozminski's heart.

A twinge of pain struck Milek's chest as he remembered how he'd spent the past year, thinking he would never see Amber again. That he would never be able to hold her. To kiss her…

And now she was here—in his arms, in his bed. Emotions overwhelmed him: relief, joy and passion. And love…

He had never stopped loving her. Even when he'd believed she was dead. His hands shook as he held her head, his fingers tangled in her hair. He moved his mouth over hers, deepening the kiss—parting her soft lips. He slid his tongue inside her mouth, tasting her sweetness.

She reached out, pressing a hand against his chest. But she wasn't pushing him away. She was caressing him, tracing his muscles through the thin material of his T-shirt. He wanted to take it off—wanted to take off her clothes, too.

He wanted nothing between them. No clothes. No secrets. No resentment or guilt.

The only thing he could realistically manage was to remove the clothes. He'd hurt her too much to expect anything more. He hadn't even expected her kiss. She'd meant it only as a thank-you, though.

Nothing more.

He knew that, but he couldn't summon his better judgment. It was gone. And he was barely hanging on to his control. He couldn't pull back. He had missed her too much and for far too long.

When he reached for her sweater and started lifting it up, she didn't stop him. Instead, she raised her arms so he could pull it up and over her head. Damn. She was beautiful—more beautiful than he'd even remembered. And he'd thought of her so often—like this. In his bed, her skin flushed with desire. Her breasts threatened to spill over the cups of her bra. They were fuller than he remembered. He reached behind her and released the clasp, setting them free. Then he touched them. With just his fingertips first, sliding them over the silkiness of her skin the way he sometimes slid them through paint on the canvas when he couldn't get just the effect he wanted with a brush.

But no matter how hard he'd worked on his art, he'd never created anything as beautiful as she was. Her nipples swelled and distended even before he brushed his thumbs across them. When he did that, she moaned and bit her lip. He leaned down and brushed his mouth over hers.

She parted her lips for him and her tongue darted out, across his lips. But he didn't deepen the kiss. Instead, he lowered his head to her breasts. He pressed kisses against the swells before closing his lips around one of those tight nipples.

A soft cry slipped through her lips, and she arched her back, pressing her breast against his mouth. He flicked his tongue over the point, teasing her.

She reached out and grasped his T-shirt again. Then she pushed her hands beneath it, sliding them over his chest and then lower when she reached for the buckle of his belt. His body tensed, his erection pressing painfully against his fly. He had to have her—had to be inside her.

It had been too long. So long that his need for her had built to a level of desperation.

Her hands trembled against his buckle, so he gently pushed them aside. And he stood up to deal with his clothes, pulling off the T-shirt and undoing the belt to drop his pants next to the bed. When he turned back to her, she'd done the same, so she lay naked before him.

"This is a bad idea," she murmured—almost as if she were talking only to herself.

But Milek knew it was a bad idea, too. She was in danger. He could afford no distractions. But the condo was safe. He and Garek had installed the highest tech security system available—one even they hadn't been able to crack. And his gun sat on the table next to the bed—within reach if he needed it.

He didn't need it.

He only needed her.

His voice gruff with desire, he forced himself to ask, "Do you want to stop?"

He regretted the question the minute he'd uttered it. He didn't want her to change her mind. He wanted her to want him as much as he wanted her.

She bit her lip again. Apparently she had changed her mind. Despite the tension painfully gripping his body, he forced himself to step back. He understood why she couldn't make love with him; she couldn't trust him—not after how badly he'd let her down.

But then she reached for him. Rising up on her knees on the mattress, she slid her arms around his neck and tugged his head down for her kiss. Her lips clung to his, nipping at them—teasing him until he opened his mouth. Then her little wet tongue slid inside, stroking over his.

He fought to hang on to his control so he wouldn't ravage her. But his body was tense to the point of breaking. He had to have her. *Now.*

But he wanted to know she was certain—that she wanted him as badly as he wanted her. So he kissed her back, sliding his tongue in and out of her mouth the way he wanted to slide his erection in and out of her body. He throbbed and pulsed, demanding release.

But he summoned patience. And tenderness.

He caressed her, trailing his fingertips along her shoulders and down her back to the sweet curve of her hips. They were fuller now than they'd once been. He found her even sexier.

She moved closer, rubbing her body against him. "Milek…"

He heard the desire in the break in her voice. She wanted him.

And her passion incited his even more. But he held tightly on to his control. And he made love to her slowly. He kissed every inch of her skin. Her lips, her cheeks, her throat…

She fell back against the bed and shifted against the sheets as he kissed her shoulders. Then her breasts…

He took his time, teasing her nipples. Moans slipped between her lips. And she reached for him again. But he moved away. If she touched him…

He might lose control.

And he wanted to please her instead. He moved his head lower, and he made love to her with his mouth. He kissed the slight mound between her legs. Then he flicked his tongue over the most sensitive part of her.

She arched off the mattress and shuddered. "Oooh…"

The taste of her passion overwhelmed him. He had to have her…

So, hand shaking, he fumbled in the bedside table for a condom. He rolled it on before moving between her legs again. Then he pushed gently inside her.

She writhed beneath him, struggling to get closer. Her legs lifted and wrapped around his waist. And she clutched at him with her hands, her nails nipping into the skin of his back.

Sweat beaded on his upper lip as he struggled for control, struggled to keep the rhythm slow and gentle—even while his body urged him to go fast and frantic. He slid in and out of her.

And his control slipped a bit with each light thrust. He moved inside her, pushing a little deeper. She arched and her inner muscles clutched at him.

He moved his hands, sliding them over her body. Reaching between them, he teased her nipples with his thumbs. Then he moved his hand lower, so that his thumb could stroke another part of her.

She clutched at him and panted for breath. Then a shudder rippled through her body, and he felt the hot rush of her orgasm. He slid slow and deep, prolonging her pleasure. Then, finally, the tension inside his body broke, and he took his own pleasure.

He cleaned up quickly before coming back to his bed. He'd been afraid she might have left it. But she lay in it yet—as if too satiated to move. That didn't mean he was welcome to join her. He'd been lucky she'd let him touch her at all after how he'd treated her five years ago.

He hesitated beside the bed. She opened her mouth. But he couldn't hear what she said because a sharp wail rent the silence—deafening in its intensity.

Her eyes—green again, since the dark contacts lay on

the table beside his gun—widened with fear. She raised her voice and asked, "What is that?"

She was already out of bed, already reaching for her clothes—while Milek had his gun clutched tightly in his hand.

"Fire alarm?" she asked.

"No." It was worse. So much worse. While he'd been distracted making love with her, someone had tried to breach the security system. What if they'd actually made it inside? It had to be a professional. Frank Campanelli?

Chapter 7

Just over a year ago, Stacy Kozminski-Payne had had hired killers trying to murder her. But that was over—it had all been a case of mistaken identity—her husband's for his twin brother. Once that had been cleared up, she had thought she would never find herself staring into the barrel of a loaded gun again.

She swallowed hard. Her own brother held this gun. She knew he'd been upset with her. But…

"Damn, Stacy!" he said as he pulled the gun away from her face. "I'm sorry."

She nodded.

"But what the hell are you doing here? How did you break in?"

Irritation flashed through her. He and their older brother, Garek, thought they were the only ones their father had taught the family trade. But he'd shown her, too—how to pick a lock. She probably wasn't as good as they were. Undoubtedly they would not have set off the alarm the way she had. She held up her lock pick kit before dropping it into her purse.

"You're lucky I didn't shoot you," he said. But he holstered the gun. He wore only the shoulder holster—no shirt. And his pants looked as though he'd pulled them on quickly and hadn't bothered with the button.

Then she looked beyond him—to the doorway to the master bedroom. A woman stood there. She had dark hair that was tangled around her face—a face Stacy had thought she would never see again.

That face was pale with fear; her eyes were wide with it, too. She had probably thought the person who'd made her run a year ago was who had broken into the condo.

A twinge of guilt struck Stacy's heart. Maybe she shouldn't have broken in. Her husband didn't even know she'd come here. He was with Garek and Candace—trying to track down Agent Rus. They thought he could explain everything.

"I called," Stacy told her brother. "And called and called. But you didn't answer." Her stomach churned with all the emotions she'd felt since her husband had told her about those empty graves. She was afraid, too, and angry and confused. "And you didn't return any of the voice mails I left you."

Milek shoved his hand into his hair. His hand shook slightly. He was obviously feeling all the things she was and probably much more.

She glanced at Amber again. Her friend was dressed. But her clothes were wrinkled—as if they'd been on the floor and had been hastily pulled back on.

Stacy remembered doing that herself—when she and

Logan had first gotten together. But Milek and Amber weren't together. After their breakup, they hadn't spoken to each other for years.

She wanted to ask about that. She wanted to ask all the questions burning in her mind. But what was in her heart—the heart that had ached for the past year—had compelled her to break into his condo. Unlike the others who'd thought Milek had taken Amber and their son and run, Stacy had known he would come home.

Just as he had when Garek had been in trouble…

If she and her brothers had learned anything from everything they'd gone through, it was that there was safety in numbers. The family was stronger when they worked together.

If only Amber had realized the same thing instead of going off on her own…

Instead of letting them all believe the worst.

She must have misread the situation between Milek and Amber. Maybe Amber had fallen asleep in her clothes. And Milek might have been in the shower. But his hair wasn't wet…

They couldn't have been together—because Stacy doubted Milek would ever be able to forgive Amber for letting him believe she and their son were dead. Amber was her best friend, but Stacy wasn't certain *she* would ever be able to forgive Amber.

"Aunt Stacy!" The shriek rang out from the other side of the condo—from the hall leading to the guest bedrooms. Then there was a flurry of movement as the little boy ran toward her. "Aunt Stacy!" He leaped onto her and flung his arms around her neck. "I missed you."

Tears stung her eyes. "I missed you, too, sweetheart." So much…

* * *

"She hates me," Amber said. She didn't blame Stacy, though. She hated herself for what she'd put her best friend through. Stacy had barely been able to look at her.

But Amber couldn't look at herself right now, either—not after what she'd done with Milek. What had she been thinking?

She hadn't been thinking—not at all. She'd only been feeling. So much desire...

Need.

For the past year she had felt so alone. So isolated. Maybe that was all she'd needed—human contact. Human closeness. And she had never felt as close to anyone as she'd felt to Milek—when they were making love.

She'd felt close. But she didn't think Milek had felt the same; she felt as if he'd held part of himself back, which she could understand if he was angry with her for faking her death. But she suspected he might have always held part of himself back from her.

He hadn't spoken to her since then or since Stacy had left the condo after tucking Michael back into bed. That entire time Milek had been on his cell, returning the voice mails the others had left him.

"You think she hates me, too," Amber concluded. That was probably why he hadn't replied—because he hadn't wanted to confirm her fear.

He was off his phone, so he must have heard her. Not that she had his full attention. Maybe she had none of it. He'd dressed. And now he reached for his leather jacket.

"Where are you going?" she asked. Fear constricted her heart.

"I need to meet with Rus," he said.

She shook her head. "You can't trust him. You can't trust anyone."

She wasn't certain she should even trust him. It had been a bad idea to come back to River City with him—for so many reasons. It was an even worse idea than making love with him had been.

"I have to talk to him," Milek said. "I think I might've hit Campanelli in the hotel parking lot."

She released a shaky breath. "It could be over…"

He shook his head. "Not until we find out who hired him."

Of course she knew that. The assassin who'd killed Gregory and was trying to kill her was only doing his job—a job someone else had hired him to do. Who?

She'd spent the past year pouring over old cases, trying to come up with more suspects for Agent Rus to investigate. But had he really investigated the names she'd given him?

She reached out to Milek, grasping his forearm. The muscles were rock hard beneath her fingers. "Please…"

"You'll be safe here," he said, mistaking her fear for her own safety instead of his.

She was scared of being left alone in the condo, though. She was scared for her son's safety more than her own. Because someone wanted her dead, he was in danger, too. It wasn't fair; he was an innocent child.

"How can you say that?" she asked him. "After Stacy broke in…"

"I'm not leaving you alone."

A noise sounded from the security panel—just a soft buzz, no piercing siren this time. And the heavy metal door slid open to another Kozminski.

Only a year had passed since she'd seen him last, but

Garek looked different to her. Like Milek, he was more muscular, but there was something newer than the muscles. There was a happiness about him that even his current concerns couldn't hide. Then she noted the wedding band on his finger.

Garek—the consummate playboy—had gotten married? She couldn't believe it. Milek had been engaged before him—before his sister—but he was the only unmarried Kozminski.

Because he'd broken their engagement...

Garek spared her only the briefest of glances before focusing on his brother. "You still have a hell of a lot of explaining to do."

She was the one who'd caused all the problems. Not Milek. She opened her mouth to defend him, but Milek was already replying.

"I brought you up to speed on the phone," he told his brother. "Now I have to see if Rus found out anything new."

"Have him come here, then," Garek suggested.

"No." The word slipped out of Amber's lips. She didn't want Agent Rus near her and Michael—not until she knew for certain he hadn't betrayed her to Campanelli. "And you shouldn't go see him alone."

Milek shook his head. "You're wrong about Nick Rus."

Garek nodded his agreement. "Nick's a good guy."

The Kozminskis probably trusted him because the FBI agent was related to the Paynes. But he hadn't been raised with them. He'd just shown up in River City right before Gregory had been killed. Was that just a coincidence?

"I'll be fine," Milek said.

She wasn't sure if he was assuring her of that or his

brother. Despite his happiness, Garek looked worried. She must have, too.

Milek stepped closer to her and started to lift his hand. But then he pulled it back to his side and shoved it into his pocket. "You'll be safe here," he promised her.

Maybe she and Michael would be safe. But what about Milek?

Milek waited until the condo door slid closed behind him before releasing the breath he'd held. Turning white, it hung in the air in front of him. The night was cold—leaving dawn with a thin sheen of frost coating the ground and every asphalt, concrete and brick surface.

There was no grass here, in the old industrial area of River City where Milek had reclaimed the abandoned warehouse and converted it into his home. Where would a little boy play here?

Not that he would be able to play outside—not with someone wanting the little boy's mother dead. They might use the kid to get to her. To coerce her to leave his protection…

He wasn't doing the greatest job of protecting her, though. He was damn lucky Stacy was the one who'd broken in earlier and not Campanelli.

Maybe Campanelli was incapacitated. He couldn't have been that close to the man and had every shot miss. Milek was a better marksman than that.

But even if he'd taken out Campanelli, there would be more—someone else hired to finish the job he'd failed to do. Someone wanted Amber dead. And to ensure her safety Milek had to take out that person, not a man already considered a ghost.

He lifted the collar of his coat, pulling it up so it protected his neck and jaw from the bite of the cold air. It was early. The sky was just beginning to lighten before the sun would rise.

Winter wasn't quite done yet. It hung stubbornly on in Michigan—outstaying its short welcome like an unwanted houseguest.

While Garek had lived with him for a while, Milek had never had houseguests. Until now.

But Amber wasn't unwanted. She was wanted. Too much.

When she'd been so upset over Stacy's refusal to speak to her, Milek had wanted to offer Amber comfort. But he knew what would happen if he touched her again. He would want her again. Hell, he already wanted her again.

Garek was right. He could have had Rus come to him. He could have even called the federal agent. But Milek had needed to get some distance between him and Amber—especially after they'd made love.

He needed to get his feelings back under control—needed to remind himself of all the reasons they could never be together again.

He couldn't be selfish. He had to do what was best for her. At the moment what was best for her was for Milek to keep her and Michael alive.

The battered pickup he'd driven from up north was parked in the garage section at the back of the warehouse. He'd brought Amber and Michael in through there to keep them safe. He had other vehicles parked back there, too, but he took Garek's instead. The black SUV was parked at the curb and already warmed up, so he punched in the code on the door and jumped inside.

Reaching under the seat, he found the key and shoved it into the ignition.

With his collar up, maybe whoever was watching him would mistake him for Garek. They weren't twins like Logan and Parker, but they looked enough alike that from a distance they could be mistaken for each other.

And Milek had no doubt someone was watching him. He could *feel* it just as he'd felt Campanelli's presence in the hotel parking lot.

It could have been him. After all, he'd told the man his name. But it wouldn't be easy to track Milek to the condo. The deed was in the name under which he'd used to paint—the name he'd incorporated years ago. *Koz.* But Campanelli had the same connections he and Garek had; maybe he had been able to find someone who knew where Milek lived.

Was Campanelli alive, though?

Milek hadn't seen his body in the parking lot. But that didn't mean he'd survived their skirmish. He could have died later.

Milek hoped not. He was worried the only way they might learn who'd hired him was from the man himself. He couldn't be dead. Not yet...

He glanced into the rearview mirror and noticed the lights on the street behind him. It was too early for there to be much traffic—especially in this area of the city. His was one of the only occupied buildings now.

His instincts were right again. Someone was following him. It really could have been anyone—any member of his well-meaning family. When he'd returned their frantic voice mails, they had all expressed the same concern— not just for Amber and the little boy but for him, as well. They were worried he would get hurt.

And probably not just physically.

That was why Stacy had been so cold to her best friend. Because she loved him so much. He needed to tell his sister the truth—he'd always known the little boy was his—even though Gregory Schievink had tried to claim paternity. Along with mourning her best friend, Stacy had also been racked with guilt that she'd kept a secret from him.

Apparently Amber had told her that she hadn't wanted Milek to come back to her because she was pregnant; she wanted him to come back because he loved her. So she'd vowed Stacy to secrecy. That had been a lie, though. She'd told him and he'd rejected her.

Had she lied out of pride? Or to protect him?

If his family knew he'd never claimed his child, they wouldn't understand. They didn't know what he was capable of—they didn't know the darkness he battled to keep at bay. The anger he could sometimes barely contain.

He felt that anger now, as the lights grew closer. Every Payne Protection bodyguard was better than this at tailing someone. He wouldn't have noticed them so quickly, and they wouldn't have gotten so sloppy as to get too close.

But then the other vehicle got even closer—as the truck nudged his back bumper. The seat belt snapped at his neck and chest, and a curse slipped through his lips.

He was alone. Surely the person had seen him get into the vehicle by himself. Amber was the one Campanelli wanted. Not him.

Unless he figured he needed to get rid of Milek so he'd be able to get to her...

He wasn't wrong.

The only way someone would hurt Amber was after Milek was gone. He jerked the wheel and turned sharply onto another street. Tires squealed as the other vehicle followed the SUV. Milek knew this area well. He could lose his tail here.

If he wanted to…

He'd rather turn the tables, though. So he turned again—purposely down a dead-end alleyway. He wouldn't be able to drive out. But he knew the area well. He could escape easily on foot—once he'd gotten a good look and maybe a shot at whoever was after him.

But he'd only just opened the driver's door when the truck turned into the alley, the lights shining at him—blinding him. Before he could focus, he heard the truck door open. Then gunfire erupted.

If it was Frank Campanelli, he wasn't carrying some revolver with a silencer on it. This was an automatic weapon firing so many bullets that Milek knew at least one was likely to hit him.

Would he survive? Or would he leave Amber and their son without his protection, without ever professing his love?

Chapter 8

She could have gone to bed. After his eventful evening, Michael was certain to sleep in until late morning. And it was barely dawn now. But Amber knew sleep would elude her. And she hadn't wanted to go into the master bedroom with Garek there—watching her so stoically. While he hadn't said anything to her yet, she suspected he would have then. And she probably wouldn't have wanted to hear it.

So she busied herself in the kitchen. Not that Milek had much food for her to prepare. His refrigerator and cupboards were nearly bare. Maybe he didn't spend much time at home. He had coffee, though. So she'd made that. And she'd scrounged up some old baking supplies. She refused to consider how old the sugar and flour might have been as she worked on a coffee cake. Baking had become almost therapeutic for her the past year, much to Michael's enjoyment and her chagrin. She'd put on some pounds. But Milek hadn't seemed to mind, when he'd looked at her, when he'd touched her...

Her skin heated and tingled as she remembered his caresses. His kisses...

She'd been right; it had been a bad idea to make love with him. Because now she couldn't lie to herself that she'd exaggerated how good it had been between them...

She knew it was better than good; it was incredible. And now it would be even harder for her to fight her desire for him. Maybe he'd felt the same way; maybe that was why he'd left.

Surely Rus couldn't be at his office yet. So where had Milek really been going?

Something beeped, and she glanced to the oven. But it wasn't warm enough yet for her to put the cake inside. Then she heard Garek's deep voice and realized the noise had been his phone.

"Hey..." There was that happiness she'd seen in his eyes and on his face; it was in his voice now along with love. She had no doubt the caller was his wife—then he cursed. "No! God, no!"

Another reason she hadn't tried to sleep was because of the fear she'd had over Milek going off alone. She'd known he was in danger—that helping her had put him in danger. She knew that fear had been realized before she even asked, "What? What is it?"

Garek spared her a glance, his silver eyes as hard and cold as steel. Stacy might not hate her, but Garek definitely did. Then he went back to ignoring her and told his caller, "I know you will. I know. But be careful. And know that I love you."

It had definitely been his wife on the phone. And he

was just as worried about her as Amber was Milek. He clicked off the cell and gripped it in a shaking hand.

"What is it?" she asked again, her voice cracking with the emotion overwhelming her. "What happened?"

His face flushed with anger, and he replied, "Someone just tried to kill my brother."

Panic pressed on her heart, but she forced herself to stay calm—to focus on the word he'd used. "Tried?" she repeated. He wasn't dead. He couldn't be dead. "Is he all right?"

Garek's eyes narrowed as he directed his anger at her. "What do you care if he is?"

"I care." More than she should have—more than was safe for the heart he'd already broken. But she didn't regret making love with him. She was glad that she had.

Garek released a shaky breath and finally relented. He must have heard the genuine emotion in her voice, which had cracked as tears threatened.

She blinked them back and studied his face—his handsome face that looked so much like his brother's. But Milek had never looked as happy as Garek had earlier, not even when they'd been engaged. Maybe he really hadn't loved her.

Maybe it had all been one-sided.

"Candace..." Despite the tense situation, his voice softened as he said the name. This was the woman he loved. "Was following Milek when someone forced him into an alley. Shots rang out. She's trying to find him."

She couldn't hold back the tears now. "So you don't know if he's hurt or worse. You don't know..."

Garek stepped around the island in the kitchen and pulled her into his arms. "I know," he said. "I know Milek's okay. He's smart and tough. He's okay."

Amber didn't know if he was trying to convince her or himself. He wasn't entirely certain his brother had survived. And if he hadn't…

Michael would never know his father. And she would never know if Milek had ever loved her…

Candace's heart ached for the concern and fear she'd heard in her husband's voice when she'd called to report the shooting. Maybe she should have waited until she'd known for certain what had happened to his brother. But she knew he'd want the news immediately—even if it wasn't good. Or it wasn't complete.

She had no idea what the hell had happened—why Milek would have turned into the dead-end alley. He knew this area of the city better than anyone. Unless he'd thought he could trap the shooter.

She'd tried. Her SUV was parked behind the truck, her windshield cracked from the bullets fired into it. She had ducked low to avoid getting shot, so she hadn't seen where either man had gone.

The driver's doors of both vehicles stood open. Her gun clutched tightly, the barrel with the light on it in front of her, Candace inspected the alley. There were spent shells everywhere.

But no bodies. No blood…

How could so many shots have been fired but nobody hit? She touched her own face—surprised she hadn't taken a bullet herself. Then a gun cocked near her, and she worried she might be about to.

"Damn it!" the man cursed, his deep voice vibrating with anger.

Candace's breath shuddered out in relief and she whirled toward her brother-in-law. "Thank God you're all right." She holstered her gun and reached for her cell phone.

Milek gripped his weapon tightly, swinging it around the alley as if ready to shoot at shadows. Could the man who'd tried to kill him be hiding in those shadows? Was he close yet?

Instead of calling Garek, she texted: Found him.

Technically he'd found her. He must have been hiding in those shadows, too. She looked at him but could see no gunshot wounds. He hadn't been hit.

She texted: He's not hurt.

"What the hell are you doing?" he asked. He wasn't hurt but he was certainly irritated.

"Letting Garek know that you're okay," she said.

"I heard you call him," he said. "You shouldn't have done that."

"Garek and I don't have any secrets," she said. Not anymore.

"The shooter could have heard you, too," Milek pointed out. "You shouldn't have even been here!"

"You honestly thought we'd let you go out alone?" she asked. "Unprotected?"

He snorted. "Of course not. At first I thought he was one of you…"

She would have been insulted—had she not been so happy he was unharmed.

"Did you see him?" she asked.

He shook his head. "It was probably Frank Campanelli." He glanced around again as if saying the man's name might have summoned him.

"We need to get out of here," she said as she led him back toward her SUV.

He pointed at the shattered windshield. "You're lucky you didn't get shot."

"He just fired a round at me—to keep me in my vehicle," she surmised. "You were the one he was trying to kill." She shuddered as she remembered all the shots fired. "You're the lucky one."

Milek didn't feel very damn lucky. If he hadn't dived behind the Dumpster, he probably would have been killed. If Candace hadn't showed up as backup...

Campanelli—or whoever had been in that alley—probably would have stayed until he'd made certain Milek was dead. While he appreciated the backup, Milek worried Candace could have been killed, too.

He had to end this before he—or someone he cared about—wound up dead. He pushed open the door to Rus's office, stepped inside and swung it shut behind him with such force that it slammed.

"What the hell!" Rus exclaimed as he jumped behind his desk.

His jaw was dark with stubble and his hair mussed. Milek doubted he'd gone home or gotten any sleep. "You look like hell," he remarked.

"Ditto," Rus said. "You look like someone's been trying to kill you."

"Someone has," Milek agreed. But he was certain Rus knew as much about those attempts as he did. Milek wanted to know more. "I need to know everything you know about the case. I need to see the official report about Schievink's murder and whatever notes you wrote down about the attempt on Amber last year."

Rus's chair creaked as he leaned back. "Why?" he asked. "You're not a detective."

"I'm not an idiot," Milek said. "I can read a damn report." He'd read the one about the desecrated graves easily enough.

"I hope you're not an idiot," Rus said as if he had his doubts.

Milek hadn't slept and he'd been shot at so many times that his hold on his temper had frayed. His hand curled into a fist, and he nearly reached for the other man. "What the hell—"

"You wouldn't be the only one," Rus said. "I might be an idiot, too." Now the detective was all self-recrimination.

Milek sighed. "Campanelli's a pro. Don't beat yourself up about his finding her or following you to the hotel." The hit man had been around a long time; he knew what he was doing to kill and not get caught.

"Campanelli is a pro," Rus agreed. "So why'd he shoot at you?"

Milek shrugged. "I'm in his way."

"But you're not," Rus said. "You weren't with her when he shot at you just a little while ago."

No. But he should have been. With Campanelli determined to kill her, Milek shouldn't have trusted her protection to anyone else. But Garek was his big brother. His idol. Garek had never let him down in the past, and he knew he wouldn't now. His brother would keep Amber and Michael safe.

Milek shrugged again. "So what are you getting at?"

Rus pushed his hands through his already tousled hair; it looked as if he'd done that before—more than once. And his jaw was clenched so tightly a muscle twitched beneath the dark stubble on his cheek. He gestured at the cell phone sitting on his desk. "That's been blowing up ever since the news learned Amber's alive."

"And?"

"The interim DA gave me a call," he said.

Milek wasn't surprised. The woman was lobbying to be elected to the position she'd only been temporarily filling. She'd want to know enough about the case to issue a press release.

"But what's bothering you?" he asked.

Rus tossed a report across his desk. "Amber..."

She'd been bothering Milek for years, but now that they'd made love again, it was worse. He couldn't get her out of his mind. And his body tensed every time he remembered how amazing it had been between them—like coming home.

That was why he'd had to leave. Because he'd known if he'd stayed, he would have wanted to make love to her again. That he would have needed to be with her.

"Why is she bothering you?" he asked. Had she and the special agent been involved a year ago? Was that why she had turned to him when she'd been in danger?

Jealousy twisted his stomach into knots. But he had no right to that reaction. He was the one who'd broken their engagement—who'd walked away from her.

"Because I'm not so sure she's the victim I thought she was," Rus admitted.

"You were there," Milek reminded him. "You saw the Ghost shoot at the van and run her and Michael off the road. He tried to kill her."

Rus nodded. "Now..."

"And a year ago," Milek said. "You matched the shells you found at the scene to the gun that killed the DA. You even said one of Campanelli's prints was on one of the shells."

"Doesn't that seem convenient to you?"

Beyond exhausted, Milek dropped into one of the chairs in front of Rus's desk. "Sloppy."

"But if Campanelli was sloppy," the FBI agent said, "he would have been caught before now."

"Arrogant." Milek suspected that was more the case with the Ghost. He believed his own hype—believed he was untouchable.

"Maybe," Rus said, but it was a begrudging admission. He obviously had another opinion.

So Milek asked for it. "What do you think?"

"When Schievink got gunned down, I looked at Amber as a suspect."

"What?"

"She would have taken over his job until the next election."

"So you think she hired Campanelli so she could take over as DA?" Milek laughed. "That makes no sense. She faked her death and went into hiding for the past year. She lost everything that mattered to her." Everything but Michael. And maybe he was all that mattered.

"Maybe she knew I was looking at her," Rus said, "and that's why she called only me about the shooting."

Milek's stomach began to knot. "So you're saying she went into hiding to avoid suspicion?"

"It worked."

"She won't get Schievink's job now. She's been gone too long. So why come out of hiding now?"

Rus shrugged. "Maybe Campanelli turned on her. Maybe he's been blackmailing her."

Milek snorted. "You're reaching. It's all too ridiculous. Amber was ambitious." That was one reason why he'd broken their engagement, so his reputation wouldn't damage her career and hold her back from all that she could have accomplished. She would have become DA without needing to kill anyone. "But what you're suggesting is absurd."

"Then maybe it wasn't about ambition."

"Why else would she kill her boss?"

"Because she was involved with him," Rus said. "Everyone believed they were having an affair."

Even Milek...

"Maybe she killed Schievink out of revenge," Rus said. "Maybe that's why Campanelli tried to kill you this morning. Maybe she wants you dead, too."

Milek laughed, but it echoed hollowly in Rus's office. "She needs to hire a new hit man, then," Milek said, "since he's been trying to kill her, too."

"Trying," Rus said. "But she hasn't been hit."

Milek shook his head. "You're wrong about her. You're all wrong. She would never put Michael's safety at risk." That was why she'd given up her career and her home and gone into hiding for the past year. For their son.

Not to avoid suspicion.

"I hope you're right," Rus said. "For my sake, but most especially for yours."

"I'm right," Milek insisted.

But Rus gave him only a pitying glance. "I wish like hell I had never told you she was alive."

"I would have found out," Milek said. "Just like everyone else has." And then he wouldn't have stopped himself from reaching for Rus and pounding on him.

"But you might not have been in the middle of it," Rus said. "You might not have been in danger."

It wouldn't have mattered when or how he'd found out. He wouldn't have stayed away from Amber when he'd learned she was alive.

"And you are in danger," Rus said.

"It's not the first time." He'd had some close scrapes helping Garek with the assignment he'd tackled for Rus.

"Campanelli is a pro," Rus said. "Until Amber, no one has ever survived a hit he's been hired to carry out."

Maybe that was another reason the special agent had become suspicious of her. Milek wished Rus had kept his doubts to himself. While he didn't believe she would put their son in danger, he hadn't needed to be reminded of her involvement with her late boss.

But even if the rumors were true and they'd been involved, she wasn't responsible for his murder. If she had ever considered hiring a hit man, Milek would have been dead five years ago—for breaking their engagement, for not acknowledging his son.

No. Amber wasn't the one who wanted Milek dead. But someone did. So now not only did he have to keep her safe, he had to protect himself. His life and his heart.

Chapter 9

Was he lying to her?

Amber studied Garek as he sipped his coffee, washing down a bite of the cake she'd made. "If he's all right," she said, "why isn't he back?"

"He left here to talk to Agent Rus," Garek reminded her. "That's what he's doing."

He'd been on the phone again. She'd thought his wife had called again. But maybe it had been Rus.

"But he was shot at," she said.

"And who better than Rus to take the report?" Garek asked. "You went to him when your house got shot at…"

And he'd turned her life upside down. Sure, he'd offered alternatives. He'd told her to talk to the Paynes, to get the family of bodyguards to protect her. But all she'd been able to think about had been how close her son had come to getting shot. She hadn't been willing to trust his safety even to her best friend's husband. And she hadn't believed Michael's father would help her.

But ever since he'd learned about the danger, Milek had put his life at risk to protect her and their son.

"I'm not so sure going to Rus was the right decision," she admitted. Her hand shaking, she set down her coffee cup. The last thing she needed was more caffeine. She was already anxious enough.

Good thing Michael was sleeping late.

"Your mistrust is mutual," Garek shared.

"What?" She had done nothing wrong. No matter how many people were mad at her she didn't regret the choice she'd made to protect her son. "Why?"

"He thinks you know more about your boss's murder than you've admitted."

"I told him everything I know. I gave him a list of suspects." Because of the volume of cases Gregory had handled himself or with her assistance, that list had been long.

"One name was conspicuously missing from that list."

She'd forgotten someone? Hope flickered. Maybe Rus had figured out who'd hired the hit man. "Who?"

"You."

She laughed. "That's ridiculous. I didn't want Gregory dead." He had been her mentor as well as her boss. He'd wanted the best for her. "Why would Rus think that? He didn't a year ago."

"He had some suspicions then," Garek said. "But then your house got shot at. And he didn't know the whole story."

"What whole story?" She was missing something—something that had Garek looking at her as he had previously, with anger and suspicion.

"That you were having an affair with your boss."

It wasn't the first time she'd heard the gossip. Anytime a man and woman worked together, people probably speculated—especially when those people were jealous of the cases she'd been given. The only thing she'd done to earn the assignments had been her job.

She uttered a weary sigh. She hadn't missed River City—and not just because of the danger. She hadn't missed the rumors that had been viciously spread about her.

"I was never involved with Gregory." He'd hinted he was attracted to her—on both a physical and emotional level. But she'd shut him down quickly.

While she'd had a serious boyfriend in college and another in law school, there was only one man she had ever loved: Milek Kozminski.

But she had respected her boss. He'd been brilliant and ambitious. And if he hadn't been murdered, she had no doubt he would have become the governor. That had been one of his goals. She suspected the White House had probably been another.

Maybe she should have been grateful it had never come to that. A political campaign would have no doubt dredged up all those vicious rumors—the kind everyone believed no matter how much she'd denied it.

"I always figured that was why Milek broke your engagement," Garek said. "Because you cheated on him with your boss."

Now she gasped. Could Milek have believed the rumors? When he'd broken up with her, she'd asked him why he hadn't wanted to marry her, but he'd never really answered her. He'd claimed he'd made a mistake to have ever proposed, and he'd apologized.

But he'd never explained...

If he'd thought she was cheating, why would *he* have apologized? She'd just figured he hadn't loved her—that he had never loved her.

But she had loved him. "I never would have cheated on Milek!"

Garek didn't look convinced. "You're ambitious," he said.

"I work hard."

"Sometimes hard work isn't enough to get you where you want to be," he said.

"It's not," she agreed. She'd worked hard at her relationship with Milek—trying to get him to open up to her. But she'd lost him. She'd worked hard the past year to figure out who wanted her dead like the DA, but she hadn't come any closer to learning who'd hired Frank Campanelli.

"So maybe it was easier having Schievink killed than waiting for the next election to run for his job..."

A whoosh of air echoed her gasp of surprise. And she turned to see that Milek had opened the door and stepped inside the condo. His silver eyes had gone stormy gray with anger. He looked furious. But she didn't know if his anger was directed at his brother or her.

"We've already made our deal," Chekov said as Nick settled into the chair across the metal table from him. "If you keep visiting, I might think you're developing a crush on me, Agent Rus."

"I keep visiting," Nick replied, "because you're not telling me everything you know."

Chekov lifted his arms as far as the chains shackling

him to the table allowed. "I've held up my end of our little arrangement."

"And I've held up mine," Nick said. "Your daughter is getting the help she needs." But Nick wasn't sure that what was wrong with Tori Chekov could ever be fixed. She was a cold-blooded killer, and he would make certain she was never free again.

"So our business is done." Chekov lifted his arms and gestured at the guard, dismissing Rus as if he was still in charge. For years the man had ruthlessly ruled an organized crime family.

"I thought you were a changed man," Nick remarked. "Capable of doing the right thing now."

Chekov chuckled. "I've only been in here a couple of months. You think I'm already reformed?"

From the crimes he'd confessed to Nick, Chekov was as cold-blooded a killer as his daughter. Nick doubted it was possible for the mobster to ever change. So maybe he'd wasted his time coming here. He started to stand.

But Chekov waved him back into his chair. "I may not be reformed, but I am actually beginning to like you, Special Agent Nicholas Rus."

Nick's blood chilled. Sometimes just the way the man said his name felt like a threat. But he'd promised no retribution for Nick trying to take him down. Could a cold-blooded killer ever be trusted?

"It must be all our visits," Nick remarked. "I'm starting to grow on you."

The old mobster chuckled. "I sure as hell hope not. I don't need to stink like a fed."

And maybe that was why Chekov refused to give up any information about anyone but himself. He'd confessed to his crimes. But he hadn't given up any other criminals. He was old-school, so he probably didn't want anyone to think he was a narc.

"Despite my stench, you like me," Nick reminded him.

"Maybe *like* was overstating my feelings," Chekov said, backpedaling.

Nick felt his opportunity to get information from the mobster slipping away.

Then Chekov said, "I respect you."

And to an old-school mobster like Viktor Chekov, respect was more important than liking. He would put up with someone he hated if he respected him.

He chuckled. "You're the only one who had the balls to take me on."

"Garek did," Nick said, although maybe he shouldn't have reminded him. But maybe that was why Chekov wouldn't help him. "The Kozminskis—"

"Aren't in law enforcement," Chekov said. "They're like me. Scrappers. You're the only fed who had the balls to try to take me down."

He was pushing his luck again but Nick couldn't resist adding, "I didn't just try. I did it."

Instead of being offended, Chekov chuckled again. "Yes, you did. You found my Achilles' heel."

His daughter. Again, that had been more the Kozminskis' doing than his. But for some reason everyone had given Rus the credit. Chekov knew the truth, though. Maybe that was why he didn't care Milek Kozminski was in danger.

"What do you want for her?" Nick asked. That was the only reason Chekov would talk—for his daughter. Nick would have to concede something. While he never intended for her to get out of the lockdown unit of the psychiatric hospital, he could offer her some small comfort.

"The best."

"She's in the highest rated facility that would accept someone who's killed."

Chekov nodded. "But the best shrink isn't there. I have someone I want her to see. I'll pay for the doctor's services. I just need for you to authorize the visits."

"I'll have to check him out," Nick said. And make sure it wasn't someone Chekov had hired to help his daughter escape.

"Her," Chekov said. "I think that's Tori's problem. She never had a mother figure in her life."

Nick hadn't had a real mother figure. And he'd had no father at all, at least not that he'd known about, but he hadn't become a killer. He refrained from pointing that out, though. "I'll check her out, then."

"So you'll consider it?"

He nodded.

"Are you here about the Ghost again?"

Nick moved his head in another nod. Last time Chekov had conceded to give him a description of the man, since the only mug shot taken of the guy had been during an arrest in his adolescence. That was how Nick had recognized him as the driver of the sedan following Amber's minivan.

"You won't find him," Chekov warned him. "He's called the Ghost for a reason."

"I know where he is," Nick said.

Chekov arched a gray brow. "If that were so, I doubt you would have bothered with this little visit of ours."

"He's in River City," Nick said.

Chekov sucked in a breath. "He's come back?"

"He tried to kill Milek Kozminski today."

"Milek?" Chekov asked, and both brows arched with

his surprise. "I could understand someone hiring a hit on Garek. But Milek…"

He was the good brother. The nice brother. Everyone still thought he was a criminal and a killer, but they liked him. No one didn't.

"You don't know why someone would want him dead?"

Chekov shook his head.

Nick voiced Milek's theory aloud. "Would Campanelli kill him just to get him out of his way?"

Chekov laughed at the thought. "The Ghost won't kill anyone for free."

That was what Nick had thought. Someone else wanted Milek dead. Amber?

"What do you know about the hit on the DA?"

"You asked me that before," Chekov said.

Solving that case was even more important to Nick than taking down Chekov had been. The crime boss had been curiously reluctant to talk about it, though.

"But we have a deal now," Nick reminded him.

"And my answer hasn't changed."

"You really don't know anything about Schievink?"

"I didn't say that," Chekov replied. "I just don't know who ordered the hit."

Maybe Nick had failed to ask the right questions the last time they'd talked. "What do you know about Schievink?"

"He was an ambitious man."

"Corrupt?"

"He was an ambitious man," Chekov repeated. "Ambitious men will often do whatever it takes to get ahead." He would know. The man had had no compunction about killing to get what he'd wanted. Neither had his daughter.

"And Amber Talsma?" Nick asked. "How ambitious

is she?" According to the interim DA, even more ambitious than Schievink had been.

Chekov shrugged. "Like I told you last time, I don't know that name."

"Schievink's assistant," Nick said. "The one who worked with him the most." Her former colleague had had suspicions about why Amber had been given all the best cases.

"The redheaded lawyer?"

Nick nodded.

"I heard Schievink was doing her, too." So even he had heard the rumors.

"What else had you heard about her?" Nick asked. "Was she corrupt?"

He shrugged. "If they were as close as everyone thinks they were, wouldn't she be?" Chekov asked. "Why else would she have looked the other way?"

Nick had nearly let Milek get to him earlier that day—with his rational defense of Amber. Of course she wouldn't have willingly put her own son in danger. Even men like Chekov cared about their kids.

But Amber wasn't as innocent as Milek thought she was. So Nick had been right to warn his new friend. He didn't want the guy risking his life or his heart on a woman who couldn't be trusted.

"Do you believe it?" she asked.

Milek glanced up from his son's bed. He'd just tucked in the little boy after spending most of the day playing with him. "I know I'm his father." Gregory claiming her baby as his had given him momentary doubts, though. Just as Rus had tried to do earlier. But after the baby had been born, Milek had gotten a look at him, and he'd known.

She shook her head. "I wasn't talking about Michael."

He rose from his crouch next to the boy's bed and barely resisted patting his head. He wanted to—but he didn't want to risk waking the boy. It had been a long day for him—of reacquainting himself with Aunt Stacy and getting to know Uncle Garek. His son still didn't know what to call him.

Still didn't know that Milek was his father.

Because he didn't want to wake the boy, he waited to speak until they'd left his room. Exhausted from his sleepless night, he dropped onto the couch. He would sleep there tonight. He wouldn't risk making love with her again—wouldn't risk falling for her again.

"We need to talk about Michael," Milek said. That conversation was five years overdue. It had been easier to believe Schievink, to accept her baby was her boss's rather than acknowledge his own paternity—even after he'd seen the child. Despite knowing the truth, he'd tried to deny it. He wasn't any more cut out to be a father than his father had been. Hell, he was worse. Patek Kozminski hadn't really ever killed anyone. Like Garek, he'd gone to prison for a crime he hadn't committed.

She nodded. "Yes, we do. But I want to talk about what your brother said—that I'm a suspect in Gregory's death. Do you believe it?"

"No." Despite Rus's efforts, he had no doubts.

She studied his face, though, as if searching for suspicion. "But you believe the rest of the rumors—that we were involved?"

His stomach began to churn with the jealousy that had eaten away at it five years ago. "Yes."

"How could you?" she asked. "You—of all people—should know better than to listen to gossip. With everything said about your family, you should have no use for rumors."

"I didn't," he said. "I heard it directly from the horse's mouth."

"I never told you…" Her eyes widened with shock as realization dawned. "Oh…"

"Yup," he said. "Good ole Gregory told me the two of you were in love, but he couldn't leave his wife yet."

"Is—is that why you broke our engagement?" she asked. "How could you believe him? How could you think that I would cheat on you? Did you know me at all?"

He'd known her. But he'd known himself better. And he hadn't trusted he wouldn't hurt her even more eventually—if he stayed with her. "Schievink didn't tell me that until after we'd broken up." That was when he'd summoned Milek to his fancy mansion—to show him everything he could offer Amber.

Her brow furrowed. "I don't understand why he would lie to you."

He could have told her what Schievink had said before the breakup, pointing out how her association with the Kozminskis would damage her career. But that had been the truth. Amber had just brought up all the horrible rumors herself. "He knew you'd told me you were pregnant, and he wanted me to know the baby was his."

With a hissing sound, her breath slipped out between her lips. "That son of a bitch," she said. "If I'd known that, I may have hired someone to kill him."

He chuckled at her reaction. Rus didn't know her at all.

Then she tilted her head as she stared at him. And he saw the suspicion in her narrowed green eyes. He was so glad she'd stopped wearing the contacts. But she didn't need a disguise anymore. Everyone knew she was alive—especially whoever wanted to kill her.

He shook his head. "If I'd wanted Schievink dead, I wouldn't have waited five years to do it." But he had momentarily lost his temper that day when he'd struck the man. Gregory had used that lapse of control against Milek, to point out that he was dangerous—too dangerous to be around Amber and her child.

"I wish you'd told me what he said."

He shrugged. "I thought you knew."

"You really thought I was involved with him?"

"What reason would he have had to lie?" Milek asked. "Married men usually don't go around admitting to affairs at all. But why would he admit to one he wasn't even having?"

Her face grew pale, and she trembled slightly. "You don't believe me."

He didn't want to believe her; he wanted a reason to keep his distance—at least emotionally—from her. "I don't know what to believe anymore," he said. "For the past year I thought you and our son were dead, but that was all a lie, too."

"You know why…"

Because she'd been scared and she hadn't thought he would help her. He'd pushed her away five years ago so well that it could have cost her and their son their lives. If Campanelli had gone after them sooner…

Before Milek had learned the truth.

He wanted to stand up, wanted to close his arms around her and give her the comfort they both needed. But he knew he'd wind up making love to her again. "I need to sleep." He said it to convince himself more than her.

"I thought you wanted to talk about Michael," she said.

He did. He wanted to figure out what to tell his son—what she wanted to tell their son. Michael obviously didn't know Milek was his father. He wanted to tell him. But was that fair? What kind of father would Milek be?

Not the one the boy deserved.

He shook his head. "Not yet…"

"You're tired," she said, as if excusing his reluctance. "You can take your bed."

"No." He pointed at the door. "I need to be out here—in case someone tries to get in." And he wasn't talking about his family.

Frank Campanelli had stepped up his attacks. He was bound to try again. Soon.

No. Milek probably wouldn't be getting any sleep tonight.

Chapter 10

People had been in and out of the condo all day. Bodyguards. Paynes. Kozminskis. They spoke to Milek and played with Michael. But barely any of them acknowledged Amber.

It was as if she was still dead. Or invisible. She sucked in a breath and pushed aside the self-pity. If none of them could understand why she'd done what she had…

Or if, worse yet, they thought she'd been involved with Gregory and with his death…

Then she didn't need them. But when the door opened to Stacy, her heart ached for the friendship she had lost. Logan was with her, standing behind her and telling her, "This is a bad idea."

Apparently there was a lot of that going around—not that she and Milek had had a bad idea since that first night.

"It's too dangerous," Logan persisted.

"With all the bodyguards around this place," Stacy said, "it's the safest place for your daughter and me to be." And she reached back and took a little girl from Logan's arms.

Her biggest regret in leaving was that she hadn't been able to see Stacy through her pregnancy—to be there with her through the pain and the joy. She wanted to see the little bundle of joy.

The little girl was in a furry pink snowsuit. Only her face with chubby red cheeks was visible. Amber gasped. "She's beautiful…"

And for a moment, Stacy softened and smiled at her. But then her smile faded as if she forced herself to remember she was mad.

Amber could handle everyone else ignoring her. But not Stacy…

"Will you talk to me?" she asked.

Stacy glanced back at her husband, as if asking him to rescue her from the discomfort. But he only took his daughter back from her hands.

"I'll get her out of the snowsuit," he offered.

"Who's that?" Michael asked as he came out of his bedroom to greet the new guests. He'd settled very well into Milek's condo. Maybe too well. They hadn't had that talk about their son yet.

But Milek played with the boy every chance he got—when he wasn't busy poring over old police reports with Logan or Agent Rus.

"This is your cousin," Stacy told him. "You can help Uncle Logan get little Penny out of her suit."

Michael's nose wrinkled in confusion. "She's not wearing a suit."

"Snowsuit," Logan explained as he carried the baby over to the couch. Fascinated with the little pink bundle, Michael followed closely behind him.

And Stacy followed Amber to the master bedroom. Not knowing how emotional they might get, Amber closed the door. She didn't want her son to see her cry. For the past year she'd waited until he was asleep before she'd wept for all they'd left behind.

"I'm sorry," she said. "I'm sorry I thought I was doing the right thing when I had Agent Rus fake my and Michael's deaths."

Stacy released a shuddery little breath. She said nothing, though.

"But most of all I'm sorry I wasn't there for you," Amber continued, "when you had your little girl."

Tears shimmered in Stacy's gray eyes.

Tears stung Amber's eyes, too. "Will you ever be able to forgive me?"

Stacy stared at her for a long moment before giving her a slow and almost reluctant nod. "I think I was angrier at you when you died than I am now."

Amber sucked in a breath as a pain jabbed her heart. "Ouch."

"I was angry at the position you'd put me in," Stacy said. "I was upset at myself for keeping Michael a secret from my brother. I never should have let you put me in that position—in the middle."

"Milek didn't want me," she reminded his sister. And except for that first night, he hadn't wanted her again. He slept on the couch in the living room—presumably to protect her. But she suspected he was protecting himself. "I didn't want to trap him."

But she had told him.

"He wouldn't have had to marry you," Stacy said. "But he could have been a part of his child's life. You shouldn't have denied him that."

"She didn't," Milek said as he stepped inside the bedroom with them. He glanced back at their son sitting on the couch playing with his little cousin before he closed the door again. "She told me. And I didn't believe her."

Stacy gasped. Then she reached out and smacked his shoulder with her hand. "That's horrible!" She turned on Amber. "And you lied to me."

"I didn't want to cause any problems between you," Amber said. But she was worried she had, despite her best efforts not to.

The tears overflowed now, pouring down Stacy's face as she pulled Amber into a tight embrace. "I'm sorry. I'm sorry."

"I get why you were angry at me," she said as she cried, too. "I would have been upset with you if you'd let me think you were dead." She would have been devastated, too. It had been so hard when her friend had been in danger a year ago.

"I should have known you were just protecting your son," Stacy said. "Like you've been protecting that jackass I call a brother."

"The jackass will leave the two of you alone now," Milek said as he slipped back out of the room.

"I can't believe he did that to you," Stacy said. "That he doubted you…"

"I know why now," Amber admitted. "He told me Gregory claimed the baby I was carrying was his."

Stacy cursed. "That son of a bitch. No wonder somebody had him killed."

Amber released a ragged sigh. "Thank you."

"For what?"

"For not thinking I was sleeping with my boss like everyone else does."

Stacy snorted. "Sure, Schievink had the hots for you. That's probably why he tried to make trouble with Milek. But you would never cheat on my brother. You were in love with him." She glanced to the bed and arched a brow. "I think you still are."

Amber shook her head. "I don't even know him anymore." She wasn't sure she ever had. "Something's going on with him." Something that kept him from sharing his bed with her again. "He either believes all the awful rumors about me and Gregory, or…"

"Or?" Stacy prodded her.

"He really doesn't care about me at all."

Stacy wound her arm more tightly around her shoulders, offering her the comfort and affection Amber had needed so badly. "You didn't see him this past year," she said. "He was devastated. He cares."

"He told you that?"

Stacy bit her lip.

Maybe Milek had feelings for her, but if he would never admit to them—to her or anyone else including himself—it didn't matter. They would never be together again—whether or not Frank Campanelli finished the job he'd been hired to do.

It was an ambush. Milek knew it the minute he stepped inside Rus's office. He wasn't alone. Garek was with him, their heads bent close together as they talked—discussing him, no doubt.

At least Logan wasn't here. He was with Amber and Michael. And Stacy. His sister had forgiven her best friend. He breathed a sigh of relief over that—glad their relationship had been repaired. He knew how much it meant to both women.

The two men looked up at him. "You came," Rus said.

"Of course," Milek replied. "You summoned me."

"Surprised you pried yourself away from her," Garek said.

Milek snorted. "You should talk—you couldn't stay away from Candace even when your presence put her in more danger."

Garek's face flushed. He couldn't deny he'd never been able to keep his distance from the woman who was now his wife. Not that Milek intended to make Amber his wife.

He'd been crazy to even consider it those years ago.

"Your situation is different," Garek said.

He couldn't have agreed more.

"Amber is the one putting you in danger."

"It's not her fault," he said.

The two men just stared at him. "You're both wrong about her," he said. "She has nothing to do with Schievink's murder or that attempt on my life."

He was disgusted they could even think that of her. And he showed that disgust, pointing at his older brother. "She's Stacy's best friend. She was there for our sister when we couldn't be…"

Because Milek had been in juvenile detention and Garek in prison.

"You know what kind of person she is," he persisted.

Garek furrowed his brow in confusion. "If you're so enamored with her, why the hell didn't you marry her?"

Milek wouldn't answer that. "That's none of your damn business."

"It is my business," Garek said, his temper snapping as his face flushed an even deeper shade of red.

His family didn't understand him; they never had. He just shook his head.

"My wife was in danger the other night, too," Garek said, his voice vibrating with anger. "That son of a bitch shot out her windshield. He could have hit her."

"She shouldn't have been following me," Milek said.

"You're damn lucky she was or you might not have survived."

Milek had already concluded the same thing. Frank—if it had been Frank—would have kept shooting until he'd hit him if Candace hadn't been there, too.

Humbled, he nodded. "I know."

Garek nodded, too—in silent agreement.

"Did you find out any more about the shooting in the alley or in the hotel parking lot?" Milek asked.

"The truck he left in the alley was stolen," Nick replied. "The gun was stolen, too—from an arms shipment a few months ago."

"Chekov's?" Garek asked.

Nick nodded. "And you'd think Campanelli would know better than to steal from him."

"Maybe it wasn't Campanelli in the alley," Milek said. "You found blood in the hotel parking lot." He hoped he'd hit the assassin. "It could be someone else."

"That's not a good thing," Garek said. "We don't need a bunch of hit men coming after you like what happened with Logan and Parker last year."

"We need to find out who hired Campanelli," Milek said.

"I gave you copies of the reports," Nick said. "Did you find anything?"

Milek hated to admit defeat. But he'd found nothing. He shook his head.

Nick sighed. "I spent the past year looking for who hired Frank Campanelli to kill the DA. Nobody on that list of names Amber gave me panned out as a viable suspect."

"That's why we need to find Frank Campanelli," Milek said. "If I hit him in that parking lot, he must have sought treatment."

"But where?" Nick asked. "Up north or here?"

Milek shrugged. "I don't know. I just know we need to find him." If he'd survived. "We can get him to tell us who hired him."

Nick snorted. "He's a professional. Even if we catch him, he's not going to give up who hired him."

Milek would make certain he did—even if he had to beat it out of him. "He'll tell me."

Garek shook his head. "The only thing Frank Campanelli is going to do is kill you."

"He hasn't tried since the other night," Milek reminded them.

Of course, he hadn't been out since then. He'd been holed up in the condo with Amber and their son, trying to ignore his attraction to the woman. Succumbing to desire that first night had been a mistake. He hadn't been able to sleep since then and not because he'd been worried about her safety.

He was worried about his heart. That was the only danger he was in from Amber—of falling even more deeply in love with her.

Despite the cold wind blowing between the buildings of downtown River City, heat suffused Frank. Part of it was that damn infection Dr. Gunz had warned he might get. He'd had to go back to the doc's mansion for a dose of IV antibiotics. The infection probably wasn't gone yet, but painkillers had taken the edge off Frank's discomfort. They hadn't affected his temper at all, though.

That was the other reason he was hot. He was pissed. Milek Kozminski hadn't given him another opportunity for revenge. He'd stayed holed up inside that fortress he called home. Until now...

But he wasn't alone. Kozminski was never completely alone. There were always other people following him— like the Amazon woman the night he'd trapped Kozminski in the alley. If not for her, this could have been over already.

Frank needed it to be over. He didn't even care right now who else was following Kozminski. Frank had taken out witnesses right in front of the US Marshals or police officers assigned to protect them. He could deal with a bodyguard or two—in order to deal with Milek Kozminski.

He had to make the most of the opportunity he'd finally been given. So he quickened his pace as he followed Kozminski down the city street. He'd just left the River City Police Department. Ignoring the throbbing pain in his shoulder, he shuddered in revulsion. That was the last place he ever intended to be.

He'd been picked up once—when he'd been a kid who'd had more balls than brains. He was smarter now. He wouldn't get caught again.

But then Milek Kozminski turned around and stared directly at him. His hand tightened around the handle of his gun. Would he be fast enough to pull it out?

Fortunately the gunshot wound had been through his

left shoulder, since he was right-handed. He'd have to draw fast because Milek's hand was close to his holster—as if he was prepared for anything. Frank would probably have only one chance to get off a shot before Kozminski returned fire.

So one shot would have to be enough. It would have to be the kill shot.

Chapter 11

Milek had been gone a long time. Too long. Was he all right? Amber closed her son's bedroom door and walked back into the living room.

Stacy and Logan had left a while ago. The former marine Cooper Payne leaned against the wall by the door now, his gun drawn. The metal creaked as the door began to slide open. He swung his barrel toward the shadow stepping over the threshold.

"Damn," Milek remarked as he pressed his hand to his chest. "Little edgy?"

"I've learned not to assume it was you just because the alarm didn't go off," Cooper said. "And you seem like the edgy one."

Milek didn't argue with the man. He just nodded. "Thanks for being careful," he said. "I can take over now."

Cooper shrugged off the gratitude. "Anytime..."

Amber waited until the other man left before asking, "What's wrong?"

Because something was. As Cooper had noticed, he was edgy—his body tense, his hands shaking slightly.

He expelled a ragged sigh. "I just had a really weird encounter."

Fear squeezed her heart. "Did Campanelli try to kill you again?"

"No…" He ran his hand along his jaw. "But I think he was close."

"You saw him?"

"I don't know what he looks like," he said. "While someone got his fingerprints off an old juvenile arrest record, there hasn't been a picture of him taken since then."

She shivered. "So he could have been close to you." The thought chilled her, and she wanted—needed—to be close to Milek, to make certain he was all right. She crossed the living room to stand beside him.

"If he was, why didn't he try to kill me again?" He stepped over to the security panel and pressed a button to bring up the monitors of the area around the former warehouse. He studied the screens.

"Do you think he followed you back here?"

Milek shrugged. "He probably didn't need to."

"You think he knows where we are?"

"You know how people talk in this city," he reminded her. "And he and I know some of the same people. By now I'm sure he knows where I live."

Her heart began to pound faster. "Then you shouldn't have brought us here."

She should have refused to come home with him. But

she'd been so scared and alone. If he hadn't arrived when he had, she would have already been dead.

But, even though he hadn't sent photos to say so, Frank Campanelli knew exactly where they were again. "We can't stay," she said.

He pointed to one of the screens. She stepped closer and peered at it. Near the back of the building, in the shadow of the Dumpster, something moved. She gasped.

"He's out there now." Panic pressed on her lungs, stealing her breath. "We need to leave."

"It's not the Ghost," he assured her. "Look again."

She turned back to the screen and studied the shadow. While long, there were curves to it. Relief shuddered through her. "It's Candace."

Milek tapped another screen. "And there's her husband, my brother."

"They're watching us."

"And maybe that's why the Ghost didn't try to kill me today." One of them must have been following him.

She heard the certainty in Milek's voice. He might not have seen him, but he was sure Campanelli had been there, too, close to him.

If not for their presence, Milek might have gotten shot at again. And maybe this time the assassin wouldn't have missed. She involuntarily reached out to him, needing to touch him—needing to assure herself that he was all right—that nothing had happened to him.

"You're really all right?"

He turned away from the monitors and focused on her, his gaze intense. "No."

"But you said he didn't try anything…"

"It's you," he said. "You're the reason I'm not all right."

And she realized where he'd been. "Agent Rus tried to convince you that I'm involved again?"

He didn't deny it—just shrugged off the suspicions. Did he believe her—did he believe she hadn't had an affair with her boss? That she hadn't wanted the man dead until Milek had told her that Gregory had claimed to be Michael's father?

"It's not old rumors that have been keeping me awake every night," he said. "It's you…"

Her pulse quickened. Then his hand was there—on the hand she'd put on his arm when she'd needed to touch him. His thumb brushed over her pulse point, making it race.

"I thought you've been awake every night because you've been protecting us," Amber said. She'd lain awake, too, but it was because she'd needed him.

He pointed toward those monitors. "They're out there. I could have slept," he said, "if every time I closed my eyes, I didn't see you—" his silver eyes darkened with desire "—naked."

"Milek…"

He lifted her and carried her across the living room— to the master bedroom that had been missing the master the past few nights. He was with her now, closing the door behind them. He lowered his head and kissed her, his lips sliding over hers.

She kissed him back, her lips pressing against his as she clung to his shoulders, her arms looped around his neck. So when he laid her on the bed, she tugged him down with her. His body covered hers.

She felt his holster digging into her side, and she tensed for a moment—remembering the danger. Remembering someone wanted her dead.

She just wanted someone to want her. No. Not someone. Milek. She wanted only Milek.

He wriggled free of her grasp, though. And he pulled off his holster and his weapon and set them carefully on the table next to the bed. Within reach if he needed them.

Hopefully he would not need them.

Amber kicked off her shoes and reached for the buttons on her sweater. But Milek's fingers were there, pushing hers aside, and he hurriedly undid them. Her cardigan parted, revealing she wore only a bra beneath it.

His breath escaped in a low groan. "You're beautiful…"

Since he was a man of few words, his compliments were always sincere and always touched her. She smiled. But he was the beautiful one—with his blond hair silky to her touch—with his chiseled features and his soulful eyes. She worked at his buttons, quickly undoing them.

His body was beautiful, too—all smooth skin and sleek muscles. She pressed a kiss to his chest. Then she skimmed her lips lower, over the rippling muscles of his lean stomach. His belt stopped her. But she reached for the buckle.

Milek's hands covered hers. He stood up to get rid of his pants and boxers until he stood before her entirely naked. She wriggled quickly out of her jeans. She wanted him. Needed him…

Even though people had been in and out of the condo the past few days, she'd felt alone. Isolated. Because she'd missed him…

"Milek…" Her heart pounded as desire overwhelmed her.

He touched her. Using his finger like a paintbrush, he swept it across her skin. He teased the pulse point in her throat and stroked the ridge of her collarbone. Then he dipped down to her breasts. His hands cupped them as his thumbs moved slowly across the nipples—back and forth.

She shifted on the mattress as tension began to build inside her. A moan slipped between her lips—then his tongue did, thrusting into her mouth. He moved it in and out, teasing her with the pleasure that was to come.

The pleasure only he could give her.

One of his fingers swept farther down her body— over the slight swell of her belly—to the mound between her legs. His fingertip found the most sensitive part of her body—stroking back and forth. He teased her until she trembled. The tension was too great. She sucked his tongue into her mouth, deepening the kiss. And she clutched at his shoulders and ran her nails down his back to his butt.

"I need you," she murmured.

Instead of thrusting inside her, of easing her ache, he pulled back. She closed her eyes on a wave of disappointment. But then she heard a drawer open and a packet tear. And suddenly his erection nudged her belly, then moved lower—prodding between her legs.

She guided him inside her, arching to take him deeper. He thrust inside her, filling her. Then he withdrew— denying her satisfaction until he slipped inside her again. In and out. In and out he stroked her.

She locked her legs around his waist and clutched his back, riding him. She moved quickly, trying to ease that tension. He felt so wonderful inside her—so right. But release eluded her.

Milek moved, lifted her and rolled so that she straddled him. Now she could set the pace—frenzied and frantic. She lifted her legs and took him deeper inside her.

Milek thrust up and moved with her—following her

frenetic pace. His hands clutched her hips, pulling her up and down—helping her until she found the release that had her crying out with its intensity. Milek's grasp on her hips tightened and he pulled her down. With a deep groan, he found his release, too.

Satiated, Amber flopped onto his chest—which rose and fell with his pants for breath. She had needed that; she'd needed him.

"It wasn't a bad idea," she mused. Not making love again had been the bad idea—trying to stay away from each other.

His fingers stroked along her spine. But he didn't agree with her. Maybe he couldn't speak yet. But maybe he hadn't understood her, because when he spoke, it was to ask, "Coming home with me?"

That wasn't what she'd been talking about, and she suspected he knew it. But she played along. "Home? It doesn't feel like home."

"It's very industrial," he admitted.

"I liked it at first," she said. "But now the brick and steel and concrete have begun to remind me of something else. Of the places the criminals I convicted were sentenced."

He tensed beneath her. And she wished back her words. Milek had been incarcerated. For six horrible months. She'd been friends with his sister then. She'd helped her through those long months of missing her brothers.

She'd tried once to talk to him about it. He hadn't been like other ex-cons she'd met. He hadn't claimed his innocence. He'd actually admitted that something good had come of his experience—his art.

"You think my home feels like prison?" he asked.

"Only because I feel like I can't leave. That I'm trapped inside." But was she trapped? She lifted her head from his chest and focused on his handsome face. "You've left."

"And I nearly got killed," he reminded her.

"But Candace saved you. And if we both went out, we would have more of them protecting us," she pointed out. "We would be fine."

Milek shook his head; he wouldn't even consider it.

Was he her protector or her jailer?

Coming back to River City PD always felt strange to Logan Payne—especially when he walked past his old desk on the way to his brother's office. The door was already open, as if Nick had been expecting him. Maybe he had been; the guy seemed to have Logan's mother's uncanny ability of knowing things were going to happen before they happened. The weird thing was that Penny wasn't the parent they shared.

"You showed the reports to Milek," Logan said. "Why not me?"

Nick didn't even glance up from his desk. He'd definitely expected Logan. "I only showed him the reports to warn him."

"About Amber?"

Nick nodded.

"She's not the danger," Logan said. "You're wasting your time investigating her."

"You haven't seen the reports."

"I want to see the reports to find out who's really behind the hit on Schievink," Logan explained. "I know Amber isn't a viable suspect."

Finally Nick looked up and met his gaze. "I can understand Milek defending her," he said. "He's in love with her.

Why are you defending her? You couldn't have known her long before she disappeared."

"Before you faked her death and hid her and her son," Logan clarified for him. He wasn't certain he could forgive him for that—for what he'd put Stacy through. Needlessly.

But Stacy had forgiven Amber. His wife was completely glowing now—with her pregnancy and happiness. But concern for her friend and her brother dimmed that happiness. Logan couldn't have that; he'd vowed on their wedding day to do whatever necessary to make her happy.

"So you don't really know Amber Talsma," Nick said.

"My wife does," Logan replied. "And I have learned to trust my wife's judgment. She's never wrong."

Nick snorted. "That's all you have? Your wife vouching for her best friend? What if this is the one time she's wrong?" His voice going deeper and gruffer, he added, "Everyone's wrong at least once."

It wasn't an apology—not in words. But in his tone, in his eyes—there was regret for what he'd done, for faking the deaths that had caused so much anguish for the people Logan loved. He suspected Nick had come to care about some of them, too.

"It happened a year ago," Logan said, reminding himself as much as Nick. "None of us really knew each other then."

"No, we didn't," Nick agreed.

But Logan suspected his brother didn't trust many people—no matter how long he'd known them. Logan had always had people he could trust—his family. Nick hadn't even been able to trust his own mother.

She hadn't been who he'd thought she was. Like Amber, she had gone into hiding—assuming another name, another identity for her and her son. At least Amber had been gone only a year; Nick had lived his entire life away from his family.

"Now you know us," Logan said. "You know we all work together. We've got each other's backs."

Nick passed a folder across his desk. He'd had it ready. He'd definitely known Logan was coming. "I hope you're as good a detective as everyone around here claims you are," he said. "We've got to figure this out soon."

Or it was going to be too late for those people Logan loved and for whom Nick had come to care.

"This is a bad idea," Milek murmured. He didn't mean making love with her. That hadn't been a bad idea at all.

This was—taking her outside the condo. Sure, they had bodyguards—ones who weren't even trying to stay inconspicuous now. But it was still dangerous.

Not just for her and him but for those bodyguards, too. If Candace got hurt…

Garek would kill him before Frank Campanelli ever got another chance.

Amber tipped her face up to the sunshine and giggled. "This feels great…"

Despite the sunshine, it was cold in the park—the wind whistling through the bare branches of the trees. But he understood her reaction. While it had been many years ago, he remembered how it had felt to be locked up—trapped. When she'd compared the condo to jail, he hadn't been able to keep her locked up any longer. Despite what Nick and Garek believed because of those horrible rumors, she had done nothing wrong. She had done nothing to deserve all she'd been through—nothing to deserve captivity.

"I feel guilty," she said. "Michael would love this park." She gestured toward the swings that although empty swayed in the brisk breeze.

He hadn't dared to risk bringing their son along, too. He hadn't wanted his focus divided. He'd managed to protect them both before, but he hadn't wanted to risk it. He wasn't sure it was just Frank Campanelli after them anymore.

"We should get back to him," Milek said.

She smiled at him—that beautiful smile that brightened her eyes and her skin—setting her whole face aglow from within. "To bring him here?"

He shook his head and reiterated, "This was a bad idea…"

He felt it again—that ominous unsettling feeling he'd had outside the hotel in northern Michigan. He'd had it when he'd noticed the truck following him the other night and again yesterday on the street. He felt Frank Campanelli's presence. The shooting began before he ever had a chance to reach for his weapon, though.

Chapter 12

Gunfire echoed inside her head, her ears ringing from all the shots that had been fired. And she couldn't stop shaking. Milek wrapped his arms around her—as he had back at the park—when he'd used his body as a human shield for hers.

"Are you okay?" he asked. "Do you think you're in shock?"

She was shocked—that they hadn't been killed. That no one had been hit.

"Are you okay?" she asked.

His chin bumped the top of her head when he nodded. "Yes."

"And everyone else?"

He uttered a heavy sigh—almost of regret—but replied, "Yes."

She eased back slightly in his arms to stare up at his face.

"Nobody hit Campanelli," he said, explaining his disappointment.

"You think it was him?"

Milek nodded. "Yeah, I think it was…"

"I'm sorry," she said. "So sorry…"

"Despite what some people believe, I know you didn't hire the Ghost," he assured her. "Why are you sorry?"

"I shouldn't have convinced you to let me leave the condo." She'd had fun convincing him—with her lips and her hands. They'd spent the entire night making love— before he'd finally agreed to take her to the park in the morning.

"Nobody got hurt," he reminded her. His arms tightened around her again, pulling her flush against his chest. His heart pounded fast and hard against hers. He was shaken, too.

"But they could have." And she'd wanted to bring Michael along…

She shuddered at the thought of what could have happened to their son. Milek hadn't let her see her little boy yet. He'd taken her directly into the master bedroom after he'd brought her back to the condo.

She didn't want Michael to see her like this, either— freaking out. It would freak him out, too. She drew in an unsteady breath, trying to ease the anxiety gripping her. She wanted to see Michael, but she had to pull it together first—for his sake.

"I'm sorry," she murmured again as she pressed her mouth to Milek's neck. If something had happened to him…

His hands clasped her back before he eased her backward. He tipped her chin up and dropped a kiss lightly on her mouth. "Nothing happened," he said again.

She drew in another deep breath. "Yes, there were a lot of shots fired but nobody got hit…"

Milek's brow furrowed, and he admitted, "He could have killed us."

She shuddered again. She hadn't been wrong. It had been a close call. A very close call.

His voice dropping to a raspy whisper, Milek repeated, "He could have killed us. But he didn't…"

"What's taking me so long?" Frank repeated the question into the cell phone pressed to his ear. He'd had a couple opportunities to end it. But Milek Kozminski was never really alone. Even if he wasn't protecting the woman and the kid, there were people protecting him.

Like the day in the city when Kozminski had been out without the lady lawyer, he still hadn't been alone. If Frank had taken a shot, he would have been shot himself. That damn female bodyguard had been there again— like that night.

Like today…

Frank hadn't wanted to kill her, though. She was just doing her job. Like Milek Kozminski was just doing his…

Maybe it was the painkillers. They'd taken the edge off his temper and made him think rationally again. He had never acted on emotion before. That was why he hadn't taken the shot when Milek had been without the woman. Frank hadn't wanted to risk his own life to take a life he wasn't even being paid to take.

He hadn't wanted to risk his freedom, either. And it was clear he'd been outnumbered in the park. So the shots he'd fired there had been at such a distance that none of them had struck a target.

There'd been only one viable target there, though. Milek Kozminski's name wasn't officially on his list.

"I don't do freebies," he inadvertently spoke aloud.

The cell crackled as the caller's voice rose with outrage. He smiled.

"Yeah, I know you paid me once and thought the job was done." He'd fooled this person once, but he didn't dare try it again. The fury was dangerously close to madness. He was getting as much money as he could from this source.

But maybe there was another one. He'd been close enough to Milek Kozminski that he'd seen the quality of the man's clothes. He'd checked out his place, too. It must have taken a lot of money to convert a warehouse to a home.

How was Kozminski able to afford all of that on a bodyguard's salary? But then, he wasn't just a bodyguard; he'd been raised a thief. Maybe Frank could get him to put those skills to use for him. Or at least for the woman the guy obviously loved so much he'd put his life in danger for hers over and over again.

Milek had never had a problem with Logan Payne being the boss of Payne Protection. Unlike Logan's brothers and sister, Milek had never coveted his job. He'd become a bodyguard because all he had wanted was to save at least one life. Not that he could replace the life he had taken—even if he'd wanted to...

Right now they were all looking at him—even Logan—as if he was the boss. He had called this meeting in his living room, but only because he'd wanted them all close to Amber and Michael.

And because he had wanted to stay close to Amber and

Michael. They were in the little boy's room. Michael was watching a movie so he wouldn't overhear the meeting. Milek didn't want him to know the bad man had tried to hurt them again.

"Nobody saw anything?"

Along with the officers Agent Rus had sent to the park, the bodyguards had also talked to joggers and dog walkers.

They all began to speak at once.

Candace: "He could have been one of the dog walkers or joggers. There was one that…"

Garek: "Was flirting with you because you're gorgeous. If it was him, you would have seen his gun."

Cooper: "I found the gun."

Parker: "An officer took it to River City PD."

Whatever else they said bled together in Milek's mind. He tried to process, but Garek and Candace had begun their own conversation simultaneously with Parker and Cooper's discussion of one of the officers.

Instead of stepping in, Logan looked to him. He knew how much this meant to Milek—how much Amber and Michael meant—so he'd stepped aside.

Milek held up a hand. "Cooper," he said—loudly enough that he drew the former marine's attention. "What can you tell us about the gun?"

He shrugged. "It wasn't the right one for the job—not at the distance he was shooting from. I found the spent shells. If he'd had a long gun—a sniper's rifle—he could have taken you out before we knew he was there."

Milek had been careful to stay close to Amber—close enough that had someone fired shots, he would have taken the bullet. So why hadn't he taken a bullet?

"Maybe it wasn't Frank Campanelli, then," he said. "He would have used the right gun."

Candace nodded. "He certainly used the right one that night in the alley."

"If that was the Ghost…"

Cooper said, "The officer took the gun back to the River City PD crime lab to see if it's from the same batch of stolen weapons as that automatic rifle."

"Good." But the gun wasn't going to lead them to Campanelli. He wouldn't have left it behind if it would. But he was cocky—cocky enough that he might have talked to one of them.

He turned to Candace. "This guy," he said. "What did he look like?"

She shrugged. "Midfifties, early sixties, average height, average build—thinning salt-and-pepper hair, blue eyes."

He'd seen guys who looked like that on the street the day before. But there had been more than one.

"Nothing distinctive?" he asked. "No tattoos? No scars?"

She shook her head.

But the Ghost would want to be nondescript. Invisible.

His cell vibrated in his pocket. He nearly ignored it.

But Logan said, "Maybe it's Nick."

Milek hadn't asked Nick to the meeting. He probably would have tried to blame the park shooting on Amber. Or maybe he was calling to concede that he'd been wrong about her. He pulled the phone from his pocket and glanced at the screen.

Private caller. An uneasy feeling lifted the hair on Milek's nape. Could it be…?

"Nick?" Logan asked.

He shook his head but he clicked on the phone. He had to know. "Hello?"

"Hey, Milek Kozminski."

His blood chilled as he recognized Frank Campanelli's voice from that night in the hotel parking lot. "Hey…"

"Shh," Frank advised. "Don't let anyone else know you're talking to me."

"Why's that?"

"Because you and I can end this now," Frank said, "between the two of us."

Milek held his hand over the cell and told the others, "I need to take this…" He ignored their surprise that he'd step away from a meeting he had called, walked into his bedroom and closed the door.

"I can talk freely now," he told Frank. "What are you proposing? An old-fashioned duel?"

"We could have had that the other day," Frank said, "when we came face-to-face on the street outside the River City PD."

Milek shivered. He'd known it—that he'd been close. He hadn't realized until now he'd actually seen the Ghost. "Why didn't you take the shot? Too close to River City lockup?"

"You weren't alone."

"I wasn't alone today, either," Milek said, "but you fired a lot of shots."

"I wasn't trying to kill anyone then," Frank said. "I was just giving a warning—like the night I fired shots into the lady lawyer's place."

"I don't know many hired assassins who give warnings." But he couldn't deny Frank had. At first Milek had thought the photos the hit man had sent to Amber were a sadistic taunt. But maybe it had been a warning. Maybe he really didn't want to kill her.

"That first time you shot at me when I was alone in the alley," Milek said, "didn't feel like a warning."

A sigh rattled the phone. "I was mad."

"Mad?"

"You hit me—that night in the hotel parking lot." He groaned as if still in pain.

"I would apologize," Milek said, "but you weren't firing warning shots that night, either."

Frank chuckled. "None of them hit *you…*"

And Milek had been close enough that Frank could have—had he wanted to. Milek had apparently hit him. Maybe that was why none of the shots since had hit anyone. Maybe Frank's injury had affected his marksmanship.

"I'm a bodyguard," Milek said. "It's my job to protect my clients."

The old hit man sighed again. "I know. That's why I got over my anger. That's why I didn't take any real shots at the lady bodyguard, either."

"I'll tell my brother you're not going to hurt his wife." Garek would be happy to know Candace was safe. What about Amber, though?

Milek glanced at the bed and remembered Amber on top of him, moving so sensually—driving him nearly out of his mind with pleasure. He couldn't lose her.

Michael couldn't lose his mother. He was just a little boy.

Frank said, "And we both know the lady lawyer is more to you than a client. The kid looks just like you."

"He's mine," Milek said. It felt good to claim his child. "So you're saying my sister-in-law is safe. And apparently you're not going to try to kill me anymore. But what about Amber?"

"That depends on what you can offer me…"

He wanted money. Of course. That was all Frank Campanelli had ever cared about—a paycheck.

"I can pay you off," Milek said—although he had no idea what the going rate was for a hit man. "But that won't stop whoever hired you from hiring someone else— maybe someone not as reasonable as you are."

Frank chuckled. "You want to know who hired me."

"Yes." Hit men were notorious for never revealing their clients. But then they weren't known for giving warning shots, either. Frank Campanelli was obviously different.

"It will cost you."

Milek didn't care how much. If he didn't have enough, he could find the rest. He hadn't forgotten everything his father had taught him. And his son's and Amber's safety were priceless.

"I want you to meet me," Frank said.

Even knowing it was probably a trap, Milek found himself agreeing. "Of course."

"Alone," Frank specified.

It was definitely a trap. But if the cost for Amber's safety was his life, Milek would gladly pay it.

Chapter 13

Her lips tingled from his kiss. As the condo door closed behind Milek, Amber pressed her fingers against her mouth. He hadn't told her where he was going.

Nerves tightened and twisted her stomach into knots. And that kiss had felt so final, as if it might be the last time he kissed her.

"Did he tell you where he's going?" Amber asked.

Candace Baker-Kozminski shook her head. Her teeth nibbled her bottom lip. Amber wasn't the only one nervous over Milek leaving. Her nerves turned into fear now, and she began to tremble.

She crossed the living room and reached for the door. Maybe she could catch him yet. Maybe she could stop him. But when she reached the door, she remembered there was no handle—no knob. Just that panel next to it. She would have to punch in a code to get the door to slide open. She reached for it but stopped. She had no idea what the code was. He had never told her.

She hadn't exaggerated when she'd told him that she felt like an inmate in his home. But she shouldn't have said that—shouldn't have risked everyone's safety just so she could feel the sunshine on her face again. But she didn't want out for the sunshine. Night had fallen already.

She wanted out to stop Milek.

"What is the code?" she asked Candace, her fingers trembling over the panel. "What is it?" He was getting away—going wherever he was going that she suspected even he didn't think he would return from. "I need to get out now!"

"You can't go anywhere," the female bodyguard said. "It isn't safe."

"It isn't safe for him, either," Amber said.

"Milek is a bodyguard," Candace said. "A damn good one. He can protect himself." But as soon as she uttered the words, her teeth nibbled on her bottom lip again. She didn't believe what she was saying any more than Amber did.

"Please—"

"Mommy, where are you going?" Michael asked. Jewel dangling from his arm, he rushed over to her.

"Your mommy isn't going anywhere," Candace answered for her. "She was just making sure the door was shut."

His chin quivering, he asked, "So the bad man can't get in?"

She'd thought he hadn't heard anything today, when they'd all been discussing the shooting in the park. And maybe he hadn't. Maybe he just remembered those other times the bad man had come after them—when he'd driven their van off the road and shot at them when they'd run for the hotel.

She dropped to her knees in front of her son and wrapped her arms around him. "Oh, sweetheart…"

Candace reached out, her hand patting Michael's head. "You're safe, little man. The bad man wouldn't dare to try to get in here." She flexed one of her impressive biceps. "He's scared of me. He knows I'd kick his butt."

Michael giggled. Then he tugged out of Amber's arms and reached out for the statuesque brunette.

A look of panic briefly crossed Candace's face. She was obviously not comfortable with children even though she'd instinctively said the perfect thing to calm the little boy's fears. Those instincts took over again as she lifted Michael into her arms.

He pressed a noisy kiss to her cheek. "Thank you, Aunt Candy."

The bodyguard's blue eyes widened with surprise. "Aunt Candy?"

Amber doubted his calling her "aunt" had shocked her; it was the "Candy."

"She's Aunt Candace," she corrected her son.

Michael's brow furrowed with confusion. "But that's what Uncle Garek told me to call her."

Candace chuckled. "Of course he did." She wasn't irritated; love brightened her eyes.

Amber envied that love—a love that was clearly reciprocated. She still couldn't believe Garek, the consummate playboy, had fallen so deeply in love, but there was no denying his feelings for his bride.

Did Milek have any feelings for her? Anything deeper than desire?

"Aunt Candy, do you want to color?" Michael asked.

He loved to draw and paint. He had inherited his father's passion for it, because Amber had no artistic abilities.

Candace looked a little freaked out again, but she nodded and replied, "Sure."

He wriggled down and ran for the room he'd claimed as his—Garek's former bedroom. When they were safe—if they were ever safe—she wondered how he'd feel about leaving this place, about leaving Milek.

Because once they were safe, Milek wouldn't want them staying with him. If he made it back from wherever he'd gone off alone...

"Don't worry," Candace said. As she had patted Michael's head, she patted Amber's shoulder now. "He's not alone out there."

A sigh of relief shuddered out, not just from Amber's lips but from her lungs. She'd been holding her breath since he'd walked out the door. "That's true. He has bodyguards, too."

Whether he wanted them or not...

"Garek will make sure he stays safe." And now respect for her husband joined her love. "He's the best bodyguard with Payne Protection."

After all the times Milek had saved her, Amber could have argued with the other woman. But she just nodded. Garek would keep his brother safe. The knots of fear and tension didn't ease, though.

She asked, "Can you check with him? Can you find out where Milek's going?"

She needed to know.

And Candace must have respected that need, because she pulled out her cell. She pressed a button and Garek's frantic-sounding voice emanated from her phone. "Honey, I can't talk right now. I think I lost him."

Fear constricted Amber's heart, and she gasped. "Milek? He lost Milek."

So he was out there—wherever he had gone—with no protection.

Garek had never been as pissed at his brother as he was now. What the hell was he thinking? And how the hell had he gotten so good that he'd shaken Garek's tail?

It was his own damn fault. He shouldn't have taught him so well. He walked into Payne Protection and slammed the door behind himself.

Nikki Payne glanced up from her desk. "What's wrong?" she asked.

"Milek…"

She leaned back in her chair. "You lost him?"

He jerked his head in a sharp nod. "Yes."

"Logan's gone," she said. "I'm the only one here."

"You're the one I need," he said. "You're going to help me find him."

Her brown eyes brightened. She didn't look like her brothers; she looked like Penny Payne. Maybe that was why Logan was so protective of her—because he hadn't been able to protect his mother from the pain she'd suffered.

"I am?" Then she nodded. "Of course I can. If I'd been at the meeting…"

But she hadn't been in the park during the shooting, so Milek hadn't called her as he had called the others to his condo. And there was no way Nikki would have been in the park. Logan was fanatical about keeping his sister away from the dangerous side of Payne Protection.

"What you do is more important," he said. "I need you to track his phone."

Her fingers tapped furiously on her keyboard. Not

only was she good, but she was fast. She shook her head. "His phone's shut off."

"Can't you remotely turn it back on?"

She tapped some more keys and shook her head again. "He must've taken out the battery," she said. "I can't track its GPS."

"Damn it!"

"But I did what you asked me last time we talked," she said, "when none of us could figure out what was going on with him and you thought he might be working for Rus." She uttered her half brother's last name with bitter emphasis.

So much had happened recently—finding out Amber and his nephew were alive—that he couldn't remember what he'd requested Nikki to do.

She smiled. "I tapped his phone."

His heart swelled, and he rushed around the desk to give her a quick hug. "If I didn't love my wife so much," he said, "I would kiss you."

Nikki shuddered. "And Candace would kill us both."

He chuckled. But Nikki wasn't wrong.

"What do you want to hear?" she asked. "I haven't played any of it yet."

"Last night," he said. "He took a call last night during the meeting. And he acted really odd afterward." He'd gotten rid of them quickly.

Nikki's fingers moved nimbly across the keyboard again. She pulled up a screen that looked like an EKG screen. But when she pressed another key, Milek's voice played.

Garek hadn't ever heard the other man's voice before, but he knew who it was. "Son of a bitch..."

The hit man had called Milek—presumably for money. But Garek didn't trust him. Why would Milek have?

Frank Campanelli didn't intend to take just Milek's money. He intended to take his life, too.

And Milek was out there alone—unprotected.

"Damn it!" he cursed. He headed toward the door but turned back to tell Nikki, "Call Agent Rus. Play him what we just heard."

"But tapping Milek's phone is illegal," Nikki protested.

"He won't arrest you." Even if she refused to acknowledge their relationship, Nick thought of her as a sister. "Call him!" He paused again and added, "Thanks."

She might have saved his brother's life. If Garek could get to him in time…

Milek had brought all the money he could get his hands on—not as much as Campanelli had wanted, though. Was it enough to get the hit man to reveal who'd hired him?

Maybe it wouldn't matter how much money Milek had. Maybe Frank had no intention of doing anything but killing him. Milek was ready for that contingency, too. He'd already drawn his gun, already clicked off the safety, as he walked toward the alley entrance to the nightclub.

It had been shut down a couple of months ago—when Viktor Chekov had gone to prison and his daughter to the psychiatric hospital. It was possible one of them had hired Frank to kill Milek. Maybe the hit man had two clients: whoever wanted Amber dead and someone who wanted Milek dead.

But wouldn't Chekov have gone after Garek or Candace or Agent Rus first? Why him? His part in that whole investigation had been minimal.

Even though the meeting was in Chekov's club, Milek

didn't believe it had anything to do with the imprisoned mobster. Schievink's murder and the attempts on Amber's life were about something else. He'd read Rus's reports. The list of possible suspects was long, longer after Rus had learned Schievink was corrupt. While he and Rus hadn't been able to tie any of those suspects to Campanelli, Campanelli would be able to.

If he really intended to talk…

Milek reached for the back door and easily pulled it open. It was unlocked—just as Frank had said it would be.

But could Milek trust anything else he'd said?

Before stepping inside, he braced himself for a barrage of bullets. He had no Dumpster to duck behind—no protection if this was an ambush. The light from the alley was faint, penetrating only a small circle of the darkness of what must have been a back hallway. Frank had said it would lead him to a stairwell to Chekov's office.

Was Campanelli trying to take over for the imprisoned mobster? Other people were apparently scrambling to try. Frank wouldn't be able to pull off the coup unless he could gain the respect of what was left of Chekov's family. Selling out would gain him no respect.

Only following through on a hit would.

Amber was safe, he reminded himself. Candace was inside the condo with her while Cooper and Parker guarded the perimeter. No one would get past them. No one would hurt her.

He was the one in danger.

He kept his back to the wall, his weapon gripped tightly in his hand. But maybe he didn't need to worry about bullets. If he had injured the hit man enough to affect his shooting, Campanelli might have switched to explosives.

The whole damn club could have been wired to blow.

Milek paused at another door. The sign above it proclaimed Stairs. The light from it reflected onto the placard below it that said Private.

He held his breath as he reached for the handle and pulled open the door. It could have been wired. Any of the steps he ascended could be, too. But nothing happened. Only his footfalls echoed as he headed up to the next level.

No explosion.

The silence was eerie.

He opened his mouth to call out but stopped himself. Maybe it wasn't a good idea to announce his arrival. Not that Frank wouldn't have heard the creak of either door Milek had opened or the metal steps groaning beneath his weight.

As he hit the landing at the top, he released a breath he hadn't realized he'd been holding. Just because he hadn't blown up didn't mean he wasn't still in danger.

Frank could have anything planned for him. And now it was time to find out exactly what. He reached for the door at the top of the stairs. His hand suddenly clammy, it nearly slid off the handle, but he tightened his grip and pulled the door open. Another trip down a dark hall and he stood outside Chekov's private office.

A lot of business had gone down inside there. Bad business. Drug dealing. Prostitution. Murder.

Was another murder about to take place?

He pushed open the door and stepped inside. It was dark; the room had no windows. He reached for the light switch and flipped it up, but nothing happened. The power had already been shut off.

Or cut...

"Frank," he called out. "I'm here. I came alone—just like you told me." Which had been foolish. He saw that now.

But Frank had made his family before. He'd seen Candace, and in the park he'd seen the others—not that they'd been trying to hide. He'd wanted the hit man to see them—to know he wasn't alone.

But he was alone now. And maybe Frank needed to know that before he'd show himself.

"We have a deal, Frank," he said. "I brought the money."

Would it be enough?

Where the hell was the guy?

The office was dark but it felt empty. He couldn't hear anyone else breathing. Just his own shallow breaths...

Was he too early?

He walked toward the desk. Maybe it would be better if he were sitting behind it when Frank showed. If he had his back to the wall...

His foot hit something, something that rolled across the hardwood floor. He knelt and reached for it, wrapping his hand around the cold metal. A flashlight. Fumbling around, he found the switch and turned it on. The beam bounced across the floor and lit the face of the body lying on it.

The man stared up at him from glazed-over blue eyes. His hair was salt-and-pepper. His features unremarkable—just like the man he'd seen on the street. Just like the man Candace had described in the park. It had to be Frank Campanelli.

He was dead. Now the Ghost was really just that.

"Damn it!" Milek cursed.

He had been going to give up the person who'd hired him. He had been going to sell out. And somehow his client had known it and beaten Milek to him.

Hinges creaked and then the metal steps as someone came up the same back stairwell Milek had and headed down the hall. He didn't really believe in ghosts. It wasn't Frank Campanelli back from the dead. It was more likely whoever had killed him.

Chapter 14

"What the hell were you thinking?" Nick asked as he fisted his hands under his desk. Even hours later, he was shaking a little in reaction. He'd nearly shot a man he knew—one he liked but wasn't certain he ever should have trusted.

If only Garek had found out sooner about that call his brother had taken—about the meeting he'd planned with an assassin…

Maybe they would have gotten to the nightclub before Frank Campanelli wound up dead.

"I was thinking I'd end this," Milek replied, his face flushed with anger. He was shaking a little, too—as he paced the confines of Nick's office.

"Did you?" he asked. Nick had asked it hours ago—in the nightclub where he'd found Milek Kozminski standing over the dead body of the man who'd been trying to kill him, the woman he loved and his child. He wasn't sure he would blame him if he had. But Frank's weapon hadn't been drawn from his holster let alone fired. Nobody would believe Frank's death was self-defense. "Did you kill him?"

"Why would I?" Milek asked. "That doesn't end this at all. That keeps it going because now we might never know who hired him."

Nick groaned in frustration.

"That's who killed him," Milek said. "The person who didn't trust him not to talk."

Campanelli had probably claimed credit and a fee for Amber dying in the car accident a year ago. So when she resurfaced, his credibility was shot. Now so was he…

Maybe it wasn't Milek who'd pulled the trigger. His gun hadn't recently been fired. Nick wanted to believe him, but he had never trusted easily. "We'll see what ballistics say…"

"You know the slug in Campanelli won't match mine," Milek said as he pulled open the door.

"I hope not," Nick said. "Until I know for sure, you know the drill…"

Milek snorted and turned back to him. "You're telling me not to leave town?"

Nick nodded.

Milek's eyes widened with disbelief. "You think I'd leave town with Amber and our son in danger? You think I'd leave them with someone still determined to kill her?"

"No," Nick admitted. "I don't think you'd leave her. But you might leave with her." He mentally kicked himself for putting that thought in the other man's head, but maybe it had already been there.

If someone Nick cared about was in as much danger

as Amber Talsma, he wasn't sure what he would do—what lengths he might go to in order to keep her safe.

And if he had a child…

He nearly snorted, too. That wasn't likely to ever happen. It was too hard for him to let anyone get close. He pushed away the fleeting thought of Annalise. That had been a mistake—one that had cost him a friendship. And Nick didn't have enough friends to risk losing any more.

"Be smart," he advised Milek. "Don't put yourself or her or your kid in danger."

"I'll do whatever I need to," he said, "in order to protect them."

That was what worried Nick.

Someone had brought up Amber's and Michael's belongings. The ones she'd packed in the back of the wrecked van. She'd been grateful to have them—until now—as she tried to hurriedly pack them again.

"What are you doing?" a deep voice asked.

She glanced up to find Milek standing in the doorway. He didn't lean against the jamb. His long body was tense; so was his handsome face, his jaw clenched.

"We need to leave," she said. Certainly he had to understand they weren't safe in River City. They might never learn who'd hired the hit man now.

He shook his head. "No, you and Michael can stay. I'll leave."

She stopped tossing items into her open suitcase and focused on his face. "You think I don't want to be here because of you?"

"I didn't kill Campanelli," he said. "That's not even why I agreed to meet him."

"I know." He'd put his life at risk to protect her and their son.

He gestured at the suitcase. "Then why are you packing? Why do you want to leave me?"

"I don't want to leave you," she said. Ever. But she couldn't deal with those fears now. She had other reasons to be frightened. "I want to leave River City."

"Why?"

"The danger's here," she said. "This is where Gregory was murdered, where I was shot at a year ago. And now the man who was supposed to kill me has been murdered here, too."

"You were found the last time you ran," Milek said. "What makes you think you won't be found again—when you're alone?"

She sucked in a breath. "You won't go with us."

"I can't," he said. "I was advised not to leave town."

"What?"

"I'm a suspect in the hit man's murder," he said.

"Agent Rus thinks you killed him?"

"I thought you thought that, too." And pain briefly darkened his silver eyes.

She hurried over to him then and did what she should have when he'd walked in the door. She threw her arms around him and pressed her head against his chest. His heart pounded hard and fast beneath her cheek.

"I thought I was never going to see you again," she murmured.

"You thought I'd let you leave here?" he asked.

She shook her head. "When you said goodbye…" Emotion choked her. "I knew you thought you might not make it back."

His arms tightened around her. "I had to take that

chance. If Campanelli was going to tell me anything, it was only if I met him alone."

"I'm glad you found him dead," she said.

He pulled back and stared down at her. "I thought you were packing because you're worried we'll never learn who hired him. If he was alive…"

"He might have killed you," she said. And she didn't know how she would have survived that. It had been hard enough on her when he'd broken their engagement. But if she lost him forever…

She needed to feel close to him—as close as she felt when they made love. So she pushed his coat from his shoulders and reached for the buttons on his shirt. She needed skin to skin—needed to feel his heart beat against hers.

He must have needed it, too, because he pulled off her sweater and pushed down her pants. Standing before him in her bra and panties, she shivered at the cool air. But the heat of his gaze warmed her as it moved over her like a caress.

He tipped her chin up and lowered his mouth. He kissed her gently at first, just sliding his lips across hers. Then he deepened the kiss.

She clung to him—with her lips and her hands. She slid her palms down his chest. Muscles rippled beneath her touch. She tackled his belt buckle next, pulling it loose. Then she unclasped his pants and reached for his zipper.

His erection pushed against the fly, against her fingers. He groaned as she released him. As she touched him, he touched her—moving his fingers beneath her panties. As he continued to kiss her, deeply, sliding his tongue inside her mouth, he slid his fingers inside her.

She'd been tense when he left—worried and on edge. Another kind of tension filled her now, making her breasts ache and her stomach muscles clench. She needed a release—the kind only he could give her.

He unclasped her bra and let it drop to the floor. Then he touched her breast, teasing the nipple as his fingers stroked her most sensitive spot. The ache intensified.

"You're driving me crazy," she warned him.

And she wanted him just as crazy. She moved her hand up and down the length of him, stroking him. But his control was stronger than hers. He didn't snap. He only groaned.

Then he lifted her and laid her on the bed. He stripped off her panties, but instead of sliding inside her, he moved down her body. He kissed her breasts and teased her nipples before skimming his lips over her stomach to the mound between her legs. His tongue flicked out, teasing that spot he'd already made almost painfully sensitive with his fingers.

She arched off the bed. As he flicked with his tongue, he slid his fingers inside her. And she came.

He pulled back. Maybe that was all he'd wanted—to give her pleasure. But then he rolled on a condom and joined her on the bed. He lifted her legs and pushed gently inside her. She wanted him as crazy with desire as he made her. So she touched him—everywhere she could reach. She kissed his shoulders and his arms. She trailed her fingers down his back and over his butt.

She arched and writhed, driving the rhythm to madness—driving herself to madness. The tension wound tightly inside her—demanding release. She nearly sobbed over the exquisite torture. Then he thrust again—deeply. And her body shuddered as pleasure overwhelmed her.

He joined her, thrusting again before his body tensed. While he came, he didn't relax. His arms were hard yet, as he wrapped them around her and held her.

She hadn't been the only one afraid he might not come back. He must have felt that way, too. But still he'd taken the risk. He'd put himself in danger for her. Maybe for their son's sake. Maybe because he'd only been doing his job.

Or maybe because he cared more about her than he was willing to admit.

Garek stood nervously inside the condo, near the front door—as if he might need to make a quick getaway.

It was late.

Milek had left Amber alone in bed so he could talk to his brother. But Garek had yet to talk. Milek glanced back toward the bedroom. Would she awake and notice him gone? Would she go back to packing to leave him?

"I don't have time for this," he said. "Say whatever you wanted to say..."

"You're pissed at me for having Nikki play that recording for Rus, for telling him about your meeting," Garek said.

Milek shook his head. He wasn't mad about that. He understood why his brother had brought in the federal agent. Nikki probably hadn't been happy about calling her half brother, though.

Garek studied his face. "Then you're pissed at me for having Nikki tap your phone?"

That wasn't the only reason he was upset, but he nodded. He couldn't believe they'd invaded his privacy like that. He knew his family had been worried about him ever since Amber's fake death. But they'd gotten even

more nervous when he'd started acting differently after
Rus told him she and their son were alive.

"It was a good thing I did," Garek said defensively. "I
can't believe you went off alone to meet a killer."

"You can't believe I shook your tail," Milek said, and
his lips twitched as a smile threatened. Usually he loved
one-upping his older brother—especially since he hadn't
had much opportunity.

Garek narrowed his eyes. "How'd you get so good?"

"I was trained by the best," Milek said. He loved his
brother; that was why he was so hurt. Not over his having Nikki tap his phone but by the look on Garek's face
when he and Rus had burst into the nightclub. He could
understand Nick looking at him like that. The guy trusted
no one.

But his brother...

"You might be better," Garek begrudgingly admitted.

Milek shook his head. "I didn't keep Frank Campanelli alive." He'd been too late to save the hit man.

"He wasn't a client," Garek said. "He was a killer."

"You thought I did it," Milek said. "You thought I
shot him."

Garek tensed.

"I saw it in your eyes..." The same look Garek had had
when he awakened fourteen years ago and found Milek
standing over their stepfather's dead body.

"If you had," Garek said, "it would have been self-
defense. Like last time..."

Milek shook his head. "Frank's gun was still in his
holster. It would have been murder."

"The guy's been trying to kill you, trying to kill
Amber and your son..."

"I didn't do it," Milek assured him—even though his

brother had never asked. Apparently he'd just assumed the worst. "You don't have to justify actions I didn't take."

"I'm sorry," Garek said.

But Milek waved off the apology. He wasn't certain what would have happened, had he found Frank Campanelli alive. He wasn't certain what he would have done had the money he'd brought not been enough for the hit man to reveal who'd hired him.

He might have beaten the information out of him. And the last time he'd beaten someone, that person had wound up dead.

Chapter 15

Logan hadn't interrogated a suspect in years, but he felt all of his old methods coming back to him. The long pause before asking a question. The unblinking stare. The blank expression to reveal none of his personal opinions.

They weren't in an interrogation room. They were in the dining room of Milek's condo. But Amber Talsma sat across the table from him as so many other suspects had during his time as a River City detective. Unlike those other suspects, however, Amber Talsma knew exactly what he was doing.

Her lips curved into a slight smile. "I see why you and Stacy fought for so many years before finally admitting how you really felt about each other."

His lips twitched but he refused to smile—even at the mention of his beautiful wife and their previously tempestuous relationship. She was in the bedroom—playing with the nephew whose death she'd mourned for a year.

He was still angry with Amber over letting his wife suffer. But because he was a father, he also understood her doing whatever necessary to protect her child.

"You're tough, Logan," she said. "You're also wasting your time."

He was protecting her, too, since Milek had left the condo to meet with his brother. Logan felt a shiver of unease. While he loved his brothers-in-law like his brothers, he didn't entirely trust them. He had only Milek's word that Frank hadn't told him who hired him.

The hit man hadn't revealed his client during the phone conversation Nikki had recorded, but that didn't mean he hadn't been able to speak when Milek arrived alone at the nightclub. Maybe he'd made a deathbed admission.

"I'm not wasting my time," he said, "if it helps us figure out who is after you."

"I'm sure Agent Rus showed you the list of suspects I already gave him. Those are the only names I can think of—the suspects Gregory and I prosecuted together."

Logan allowed a crack in his detective mask and sighed. "Nick spent a year trying to find a connection between one of them and the Ghost." And despite how stubborn and determined his brother could be, he'd turned up nothing.

"Frank Campanelli was a professional," she said. "While he's been credited with many murders, it's never been proved who hired him."

Logan let a groan slip out. "I tried," he murmured, remembering one of his biggest frustrations from his years on the force. Knowing someone had killed and not being able to prove it. "There was this doctor..."

She leaned forward and asked, "The one who had his malpractice case thrown out when the witnesses died?"

He nodded.

"I was going to prosecute the malpractice case," she said. "I was pushing to increase the charges to manslaughter, though. The guy was drunk. He shouldn't have been operating. The anesthesiologist and surgical assistant were going to testify to his condition…"

"Until they wound up dead."

"It was too great a coincidence," she said. "It had to be Dr. Gunz."

Logan nodded again. And something else occurred to him. "Frank had a gunshot wound."

"That's what killed him," she said.

"Not that gunshot wound," Logan said. "Milek got him in the shoulder in that hotel parking lot. Someone treated that gunshot wound—stitched him up…"

And maybe a doctor's stitches were like fingerprints. "I need to call Nick."

She nodded, and there was a spark in her green eyes. "I hope you can link Dr. Gunz and Campanelli." But that wasn't all she hoped. It was obvious she wanted to be the one who finally brought the doctor to trial.

But in order to do that, she needed to stay alive.

"My mother-in-law wants to meet you," Stacy said.

Amber knew Penny Payne was more than a mother-in-law to her friend. Even when everyone thought Stacy's dad had killed her husband, Penny had cared about the Kozminski kids. She'd become a surrogate mother to Stacy because the woman who'd been her mother hadn't deserved the honor.

"I would love to leave here," Amber said. But only if it was safe. Despite Campanelli's death, it wasn't safe. She sighed. "But I don't think anyone from Payne Protection will allow that."

Until the person who wanted her dead was behind bars, Amber was the one imprisoned. The condo was beautiful. But she needed fresh air and sunshine that didn't come through reinforced glass.

The sunshine had nearly cost her dearly, though. If Campanelli had been any closer when he'd fired those shots...

Milek might have been killed. Or any of the other people she'd come to care so much about...

Stacy's extended family felt like hers now.

"Nobody would let you leave," Stacy agreed. "And nobody thinks Penny should visit you here, either."

As much as they all loved and protected each other, they loved and protected the family matriarch even more. "They don't want her in danger."

"No."

"I don't want anyone in danger because of me, either," Amber said, and tears threatened, stinging her eyes. She'd nearly lost Milek more than once. She wouldn't take a chance with anyone else. "Maybe you shouldn't have visited."

"Logan will keep me safe," Stacy said with full faith in her husband.

Amber envied that—just as she'd envied the love between Garek and Candace.

"He'll keep Michael safe, too," Stacy added.

"Of course." Uncle Logan treated the little boy as if he was his own.

"So you wouldn't mind if I took him with me?"

Amber had missed something. "Where?"

"To see Penny."

"You want Michael to meet your mother-in-law?"

Stacy smiled. "Yes, he will love her. And he'll get to see little Penny again. Her grandmother is watching her."

Amber's mother had died of breast cancer when Amber was in law school. Her father had died a few years later from heart disease. Amber figured it had just been broken from losing her mother—the love of his life. Amber had understood that pain when Milek broke their engagement. She'd never thought she'd be able to give Michael the family he deserved.

But her son had a cousin now. He had aunts and uncles. He still didn't have a father. Milek had yet to broach that conversation he'd claimed he wanted to have about their son. Usually when they were alone they made love—giving in to the passion that always burned so bright and hot between them.

Amber nodded. "Of course you can take him." He wasn't in danger when he wasn't with her. Maybe she should have left him behind a year ago—left him with Stacy then for protection. He would be safer without Amber than with her.

But she hated letting him go—even for a short visit. Her arms ached from the hug she gave him before he walked out the door with Aunt Stacy and Uncle Logan.

"I can send Cooper or Parker inside," Logan had offered.

But she'd refused. For the first time since she'd opened that envelope of photos Frank Campanelli had taken, she was actually alone.

She needed the solitude. She needed to be able to think. To remember who she was.

She hadn't been a lawyer, a real lawyer, for the past

year. Until Logan's interrogation earlier, she hadn't realized how much she'd missed it. How she needed it…

Maybe it was because she finally felt like a lawyer again that she needed to investigate. Not that she suspected Milek of anything nefarious.

She believed he had nothing to do with Gregory's murder. Or Frank Campanelli's…

But she wanted to check out his place—to see if she could find some clue to the secrets she was sure he was keeping from her. Why had he broken their engagement?

How could he make love to her the way he did if he didn't care about her?

He had to have feelings for her. It couldn't be all one-sided.

She knew there was nothing in his bedroom; she'd spent too much time in it to have missed anything. But there was another door down the hallway past the room in which their son slept. It looked like a back door. But it didn't open to the outside. It couldn't. The warehouse was big and only a portion of it had been converted to the condo. What about the rest of it?

She stopped in front of that door. The access code was written on the panel beside it. Not in Milek's handwriting. The scrawl was bolder—sloppier. Garek's.

Her heart rate quickened when she read the number. The date Milek had proposed to her. If he'd regretted proposing—as he'd told her—why would he have wanted to remember it?

Her fingers trembling, she punched in the code, and the door slid open. Cold air rushed over her. This area of the warehouse hadn't been converted. But it wasn't the garage. That was on the other side. What was back here?

She moved through the open area until she found

another door. There was no lock here; it wasn't even shut tightly, so she pushed it open.

Sunshine poured through the skylights in the metal roof—illuminated the space. Dust danced in the light. Nobody had been here for a while.

But she could see what it was used for.

Paint spattered the concrete floor. It was dry. Like the paint on the canvases leaning against the walls. They covered every wall except for the area where he'd put a desk. Only a few papers sat atop it.

She walked over to find what he kept here. Some old receipts for paint supplies and a few sales. And a review. She picked up the yellowed paper and read. *There is an angry energy in the brushstrokes and colors Koz uses in his work. If the rage in his paintings was ever unleashed, he could prove a danger to himself and others.*

She gasped at the reviewer's audacity. It was one thing to judge the art. But to judge the artist?

Why had Milek kept such garbage? She rummaged through his desk but there were no other reviews—none of the ones she had kept in a scrapbook for him. Those reviews raved about his brilliance—about his use of vibrant colors to express emotion—to bring his art alive.

Why keep the one bad review and ignore all the good ones? She looked at the article again. Was the reviewer someone he knew? Respected?

She didn't recognize the name. But she recognized the date—the day Milek had ended their engagement. Had that review had anything to do with it?

Had he actually believed he could be a danger?

Metal creaked and groaned. It might have just been the roof. Or the walls...

Or the wind blowing around outside. Amber shivered.

It was cold in here. But the chill Amber felt was within—because she didn't think those noises were the weather or the warehouse. But a real danger…

"Frank's money must have been running low," Garek commented as he pushed open the door to the studio apartment. It had taken him only seconds to pick the lock.

But then, a notorious assassin like the Ghost wouldn't have had to worry about security. Nobody would have dared sneak up on a man who'd killed so many.

So, who had shot him in the nightclub? Who had he trusted enough to get that close to him?

Milek followed his brother inside and glanced around the place. The furnishings were minimal. A bed. A table. One chair. But then Campanelli probably hadn't planned on staying long.

He'd wanted to kill Amber, collect his fee and leave River City.

"Would you have done it?" Garek asked.

"Killed the doctor?" He wasn't even sure what he'd have threatened Dr. Gunz with—death? That probably wouldn't have scared the man. Surgeons like him thought they were God. He'd threatened him with exposure and that had been far worse. Of course, they'd had nothing but the word of other criminals that Dr. Gunz was the one who'd treated Frank's gunshot wound. They couldn't have gone to the authorities. But the media didn't care about little things like facts and evidence.

"No," Garek said. Maybe a little too quickly. "Would you have stolen to get Campanelli more money?"

Milek met his brother's curious gaze. And nodded. "I would have done whatever's necessary to find out who's trying to kill Amber."

They had. They'd reached out to old contacts—to friends of their father and uncle—to find out what they'd known about Frank Campanelli and who might have patched him up. Dr. Gunz. He hadn't known much; it was his chauffeur who'd driven Frank from the doctor's mansion to the tiny studio on the other side of River City.

Maybe it wasn't so bad being a Kozminski after all. Since those contacts had led them to where Campanelli had been staying.

"I would have helped you," Garek told him. "Get whatever you needed…"

Milek grabbed his brother's shoulder, squeezed it.

"We should have told Nick, though…"

"That we're going back to our lives of crime?" Milek asked. He moved around the place, opening drawers—cupboards.

Garek checked the usual places. The toilet tank. The freezer. The flour jar. Boxes of cereal.

Milek riffled through books. Then he flipped out his switchblade and went to work on the mattress.

"That we found where Campanelli had been staying," Garek said.

"He'll find it, too," Milek said. But he'd wanted the head start—in case they found something that led to the person who wanted Amber dead.

Garek chuckled as he looked around at the destruction. "He'll be pissed."

"Yeah." Milek was pissed, too. They'd found nothing. As he headed toward the door, a board creaked beneath his foot. He paused. It gave more than it should. It wasn't just old.

Garek met his gaze. Then they both dropped to the floor. Milek used the blade of his pocketknife to pull up the board. A small metal box lay in the space between the trusses.

Garek laughed at the lock as he disposed of it. Then he handed the box to Milek to open.

A book lay inside, its leather cover fraying at the edges. He pulled it out and scanned through the pages. There were names. So many names. But they weren't easy to read—not with the line meticulously drawn through each.

He didn't recognize many of them, either. Until he got toward the end. Then he found one: DA Gregory Schievink. The name was visible despite the line scored through it. All the names had lines through them but for two on the last page.

Frank had never failed to kill any other targets but those last two.

Seeing the names like that, in Frank's careful handwriting, chilled Milek's blood even while his heart began to pump hard and fast with fear.

Amber Talsma.

Michael Talsma.

Someone didn't want just Amber to die; they wanted her son—their son—dead, too.

Chapter 16

Candace glanced in the rearview mirror, but something distracted her from the road behind her. Michael met her gaze and smiled.

"Hey, Aunt Candy!"

"Hey, little man."

Stacy reached over the center console and squeezed Candace's hand. "Thanks for driving us out to Penny's when Logan had to go talk to Nick."

"I'm happy to—"

"It's not necessary, though," Stacy said. "We're not in any real danger."

Candace wasn't so sure about that—not when she glanced into the rearview mirror again. She'd noticed that truck before—back at Milek's condo. Someone was following her.

But that discreet distance the driver had maintained was closing. Of course, she would have made the tail anyway. The road to Penny's wasn't as traveled as the streets of River City.

Who was it?

Campanelli was dead. But he wouldn't have followed her. He'd seen Amber's new appearance. He wouldn't have mistaken either her or Stacy for the former assistant district attorney. Whoever had replaced him probably didn't know what Amber looked like now.

Maybe he had mistaken Stacy for her. There were streaks of red in her hair, along with blond and brown, and she was nearly the same build as her curvy friend.

Or maybe it wasn't a bad man—as Michael would say. Maybe it was one of Rus's men. He might have stopped trusting them after Milek had slipped away to meet Frank alone.

The guys had gone off alone today, too.

She knew where. She and Garek had no secrets. She reached for her cell phone. She should probably call him now—let him know she'd picked up a tail. He could check with Rus to make sure it was one of his men.

But the truck kept coming. An agent or an officer wouldn't have been driving so fast. So carelessly...

No. This was a bad man.

The truck slammed into the rear bumper of the SUV. Despite Candace's grip on the steering wheel, it spun out of control.

Panic gripped Milek. His heart pounded fast and frantically. His hand shook as he punched in the code on the panel outside his condo. He couldn't wait for the door to open fully before squeezing between it and the jamb. "Amber? Amber?"

His voice echoed in the empty living room. He could

see through it to the kitchen and the dining room. They were completely empty. His footsteps echoed off the concrete floor as he rushed across the living room to the open door to the master bedroom suite. Had she been inside, she would have heard him. So he wasn't surprised to find it empty.

But a creak from the living room had his breath easing from his tightly constricted lungs. "Amber?"

"She's not here?" Garek asked.

Ignoring his brother, he hurried to the hall on the other side of the living room. The first door off it was a bathroom. It was empty. He moved down to the next door—to Michael's bedroom. The bed had been made but the little bear that was always sitting on it wasn't there. Jewel was gone.

He remembered the night he'd found her packing. Should he have trusted that she'd stay? "She took off..."

Garek shook his head. "No. Cooper said nobody left the warehouse since Stacy and the boy."

"The boy?" he repeated. Logan had been here when Milek had left, but Cooper wouldn't dare call his older brother *the boy*. "Michael?"

Garek nodded.

And a pang of pure fear struck Milek. "He's out there—where the killer can get to him?"

Garek reached out and squeezed his shoulder. "Candace is driving him and Stacy out to Penny's. They're safe."

He would have believed that, too—had he not seen Frank Campanelli's kill book and those two unlined names.

"And where the hell is Amber?" If nobody had seen her leave...

"She's gotta be here," Garek insisted. "Cooper wouldn't

have missed her. He couldn't have survived all those tours
of duty if he wasn't observant. He wouldn't have missed
her slipping out of the condo."

"Not the condo…" Milek murmured.

"What?"

"He didn't see her slip out of the *building*." There was
more to the building than the portion that was his condo.
There was his studio space and the place where he stored
old canvases. That area wasn't as secure as the condo,
though. If someone had managed to slip past the perimeter guards, they might have been able to get into that
part of the warehouse.

His pulse racing, he hurried down the hall to the door
at the end. Like the front door, it had a security panel.
He hadn't been out to his studio in a year, so he'd forgotten Garek had written the code on the panel. His brother
knew he painted; he didn't know about the shows and
the reviews, though. He just thought it was a hobby—
one he'd worried had consumed Milek. So he'd wanted
the code to get into the studio so he could remind Milek
to eat and to drink and to sleep—for those times when
his art had consumed him.

He didn't need to see the code. He would never for-
get it. The date he had asked Amber to marry him. The
date she'd said yes.

What had she thought when she'd seen it? If she had
seen it?

Had she punched it in? Was that where she'd gone?
He should have been furious if she'd invaded his private
space, if she'd put herself in danger in the less secure
area of the building…

But all he wanted now was to see her. His hand shook

as he punched in the numbers; she had to be there. She had to be safe.

Before he could step through the door, Garek's cell rang. His brother fumbled it out of his pocket. His breath shuddered out in relief. Despite his assurance, he'd been worried, too. "It's Candace."

He pressed the phone to his ear. But as he listened his smile faded and his eyes darkened with concern.

Whatever he'd learned was not good news...

Pain struck Amber—so hard she sucked in a breath. Until he'd found them living in that lakeshore town under assumed identities, Milek had had no interest in their son or her. Or so she'd thought...

She'd thought he had never even seen the baby they had created together.

But if not...

How had he created a portrait so vivid it brought Amber back to those early days, to the smell of talcum powder and baby shampoo? And the warmth and comfort of holding her baby in her arms, against her heart?

She'd thought Milek had missed all that—that he'd wanted nothing to do with his son. But somehow he'd painted this portrait. She reached out and touched the canvas, expecting to find it as warm and soft as their infant son had been. But the paint was hard and as cold as the low temperature in the old warehouse.

Nothing had been converted from the original structure here. The walls were metal and brick and apparently uninsulated. The ceiling was metal, too. Maybe it was the source of the noises she'd heard earlier, because it creaked and groaned above her with the weight of the snow left from winter.

And the floor was bare concrete but for all the spatters of paint Milek had left on it. He worked here?

In the cold.

It was where he'd put himself when he'd broken their engagement. Out in the cold…

Maybe that was why he'd used the date of their engagement. To remind himself of what he'd given up.

But why? Why had he stayed away from her? From Michael?

Because of that silly review—that bullshit that he might be a danger to anyone…?

She wasn't in danger from him. But she was in danger.

She heard another creak, but it wasn't overhead. She glanced toward the door and saw him standing there. A gasp slipped through her lips and hung on the cold air between them like a ghost. She pressed a hand to her racing heart.

"You scared me."

He said nothing. Just stared at her.

Maybe he was angry she'd invaded what was obviously a very personal space to him—with very personal things. She couldn't help it, though. She had had to pry—had to know everything about the man she'd once loved so desperately. "I didn't know you painted anymore."

He didn't reply. Maybe he thought it was none of her business what he did. They weren't together—not really. He was only protecting her and their son.

But there was something about his silence that unnerved her. It wasn't as if he was angry with her. It was worse. "Milek?"

The look on his face scared her as much as his sudden appearance had. "What's wrong?"

He shook his head—not as if he was claiming nothing was wrong. But as if it was too awful to speak aloud.

"Milek, what is it?" She had to know—no matter how terrible. She glanced at that portrait of their infant son— at all those loving brushstrokes. And she realized the only thing that would have upset him so much. Her knees began to tremble, threatening to fold beneath her.

She might have collapsed right on that paint-spattered concrete floor if he hadn't vaulted forward and caught her. His arms closed tightly around her—as if he could hold her together.

But if what she feared had happened, there would be no holding her together—ever again. "Tell me," she implored him. "Just tell me…"

"Amber…"

"Tell me!" she shouted at him. "Tell me what happened to our son!"

"There was an accident…" But his eyes were dark— almost black with rage. There was the anger now—the anger she'd missed because she'd felt only his devastation. His loss…

And she knew it had been no accident. Whatever had happened to their son had been intentional. Someone hadn't been trying to kill just her. They'd wanted her son dead, too.

Had they succeeded?

Chapter 17

Penny Payne forced a happy smile. She was used to faking it. To pretending nothing was wrong when everything was. She'd done it when she found out years ago her husband had cheated on her. She'd pretended she'd forgiven him even before she'd found that forgiveness within her heart. And when he'd died, she had forced herself to be strong—for her devastated children.

She summoned that strength now and wound her arms around her daughter-in-law. Stacy's slender shoulders bowed with guilt. "I shouldn't have taken him out of the condo. I should have left him with his mom. She'll never forgive me…"

Penny suspected Amber would forgive her best friend before Stacy forgave herself. "It's not your fault."

It was the fault of the sadistic bastard who'd rammed his truck into the SUV carrying a child and a pregnant woman and Candace.

White-faced, the female bodyguard stood against the wall of Stacy's hospital room. She had no reason to feel guilty, either. But Penny wasn't the one who could absolve either woman of guilt.

The door to the hall opened, and as it did, Candace drew her gun. But a big hand wrapped around it, bending it down to her side as strong arms closed around her.

"You're all right!" Garek said as he hugged his wife. "Thank God you're all right."

Milek and a woman rushed into the room behind Garek. Their faces were as pale as Candace's until the little boy sat up in the bed Stacy had tucked him into—the bed she was supposed to be in herself while she waited for the doctor to release her.

"Hey, Mommy," he said.

The dark-haired woman ran to the bed and enveloped him in a big hug. Tears streamed down her face. "Are you really all right?"

He wriggled free and stared up at her, his little brow puckered with confusion. "I'm not sick," he assured her. "Aunt Stacy is. This is her bed."

But she had been too upset to sit, let alone lie down— no matter how badly she could have been hurt. How much she could have lost...

Stacy was pregnant. Penny was about to be a grandmother. Again.

"I heard you were in a car accident," the little boy's mother said, her voice cracking with emotion. "And that you'd been brought to the hospital."

He shook his head. "Aunt Candy is a better driver than you are. She didn't run off the road when the bad man hit us."

Instead of being offended, his mother laughed and

hugged him again. Her breath shuddered out in a sigh of relief.

Garek laughed, too—a laugh cut short when Candace jabbed his side. "Thanks a lot."

Somehow Penny didn't think the tough female bodyguard really minded her nephew calling her Candy. She'd done her best to protect him. She'd wrestled her SUV under control instead of rolling it, and she'd outrun the truck that had tried to overtake them.

"Thank you," Milek told his sister-in-law. "Thank you for keeping him safe."

Her throat moving as she swallowed her emotion, Candace nodded.

Another man came through the door. And, as always, Penny's heart constricted at how much Logan looked like his father. But then, all her sons did—even the one she hadn't borne but who was every bit as much a Payne as Logan and his brothers. Nick wasn't here yet, though. He would be—he always came when his family was in trouble even though he struggled to accept he was family.

His hands shaking, Logan reached for his wife. "Sweetheart, are you all right?"

She nodded.

"And the baby?"

"Both of them are fine," Stacy said.

Logan's brows lowered with confusion. "Penny wasn't in the car. We didn't bring her with us to Milek's condo. Mom was watching her…"

Her namesake had been with her. Now the baby was with her aunt Tanya—Cooper's wife.

"She wasn't," Stacy assured him.

"Then…" And realization finally dawned. "We're having twins?"

Stacy nodded.

"That's wonderful," Amber told her friend—her joy sincere.

Stacy tugged free of her husband to face the other woman. "Are you okay? You're not angry at me?"

"Of course not," Amber assured her. "It wasn't your fault."

"It was the bad man," Michael said. While he was young, he was wiser than the others. He knew where the blame really lay—with the person who'd tried to harm them. He turned toward Milek. "We need to find the bad man."

"We will," Milek assured his son. "We will."

Penny hoped it was soon—before someone tried to harm the boy again. She didn't like when someone tried to hurt her family. And although she hadn't officially met Amber and her son, they were family now—because Milek was.

Milek had never felt so sick. He was still as tense and fearful as he'd been when he hadn't been able to find Michael and Amber—because even though they were with him now, he knew how easily he could have lost them.

How easily he once had...

And just like that last time, he would have no one but himself to blame.

Keeping his voice low, he spoke into the cell phone pressed to his ear. "It's because of me."

He didn't want to wake his son or Amber. They'd already been through too much. So he sat alone in the living room—watching the door to make sure no one tried to get in.

"What's because of you?" Agent Rus asked. He sounded tired—as if Milek had awakened him.

Maybe he had. He didn't know what time it was. He hadn't even tried to sleep because he knew it wasn't possible—not with the realization he'd had.

"Someone's trying to kill Amber and Michael because of me."

"Why would you think that?"

Because if someone wanted to hurt him—really hurt him—he would take away the two people who mattered most to him: the woman he loved and his son. "The same reason we thought Chekov was trying to take out Candace…"

Because she was Garek's weakness—just like Amber was his. Rus apparently had no weaknesses, because he said nothing for a long moment. Then, finally, he spoke again. "It can't be Chekov. That first attempt on Amber's life was made a year ago—before you and Garek helped me take him down."

"It's not Chekov," Milek agreed. "So there's someone else."

Someone who hated him so much he wanted to completely destroy him. When had he made such an enemy? He could only remember two people whom he'd really hurt in his lifetime. One of them was dead. The other was Amber.

He glanced toward the master bedroom and found her standing in the doorway, leaning against the jamb. Bathed in the moonlight streaming in through the skylights, she was beautiful. So beautiful his body ached to possess her…

Rus said something but Milek didn't hear it—not with blood rushing through his ears—rushing low in his body.

Then she asked, "Who are you talking to?"

"Agent Rus…"

"Why so damn formal?" the FBI agent asked, as if annoyed.

Milek was never sure what to call the other man. He wasn't even sure what they were to each other. Were they friends? Family?

Rus wasn't entirely convinced Milek hadn't murdered the hit man. But that didn't mean anything. His own brother had suspected the same thing.

"I was telling Amber who's on the phone," Milek explained. He hoped his talking hadn't awakened her. He hoped she hadn't overheard his fear. She would probably hate him even more if she knew everything she'd been through, every bad thing in her life, was likely because of him.

Amber felt the tension in Milek even from across the room. He clicked off his cell phone and slid it into his pocket. "It's late," she said. "Why aren't you sleeping?"

He gestured toward the door. "I need to keep watch…"

She shook her head. She'd heard Logan at the hospital. He'd pulled every Payne Protection bodyguard from other details in order to guard them. "We're safe."

For the moment…

He stepped away from the door—finally—as if he believed her. But then he said, "You won't be safe until we figure out who hired Campanelli."

"Whoever it was must have hired someone else," she remarked. Apparently even assassins were replaceable. Maybe she shouldn't have been concerned that another assistant had taken over as the district attorney. Maybe the job never would have been hers—even if she had stayed in River City.

And with the reports on the news making her sound complicit in faking her death, and her rumored affair with her boss, she would probably never have a career again. Too bad she had just realized how much she missed it.

"We'll find out who it is," Milek said with grim determination. He stepped closer to her, but he didn't look at her—as if he wasn't quite able to meet her eyes.

"You won't," she said.

And he flinched.

"Not if you're going to waste your time thinking it's someone trying to hurt you."

He looked at her then, his eyes narrowed. "You heard what I told Agent Rus?"

She nodded.

"I'm sorry," he said, his voice gruff with guilt. "I'm sorry I've put you and Michael in danger."

She hated seeing him like this—beating himself up over something that wasn't his fault. She stepped closer and slid her fingertips along his clenched jaw. "It's not your fault. This has nothing to do with you."

"I hoped not," he said. "But to want to kill Michael, too…"

"And Schievink," she reminded him. "You didn't particularly care for him."

His lips curved into a slight smile. "No, I didn't…"

"And who would think you particularly cared for me?" she asked.

He released a sharp breath—as if she'd sucker punched him. Maybe now he knew how she'd felt when he broke up with her.

"You dumped me," she reminded him. "You had

nothing to do with our son. How would hurting either of us hurt you?"

He shrugged, and his broad shoulders slumped as if he carried a heavy burden.

She hadn't lessened his guilt. Maybe she'd even made it worse. But she couldn't absolve him of the pain he'd caused her—especially when she'd never understood it.

"Why?" she asked. "Why did you break up with me?"

"I had my reasons," he said.

"Schievink?" she asked. "But you said he hadn't claimed Michael as his until after you'd broken our engagement." And her heart.

"We need to focus on who's trying to hurt you and Michael," he said. "We both already know that I have." The guilt was in his voice. "I'm sorry…"

She believed him, but she doubted it would have changed what he'd done. "I loved you…"

Unfortunately she suspected she still did.

"Amber…"

"Did you ever feel the same?"

"You know…"

"What?" she asked. She knew nothing. He'd shut her out five years ago and he'd never let her back in.

But then he reached for her, dragging her up against his hard body. His head lowered, and he covered her mouth with his, kissing her deeply—passionately. Maybe this was his way of showing her what he couldn't tell her.

At least, that was what she wanted to believe—that he still cared. So she clutched his shoulders. And she kissed him back.

He lifted her and carried her back to the bedroom—to the bed. She wore only a robe, which he quickly untied and pushed from her shoulders. His breath caught as he stared at her breasts. "You're so beautiful…"

He wasn't the only man who'd ever told her so. Old boyfriends had. Dates. Gregory…

But it mattered most when Milek said it—as he had before. As an artist he created beauty—beauty beyond anything she'd imagined. That portrait of their son…

It had brought her to tears.

And the way he touched her, almost reverently, nearly brought her to tears, too. She blinked and focused on his face. He was the beautiful one, his features too perfectly chiseled to be handsome. She traced her fingers along every line of his face.

When she touched his lips, he kissed her fingers. Then his mouth skimmed down her arm to her shoulder. He kissed her neck, and she shivered as her skin tingled.

"Are you cold?" he asked.

The heat of passion flushing her body, she shook her head.

But he covered her anyway—with his body—after he'd pulled off his clothes. Naked skin slid over naked skin. He was as warm as she was. His erection pushed against her belly, and she could feel it throbbing. He needed her as badly as she needed him—even if he wouldn't admit it.

She stroked her fingers over the tip of him, and he groaned. Then his mouth covered hers, and he kissed her passionately. His tongue slid between her lips as he deepened the kiss.

His hands caressed her, gliding over her back to her hips and her butt. She was rounder than she'd been when they were together before. But he seemed to appreciate her new curves, since he kept stroking them.

A moan slipped through her lips. She was surprised she wasn't purring from his touch. Her desire intensified. She needed him now. She wrapped her fingers around his erection and stroked him.

"Amber..." He groaned her name almost as a warning.

She took it as encouragement. She wanted him to lose control. But he always held on to it—somehow. The way he now caught her wrist in his hand and pulled her fingers away from him.

She murmured a protest, but his mouth covered hers. He kissed her. And the passion was in his kiss. But a kiss wasn't enough. She shifted beneath him, rubbing her skin against his. His erection throbbed again, pulsing against her.

He moved his hands to her breasts, teasing her nipples— pushing her to madness. He kept one hand on her breast as his other hand trailed down her body. She arched against his hand—wanting more.

But his fingers weren't enough. The pressure kept building. She wanted him. Badly.

So badly...

"Milek, please..."

Finally he relented. He parted her legs and pushed inside her. She arched, taking him deeper. Then she locked her legs around his waist and moved against him. He matched her rhythm, as if he instinctively knew what she needed. He gave it to her—slow, deep thrusts.

Her body shuddered as she came. Moments later, with a deep groan, Milek joined her in pleasure. She'd needed the release more than she'd realized. She wasn't nearly as tense as she'd been. Milek was, though. His body was rock hard next to hers, his heart beating fast.

Then she heard what he must have already. Something

creaked and then clattered as it tumbled across the hard-wood floor in the living room.

Despite all that security, someone had made it inside the condo.

Chapter 18

"What were you doing?" Milek asked his son as he carried him back to his bedroom. Had the little boy been sleepwalking in the dark? He'd bumped into the coffee table and sent a water glass clattering across the floor. He'd also sent Milek's heart into overdrive.

Not that it hadn't already been after making love with Amber.

Michael's arms looped around his neck as the little boy cuddled close and sniffled. Milek had never known such pain; his son's tears affected him like someone reaching inside his chest and squeezing his heart.

"I had a bad dream," Michael admitted.

Milek's arms tightened around his son. He could protect him from physical danger—he hoped. But what psychological damage was being done to the child? What fears and insecurities would he have because of this ordeal? A year ago he'd had to leave his home, his school, his friends and pretend to be someone else. And that was after someone had fired shots into his home.

Then he'd been run off the road and shot at again. It was a miracle he hadn't had more nightmares after what he'd been through.

"It was just a dream," Milek assured him. But he worried it wasn't—that it was, instead, the boy's memories of the nightmare he was living. He wanted to promise that nothing bad would happen again. But that was a promise he couldn't keep—not until they figured out who'd hired Campanelli to take out the mother and the child.

What kind of sick son of a bitch would order a hit on a little boy?

Milek pulled back the blankets and laid his son back in his bed. But Michael's arms stayed locked around his neck, pulling him down with him.

"Can you stay with me?" he asked.

"Sure…" Milek would do whatever necessary to make the little boy feel safe again.

Michael scooted over and patted the bed beside him. "Lie down with me like Mommy does."

Milek had watched Mommy do that—had watched how well Amber soothed all the little boy's fears and made him feel secure again. Milek wasn't sure if he was capable of the tenderness she showed their child.

But he lay down next to him. Michael snuggled against his side. And Milek felt the little boy staring up at him. He turned to his side to face him. Michael looked so much like him—with those thickly lashed silver eyes.

Michael blinked—fighting sleep. Probably because he was afraid he would have another bad dream.

Milek searched his mind, trying to come up with a

story to tell his son. But all the fairy tales he remembered were more violent than the scrapes the little boy had had with the bad man. Milek could draw pictures with him, but he would need to get out of bed to retrieve the crayons and paper. And it felt very right lying next to his son.

"You're Aunt Stacy's brother?" he asked.

Milek nodded.

"Like Uncle Garek," the little boy said. "So doesn't that make you my uncle, too?"

"No," Milek replied.

And maybe he should have had this discussion with Amber first; maybe he should have gotten her permission. But like so many times before, he ignored what was probably the right choice and said, "I'm your father."

The little boy's eyes widened, but it wasn't with surprise, because he said, almost exultantly, "I knew it! I knew it!"

His arms locked around Milek's neck again as he clung to him. "You're my daddy!"

His hand trembling slightly, Milek patted the little boy's head. "Yes, I'm your daddy."

A slight noise drew his attention to the bedroom doorway. Amber stood there, tears streaming silently down her face. His stomach lurched with dread.

Was she upset with him?

He hated that he'd made her cry again—the way he had five years ago. He'd never meant to hurt her then. Or now. He'd only been trying to keep her safe. Then.

And now.

The bedroom door creaked open, and Amber tensed. She knew it was Milek, though. Nobody else would get past security. Or him.

After seeing him cuddling with their son, she'd hurried back to the master bedroom. She hadn't wanted Michael to see her crying as Milek had. She wasn't certain she could talk even now, with emotion overwhelming her.

He settled onto the bed next to her, the mattress dipping beneath his weight. He didn't believe she was sleeping—despite her efforts to be still—because he asked, "Are you angry I told him?"

Amber shook her head. She was relieved. She'd thought Milek might never claim his son. She was also overwhelmed. It wasn't just a suspicion anymore. She knew without a doubt she'd fallen in love with Milek all over again.

Or maybe she'd never gotten over him. Despite Schievink's best efforts, she'd never been tempted to cross the line with him. Of course, he'd been married, and she would never commit adultery. But even if he'd been single, she wouldn't have been tempted. She had only ever really loved one man: Milek.

"No, I'm not angry," she said. "Our son deserves to know who his father is."

"He deserves a better father," Milek murmured.

Maybe that horrible review had affected him. Or all the rumors that had always circulated about his family. He had to know he wasn't the man any of that stuff had painted him as being.

"You've saved his life and mine over and over," she reminded him. "That's what a good father does—he protects his child."

He touched her then, brushing her tears away with the pad of his thumb. "You did that," he said. "You gave up everything—the job you loved, your friends, your home—you did everything you could to keep him safe."

"You've nearly taken a bullet for us," Amber said. "You're a good parent, Milek."

He shook his head. "I'm afraid I'll disappoint him. That I'll let him down…"

Her heart ached for the fear in his. He was really afraid of being a father. He hadn't denied his son because he hadn't loved him, but because he had.

"I need to find out who's after you both," Milek said. "That's the only way I can really protect you—the only way you'll be safe."

Remembering what she'd heard him tell Agent Rus earlier, she assured him, "We're not in danger because of you."

"You made that clear, counselor," he said with a slightly bitter chuckle.

She had been pretty brutal in her argument with him earlier. But then she'd been accused of being a ruthless assistant district attorney. She hadn't shown much leniency. But she'd learned that from Gregory. Tough sentences for tough crimes.

There had been only one time they'd disagreed. But she'd had to accede to his decision, since he'd been her boss. Not that the judge would have listened to her anyway. Both he and Gregory had been determined to send the perpetrator to prison. He had been convicted of two counts of manslaughter—after driving into a crowd outside a nightclub. He'd been drunk, his first offense. She'd wanted to send him to rehab. She'd known he wouldn't last in prison.

She hadn't known the reason he wouldn't last was that he would take his own life. He'd been sentenced to five years. He hadn't made it five days.

She'd gone to his funeral. His father had been inconsolable that he hadn't been able to protect his son. She flinched as she remembered the ugly scene. She hadn't meant to cause trouble. She hadn't meant to…

"I know who wants us dead," Amber said with sudden clarity.

Milek studied her face, his brow furrowing slightly. "One of the names from your list?"

She shook her head. "I didn't think of him. He wasn't a suspect. We hadn't prosecuted him."

"Then who?"

"A bereaved father," she said.

And Milek nodded. He obviously understood and agreed.

Who else would want to hurt her son but someone who thought she had hurt his?

Could no one do what they were hired to do anymore? Were they too lazy or too inept to complete the job? So much money had been spent with no results yielded. No deaths.

At least, not the deaths that mattered. The ones that were overdue.

Not that Frank Campanelli hadn't deserved to die— the mercenary double-crosser. That had been the mistake. Hiring someone whose only stake had been financial, money his only motivation. And when that "fatal" accident had been staged, he'd been only too happy to take credit for it.

He hadn't really cared about killing—until he was the one dying. Remembering the look of shock on Campanelli's face as the bullet had struck his heart brought a surge of satisfaction.

He hadn't expected it.

Amber Talsma would, though. She knew it was coming. Despite her bodyguard boyfriend and his family, she couldn't keep escaping death. They couldn't watch her every minute. They couldn't protect her every minute.

Sooner rather than later, she and her little bastard were going to die…

Chapter 19

Nick nodded in agreement. "I think we have a real viable suspect." Finally. He'd spent the past year checking out all those other names she'd given him.

If it had been one of them and he'd missed it...

But she hadn't mentioned this one. She wouldn't have thought of him until she'd learned her son's name was on Frank Campanelli's hit list.

Irritation nagged at him. He hadn't been happy Milek and Garek had found that book. The apartment had been unlocked—his ass. There wasn't a lock created that at least one of the Kozminski brothers wasn't able to pick.

Nick needed to learn some of those skills...

"What are you going to do?" Milek asked.

Nick had been asking himself that a lot lately. With the interim district attorney breathing down his neck, and having to run everything through the Chicago FBI division and deal with the River City mayor, he felt more like a politician himself than a lawman. He wanted the freedom the Kozminskis and the Paynes had—the freedom to investigate without worrying about the consequences.

"Nick?" Milek prodded him.

He forced himself to focus again. "I'll have him picked up and brought in for questioning." He tapped his keyboard and dispatched the order to have a uniform go to the last known address of Brad Jipping.

"I want to talk to him," Amber said.

"Absolutely not."

"I've questioned suspects before," she said. "I'm an assistant DA."

"Not anymore," Nick reminded her. She'd given up her career to protect herself and her son. He turned to Milek. "You shouldn't have brought her here." It was dangerous. Every time she was out in public, shots were fired.

He was getting sick of writing up damn reports, too.

"She insisted," Milek said.

"I could have come to the condo," Nick pointed out.

Amber shook her head. Her hair was still dark but there were streaks of her natural red color coming through now. She'd ditched the brown contacts, too. The disguise he'd given her, and the life, were gone.

"We needed access to the police computers," she explained. "To my records…"

"I'm pretty sure Nikki could have accessed the computers remotely for us." For them. Nick's half sister wasn't likely to help him do anything. While his half brothers didn't blame him for their father cheating on their mother, Nikki did. She had—albeit begrudgingly—

called to play him the recording of Milek and Frank
Campanelli, though.

Maybe he was making progress with her.

"I want to be here when you bring him in," Amber
said.

He shook his head. "We don't know how long it will
take to find him." And he didn't want them hanging
around his office. If the interim DA saw her there...

She'd do something crazy—like insist Nick arrest her.

Amber glanced nervously at Milek. "We can't stay
away from Michael that long."

Nick was surprised they had left their son at all. But
the whole Payne family had gathered around to protect
him—to protect her and Milek, too. He almost pitied
whoever was trying to kill them. They were bound to get
frustrated—maybe so frustrated they'd slip up.

"I'll let you know what Brad Jipping has to say," Nick
said, "after I interrogate him."

Amber gave him a skeptical glance. He'd heard she'd
been a good assistant DA, maybe even one of the best.
That hadn't come from the acting DA, though. Evelyn
Reynolds had had nothing complimentary to say about
Amber. Other lawyers, judges and even the mayor had
sung her praises.

"You going to go after your job again?" he asked.
"Once we find whoever's been after you?" She had a
pretty damn good chance of getting it—if she talked to
the right people.

She glanced at Milek again. And the nerves were still
there. She wanted to know what he thought of the idea,
but Kozminski's expression revealed nothing. And he was
usually the easier of the two brothers to read. Nick had

certainly had no problem seeing how much pain it had caused Milek, thinking Amber and their son were dead.

Instead of answering his question, Amber just shrugged. "It's not a possibility now. Not with the danger Michael and I are in."

Nick didn't make promises. He didn't claim he would find whoever was after her. All he could say was "I'll let you know when I talk to Jipping."

She opened her mouth to protest, but Milek escorted her out of Nick's office. The door had been closed for just a minute before it opened again.

He uttered a weary sigh. "You can't seriously think he's being brought in already..." He glanced up and stopped.

"Who?" Penny Payne asked.

He could have refused to answer but she'd find out anyhow. She always found out everything. "A suspect in the attempts on Amber and Michael Talsma's lives."

"That's great." She smiled. "You've made progress, then."

He shook his head. Too many people had given him credit for things he hadn't done. He'd been too busy pushing papers to do the hard work. The dangerous work.

"Amber came up with the guy," he said. "He's a good suspect, though."

"Hopefully this will all be over soon," she said. "And Amber and her son can take their lives back."

"Is that why you stopped by?" he asked. "To check on the investigation?"

She reached into her purse—which was voluminous—and pulled out a large plastic bag full of chocolate chip cookies. "I brought you these," she said. "Your favorites..."

How had she known? His own mother hadn't known what he liked to eat. Not that she'd cooked very often.

She'd usually sent him down to a fast-food restaurant to bring them back a meal—when she hadn't spent all of their money on drugs or booze.

"They're the ones with the sour cream in the batter to keep them soft," she said.

"And the big chunks of dark chocolate," he murmured. It had been a while since he'd been with a woman when he could feel lust for a cookie. But Penny Payne was a master baker. She didn't use those measly little chips of chocolate. She used chunks, and a lot of them. "Thank you."

She smiled again.

He wasn't sure what she wanted from him. She had his gratitude. Nobody had welcomed him more than she had. "Why?" The question slipped out without his volition. "Why are you so nice to me? Why do you bring me cookies? Why do you treat me like I'm one of your kids?"

"You're a Payne," she said.

He shook his head. "I'm a Rus."

"That's not your real name. That's a name your mother assumed when she went into hiding."

He shrugged. "So it was something else before Rus." He didn't care. "It was never Payne."

"It should have been," she said.

"I've made a life for myself," he said.

"You've made a career for yourself," she said as she glanced around his office. "You haven't made a life, Nick. Not yet…"

Without another word, she turned and walked out. But she left more behind than the cookies she'd baked for him. She'd left him with a confusing myriad of emotions. He didn't have time to sort them out now. He had a case to solve.

* * *

"Would you do it?" Milek asked. "Would you go back to your old job if you weren't in danger?"

She felt him studying her face as if her answer really mattered to him. But when she glanced across the console, his attention was back on the road.

"I wouldn't have left it if I hadn't been in danger," Amber replied.

"You'll be able to get it back," he assured her.

She chuckled. "Not likely. The new DA would never hire me back."

"Why not?"

"She resented my relationship with Gregory."

A muscle twitched along his tightly clenched jaw.

"My working relationship," she clarified. "That was all we had."

"It wasn't all he wanted."

She couldn't argue that. "I think Evelyn Reynolds thought there was more between us."

"She wasn't the only one."

"She wasn't happy about it at all…" Amber tensed as she remembered the older woman's viciousness. Lawyers were usually competitive and ambitious. But Evelyn Reynolds had taken it to a whole new level.

Milek reached across and slid his hand along her thigh to her knee. Maybe he'd meant it as a comforting gesture. But her skin tingled. "How unhappy?" he asked. "Unhappy enough to do something about it?"

During her years with the DA's office, Amber had seen too much to rule out anyone as a suspect. Grandmas had killed for gambling money. Teenagers for shoes. Would Evelyn have killed for a job?

Maybe. But then, why go after Amber and Michael?

She was no longer a threat to her position. Evelyn had it all now, but maybe she still wasn't happy.

"I don't know…"

"Maybe we should talk to her and find out," Milek suggested.

She'd insisted on leaving the condo because she'd wanted to interrogate Brad Jipping. But she had been away from Michael for a while. Too long…

He squeezed her knee again. "He will be okay," he assured her—instinctively knowing why she'd hesitated, about whom she was concerned. Because he was concerned about him, too. Milek might not love her, but he loved their son. "Everyone is watching him."

"Then who's watching us?" She didn't only want her son to be safe; she wanted to live to see him again.

The killer. That was who Milek suspected he'd seen in his rearview mirror, driving a truck with conspicuous front-end damage. From slamming into Candace's SUV, from trying to run her and Michael off the road. Milek could see the truck, but he couldn't see the driver—only a shadow slouched behind the steering wheel. That truck had been following them since they'd left River City PD.

Was it another hired assassin? Or was the person who'd hired Campanelli so determined Amber and Michael die that he had decided to carry out the job himself?

Milek hoped so. Not that he wanted Amber in danger. But maybe Parker or Logan could catch him. The twin bodyguards were following him today. He would have noticed their tailing him even if they hadn't told him they had personally taken on protection duty for him. They were good, though, so the killer was probably totally unaware of their presence.

"He's back there, isn't he?" Amber asked as she glanced over her shoulder at the street behind them.

Milek squeezed her knee. "Don't look," he advised her.

"You don't want him to know you noticed him?"

"I don't want to lose him before Logan or Parker has a chance to get a better look."

But tires squealed behind them as the truck made a sharp U-turn. He murmured, "Too late..."

An engine revved as a black SUV made the same sharp turn and pursued the truck.

"Follow them," Amber said.

Milek shook his head. "I'm not putting you in more danger. I'll let Parker and Logan handle it." They were good—hopefully good enough.

"If Evelyn is behind Gregory's murder, she won't be the one behind the wheel. She would have hired someone."

"And she'd have some resources," he said. "Maybe a criminal she cut a break who owes her a favor..."

He wished he were following the truck, that he could catch the man who'd tried to hurt his son. If not for Candace's expert driving, Michael could have been hurt. Stacy and her unborn children could have been harmed, as well. Reminding himself that they were all right, he released a shuddery sigh.

Amber's hand covered his on her knee. "It's okay," she said. "They'll catch the driver. You and I can catch the killer. Let's talk to Evelyn—see if she's a viable suspect."

He nodded. At least it was something to do—something to occupy his mind until he heard back from Parker and Logan. Since the police department was downtown, the city courthouse was close. In minutes he pulled into its parking structure. He had to drive up several levels before he found a space, and with each level Amber's grip on his hand tightened more.

After finally finding an open spot, he pulled the SUV into it and turned toward her. She'd gone deathly pale, and her nails dug into the back of his hand. He pulled his hand free to put the SUV into Park and remove the key from the ignition.

But all his attention—all his concern—was focused on her. "Are you all right?"

She shook her head. "I used to love coming to work," she murmured. "Loved fighting for justice…"

That was why he'd broken their engagement; he hadn't wanted to jeopardize the career for which she'd worked so hard and that she loved so much.

"Shouldn't you be happy to be back here, then?" he asked.

She shook her head. "I'm not back."

And it was clear she was worried she would never be able to come back.

He reached for the keys. "This was a bad idea…"

And not just because coming here had upset her, but because something else had occurred to him. With Parker and Logan pursuing the truck that had been following him, nobody was protecting him and Amber anymore.

He was her only protection. He'd handled a lot of assignments on his own and had never lost a client. But this wasn't an ordinary assignment.

This was Amber.

He couldn't lose her. Not again…

She grabbed his hand and stopped him from turning the key. "Don't leave," she said. "I'm fine now. It was just weird coming here and not working here anymore. We still need to question Evelyn."

"We don't even know she's going to be available," he reminded her.

"We'll wait, then."

"You want to be away from Michael that long?" he asked. Because he didn't.

She shook her head. "No. But like you said, he'll be okay. And with all the attention he's getting from his aunts, he won't miss me."

Milek's blood chilled. Maybe their son wouldn't miss her for an hour or two. But what if something happened to her? What if she never made it back to him?

He would miss her. Thanks to Milek, Amber was the only parent the little boy had ever known. He had to make sure he got his son's mother safely back to him.

"We're going home," he said as his uneasy feeling persisted.

Maybe she felt it, too, because she begrudgingly nodded her agreement. "Okay…"

Was it home to her? Had his condo begun to feel that way to her? While he wanted her to be comfortable there—to no longer feel as if it was a prison—he didn't want her to settle in too completely. Despite all the times they'd made love, nothing had really changed.

He wasn't a good enough man to be her husband or Michael's father. It wasn't just her career that could be jeopardized by being with him.

He turned the key and glanced into the rearview mirror to back out. And that was when he saw the movement—the flash in the shadows. He pushed Amber's head down just as the back window exploded from the gunshot. Glass flew—raining into the front seat and around his face and hands.

He reached for his gun as more shots rang out. But it was too late…

Chapter 20

He'd made a rookie mistake. He'd fallen for the decoy. Self-disgust twisted Logan's guts into knots. Stacy would never forgive him if her brother and her best friend were killed on his watch.

He would never be able to look at himself again. He could barely look at Parker as his twin clicked off his cell and shoved it into his pocket. "Milek's not answering."

Logan turned back to the kid he'd pulled from the battered pickup truck. "If anyone's been hurt—or worse—you're an accessory," he warned him, pushing the kid against the side of the pickup box. "You better tell me what the hell you know right now!"

The teenager's tough facade crumbled as tears rolled down his dirty face. "I don't know nothing!"

"You're driving a truck that ran my pregnant wife off the road a day ago," Logan said. He'd felt so helpless—

so angry—that he hadn't been there, that he hadn't protected the woman he loved. Candace had. But *he* should have been there.

"I didn't run nobody off the road," the kid said. "I just had to follow that SUV."

"Why?"

"Cuz I got paid to." He moved his hand toward his pocket. But Logan grabbed him.

He checked the pocket himself. He didn't expect a gun, or the kid would have already pulled it. But he could have carried a knife. Instead Logan found some crisp bills. Two hundreds. Frank Campanelli wouldn't have done anything for that amount. Maybe, like so many older executives, he'd been replaced with a kid who would work cheap.

"Is that how much you got paid for the other day—for trying to kill a little boy?"

The kid shook his head, and his knit cap slid off his greasy hair. "I'm no killer. I just got paid to drive the truck."

To be the diversion. Logan's guts knotted, and he glanced at Parker, who was back on his cell.

"Who paid you?" Logan asked.

The kid shrugged. "I don't know 'im."

"A man?"

"I think so," the kid replied.

"Tall? Thin? White? Black?"

He shook his head. "I don't know..."

"This person gave you two hundred dollars and you didn't notice anything about him?"

"He was wearing a hoodie and big glasses and talked really funny," the kid said. "He even had on gloves."

So there would be no fingerprints besides the kid's inside the truck, which Logan had already discovered was reported stolen. The police were on their way to pick up the kid for driving a stolen truck. That was probably the only thing they'd be able to charge him with, though.

The tears surged again, streaming down the boy's face. "I wish I could tell you more…"

So did Logan. "Why'd you turn around?" he asked.

"The person told me to—"

Logan patted down the kid's pockets again. "He was talking to you? Through a cell?"

"No, he said I just had to follow the SUV for a few miles—then I could turn around…"

Because the killer—the real killer—had known Milek wouldn't be out alone, that he would have someone following him. The kid hadn't made him, but the killer had known he'd be there. And he'd wanted to get rid of him.

"Son of a bitch," Logan murmured.

"I'm sorry." The kid sobbed. "I'm so sorry…"

So was Logan when Parker shook his head again. Milek still wasn't answering his phone. That wasn't good. That meant something had happened. Something bad.

"Are you all right?" Milek asked again—but for a different reason than when they'd first entered the parking structure.

Glass had rained in on them. Fragments sparkled in Amber's hair. He reached out to brush it away, but the sharp edges cut into his skin.

"Don't," she said. "You'll get cut."

He snorted. He wasn't worried about the glass—not after the barrage of bullets that had been fired into the SUV. "Are you okay? Did you get hit?"

She paused a moment and stared down at her body—

as if she had to visually inspect it because she couldn't feel it.

Fear constricted his heart. Had a bullet gone through her seat? Into her spine? Hadn't he shoved her below the dash in time?

"Amber!"

"I'm fine," she said. "Did you hit him?" She swiveled in her seat and looked out the rear window.

All the glass was gone. And so was the shooter.

Milek had returned fire. He hoped like hell one of his shots had connected. If the killer was injured…

Maybe they'd be able to track down the son of a bitch; they'd tracked down Campanelli—through his doctor. Dr. Gunz had been arrested, though. This guy would have to find another corrupt physician. Milek reached for the door handle, but as he did, he heard another gun cock.

"Hands where I can see them," a security guard told him.

Milek moved his hands to the steering wheel. Fortunately he'd holstered his gun after seeing the shooter was gone. Otherwise the nervous guard might have shot him.

"Don't move, don't move," the older man said.

Milek wasn't entirely certain the man wouldn't shoot him yet. Then tires squealed as more vehicles careened into the structure.

And a familiar man alighted from an SUV. "Put down your gun," Agent Rus told the guard as he flashed his badge at him. His breath hissed through his teeth as he inspected the shot-up vehicle. "Are you both all right?"

Milek still wasn't certain Amber hadn't been hit. While he saw no blood, she was so quiet. Maybe she was in shock. "You should call for an ambulance," he said. "We should bring her in."

"I'm supposed to," Rus said. "I've been told to take her to the police department."

"You found Brad Jipping?" Amber asked, and finally she moved, leaning across the console and Milek in order to speak to Agent Rus.

Rus shook his head. "Not yet."

Maybe when they did, he would have one of Milek's slugs in him. Maybe the nightmare Amber had been living would finally be over.

"If you haven't found him, why are you supposed to bring me in?" Amber asked.

"The interim district attorney filed charges against you," Agent Rus said.

"What charges?" Milek asked the question in disbelief. What the hell was going on?

"Obstruction of justice," Rus said. "She also wants to question you on suspicion of murder."

"Gregory?" Amber asked.

Rus nodded.

Milek pushed open the driver's door and shoved the FBI agent back. "I thought you'd realized you were wrong about that! That she had nothing to do with Schievink's death!"

"I didn't ask her to file these charges," Rus replied. "I had no idea they were coming…"

The DA had blindsided him. She obviously had a vendetta against Amber. Maybe Amber had been right about her after all. It hadn't been enough for Reynolds to get Schievink's job. She wanted to destroy Amber entirely. Maybe that was how she thought she would hang on to the position when it came up for election—by eliminating her competition.

"She's even bringing Amber in to question her about Campanelli's murder."

Milek snorted. "Well, Amber has witnesses and surveillance footage to prove she was nowhere near the nightclub. There's nothing to tie her to Frank's death."

"There's you," Nick said.

"Ballistics will prove—"

"Ballistics aren't back yet," Rus said. "I have to bring her in." He withdrew his handcuffs. "And I've been told to do it by the book."

Milek cursed him.

"It's all right," Amber said.

But it wasn't. Seeing her being handcuffed and put into the back of a police vehicle took Milek back all those years ago to when Stacy and Garek had been arrested along with him—for something he'd done. They hadn't been responsible—just as Amber was not responsible for anything she was being charged with.

And, just like then, guilt overwhelmed him. Logically he knew none of what happened was his fault. He hadn't killed Schievink or Frank—no matter how much he might have wanted to. But he hadn't protected Amber, either. He hadn't been there when she needed him.

Before Rus closed the door on her, she met Milek's gaze and implored him, "Take care of our son."

He nodded. He would take care of Michael. But he intended to take care of her, too. He'd make sure she was cleared of all these ridiculous charges. And he'd make sure the real guilty person paid for all the hell he or she had put Amber through...

"I wanted to talk to you," Amber admitted.

"That's why you faked your death and have been living under an assumed name for the past year?" Evelyn asked facetiously. The lawyer was cocky—because she'd always thought she was better than she actually was, that she was better than everyone else.

"I did it to stay alive," Amber replied.

Evelyn shook her head, but not a single blond hair strayed from her tight bun. "It doesn't seem like you're the one who has trouble staying alive, but everyone else around you…"

Amber laughed at how obtuse the woman was being. "You had me picked up at the scene of the latest attempt on my life. How can you deny I'm in danger? You have Frank Campanelli's hit list with my name on it."

And Michael's. Fear tore at her heart. Her son was safe. He had his father now. Finally…

Milek wouldn't let anything happen to their little boy. He would protect him with his life. Not that she wanted to lose Milek, either. Again.

Still.

Evelyn shrugged her bony shoulders. The woman was thin—thinner than Amber remembered, almost as if she never ate or was too stressed to keep anything down if she did. Stressed with guilt, or the job she really wasn't qualified to handle?

"We have no proof that's Campanelli's book," she said. With a sneer, she added, "Especially since your *baby daddy* was the one who brought it in to the authorities."

Everyone was always so quick to think the worst of Milek and his family. Hadn't they proved themselves yet? They were not the men their father and uncle had been. They weren't thieves; they were honorable people who saved lives and brought real criminals to justice. Apparently Evelyn knew nothing about that. But then, she hadn't been able to prosecute Viktor Chekov because he'd confessed and worked out his deal with Nick Rus.

"You're a fool," Amber told her former colleague. But she actually hoped that was all Evelyn was. A fool and not another link in the chain of corruption in River City.

Evelyn's pinched face flushed with anger. "How dare you—"

"How dare you," Amber replied, "pretend to know what you're doing. You should be doing everything in your power to authenticate that book. It's a gold mine of evidence linking Frank Campanelli to a slew of unsolved murders."

"Trying to get your job back?" Evelyn asked.

Amber shook her head. "I don't want my job back," she said with sudden realization. "I want yours."

"Are you going to have me killed?" Evelyn asked. "Like you had Gregory killed?"

Amber shook her head. "I don't need to kill anyone. I just have to wait for the next election and prove how incompetent you are at this job."

Evelyn's face turned a brighter shade of red.

Maybe inciting her temper wasn't Amber's smartest course of action. But if she made Evelyn angry enough, maybe the woman would let something slip—would reveal how much she hated Amber—enough to try to kill her even after she'd no longer posed a threat to her job.

"You're never going to get this job," Evelyn told her, her voice sharp with an icy rage.

"Why's that?" Amber asked. "You're going to keep hiring hit men until one of them actually succeeds at killing me like Frank Campanelli killed Gregory for you?"

Now all the color drained from Evelyn's face. "You're accusing me of his murder?"

"You're the one who gained the most," Amber pointed out. She should have realized that before. "The mayor appointed you to fill this position until the next election. Is that why you're trying to have me killed? So I can't run against you?"

But why Michael?

Why would she want to hurt an innocent child? Surely even Evelyn wasn't that vicious.

"I welcome you to run against me," Evelyn challenged her, "because you're never going to get this job."

Yes, the blond attorney still thought she was the smartest one in the room.

"Why's that?" Amber asked.

"Because of your association with known criminals," Evelyn replied. "With a killer…"

"Your charges are ridiculous," Amber said. "I never associated with Frank Campanelli."

"I wasn't talking about him. The father of your kid is a convicted killer," Evelyn said. "You think that's going to win you any votes?" The woman shook her head again— pityingly. "I don't need to kill you to keep my job."

Amber shook her head. "You're delusional if you think you're going to keep it after having me arrested for obstruction of justice."

During the drive to the police station, Agent Rus had assured Amber that he would go over the DA's head to have the charges dropped. Since he'd helped her fake her death, she'd been under federal protection. She glanced to the door of the interrogation room. Where was he?

She'd been fingerprinted and processed and brought into this tiny room for questioning. Evelyn had even Mirandized her and asked if she wanted a lawyer.

"You were a suspect in Gregory's murder," Evelyn

said. "And instead of staying to face possible charges, you fled."

"I fled to save my life and my son's," Amber said. "I had nothing to do with Gregory's death, and you know that or you would have brought charges against me for it."

Evelyn's already beady eyes narrowed as she studied Amber's face. "Really? You had motive."

"You're the one who has his job," Amber pointed out.

"Your motive wasn't his job," Evelyn said. "It was revenge."

It might have been—had she known the things he'd told Milek, that he'd claimed her baby was his. She'd known Gregory had found her attractive, but she hadn't known the attraction had gone further than that. Had he been obsessed with her?

"Revenge?"

"He wouldn't leave his wife for you," Evelyn said. "Apparently you got tired of waiting any longer for him to keep his promise to you. So you killed him."

Amber laughed. "You're definitely delusional. There was nothing going on between Gregory and me."

Evelyn snorted now. "That's why you got all the best cases."

She had gotten all the best cases, but that wasn't because she'd been sleeping with him. But maybe it had been because he'd wanted to sleep with her. And Amber had just thought she was the best assistant DA for the job. Maybe she was more like Evelyn than she'd thought; maybe she thought she was better than she was.

But then, she'd won those cases. She'd won the case against Brad Jipping's son and sent him to prison, where the young man had killed himself.

"I was not having an affair with our boss," Amber

said. She understood now how Milek felt having people talk about him, act as if they knew him based on rumors and unearned reputations.

"His wife says otherwise," Evelyn said. "She knows he chose her over you and that you weren't happy about it."

What the hell had Gregory told his wife? Had he lied to her the way he'd lied to Milek?

Why? For what purpose?

"She's wrong," Amber said. "And whatever she says will be hearsay only, so you don't have a case against me. Drop the charges now before you embarrass yourself any further."

"I'm not the one who'll be embarrassed," Evelyn said. She stood up and opened the door to the interrogation room. To the uniformed officer standing in the hall, she said, "Bring her down to holding until she's arraigned and bail can be set."

"Evelyn—"

"You might have some trouble making bail, huh?" Evelyn taunted. "Heard you weren't doing much this past year."

How had she known what Amber had been doing? Was she the one who'd hired Frank Campanelli?

"But maybe your boyfriend can steal something to make your bail," Evelyn said.

She'd already called the woman delusional. Now she called her something else.

Evelyn's hand connected with her face with so much force that Amber's head snapped back. Instead of being mad, she smiled. "Oh, I will definitely have your job."

The interim DA glanced nervously at the guard, who could not have missed the slap. "Take her down to the holding cell!"

Amber hadn't thought it would go this far. Where was Rus? Why hadn't he gotten the charges dropped yet?

"It's late," Evelyn said. "So even if your boyfriend can make bail for you, you'll probably have to spend the night behind bars—waiting for arraignment."

That was what Evelyn wanted. To embarrass and maybe to endanger Amber...

Moments later the cell door slid closed with Amber where she'd never expected to find herself—with criminals she would have been getting ready to prosecute had she not been forced to leave her job.

Her life.

The cell was crowded. At least ten other women were in the cell, some sleeping on cots, some pacing...as Amber wanted to pace.

Nicholas Rus had to come through for her and keep his promise to free her.

A woman stepped into Amber's path, stopping her. "You're that lady lawyer," she said. "The one who's been all over the news."

Amber breathed a slight sigh of relief. That was the only reason the woman had recognized her—because of the media coverage.

"Don't you know me?" the woman asked.

"Should I?"

"You prosecuted me two years ago," the woman said as she stepped closer. She was big—far bigger than Amber. Taller and heavier and strong.

She'd be able to hurt Amber, or worse, before a guard ever stepped into the cell to help. As the woman moved closer, so did the others. Amber didn't like her chances.

Milek couldn't protect her here. Amber was on her own.

Chapter 21

"Where's my mommy and daddy?" Michael asked. The little boy's thick lashes fluttered as he fought to keep his lids open. His eyes were so like his father's—like his uncle's—that Candace's heart warmed with love.

She'd already fallen for her nephew, though—probably the first time he'd called her Aunt Candy. Damn Garek...

She loved him so much. He didn't irritate her nearly as much as he used to. Thinking of him made it easier for her to force a smile for their nephew. "Your mommy and daddy will be home soon," she promised. They had to be.

Amber was a victim—not a suspect. She hadn't obstructed justice when she'd fled with her son. She'd kept him alive.

"I'll wait for them," Michael insisted as he dragged his lids up again with a flutter of those thick lashes.

"It's late, sweetheart," Candace said as she tugged the blankets up to his quivering little chin.

Tears sparkled in his silver eyes, and her heart constricted over his sadness.

"Mommy tucks me in," he said. "Every night."

But tonight...

Because she was in a jail cell. What if something worse had happened? What if one of the bullets fired into the SUV had struck her?

She had had too close a call in that parking garage. She could have a close call in jail, too, if anyone recognized her as a former assistant district attorney. But Amber's appearance had changed over the past year.

Hopefully no one would recognize her. Hopefully she'd make it safely back to her son.

The little boy couldn't lose his mom.

"She'll tuck you in, too," Candace promised. "When she gets home, she'll come in and give you a kiss." And she leaned down and kissed his puckered brow.

"The bad man didn't get Mommy?" the little boy asked, his voice cracking with fear.

Candace dropped to her knees beside his bed and wrapped her arms around him. "Of course not. Your daddy won't let anyone hurt your mommy."

Just as Garek hadn't let anyone hurt her when she'd been in danger. Kozminski men protected the women they loved. They were heroes. That should have been their reputation—instead of the notorious one they hadn't earned.

Michael drew in a shaky breath and nodded. "Daddy will get the bad man."

"Yes, he will..." Or he'd die trying.

It was the *die trying* part that Candace worried about. They'd nearly lost Milek once—to his grief. Now they might lose him to a killer.

Finally, snuggled in Candace's arms, the little boy succumbed to sleep. She waited until he was breathing deeply before settling him back into his bed. Rising from his bedside, she pressed another kiss to his forehead. Maybe he would think it was Amber—that his mommy had tucked him in just the way she had every other night of his life.

She rose, turned toward the door and gasped at the shadow standing there. But she instinctively recognized that long, hard body even before Garek leaned into the glow of the night-light beside the child's bed.

"So, we going to do this someday?" her husband asked, gesturing at the little boy she'd tucked into bed. "We going to make one of those?"

Emotion choking her, Candace could only nod—quickly and definitely. She wanted a baby with her husband.

"I'll tell Stacy to get started on another bear."

She pressed a hand over her stomach, thinking of their child growing inside her. And Garek's hand covered hers. His shook slightly. But then he was worried about his brother and Amber—just as she and Michael were.

"Did you hear from Milek?" she asked.

He shook his head. "Not yet."

"He's okay," she reminded him. He'd survived the gunfire in the parking garage.

"He won't be if Amber's not," Garek said.

She had to be okay. Candace glanced back at the little boy. He slept, but his brow was still furrowed. He wasn't sleeping peacefully. He needed his mother.

Milek didn't know if Nick Rus had done him a favor or a disservice when he'd let him watch the interim district attorney interrogate Amber. The woman wasn't as delusional as Amber thought. She was right about him, just as Gregory Schievink had been right. Amber would never be elected if she was with him. His reputation would destroy hers and any chance she had of winning the job she wanted.

And now he knew for certain she still wanted it—even after having to take a year away from the courtroom. Maybe the year away had made her want it even more.

But if she wanted to run for that position, she needed to be able to stop running for her life. Milek had to find who was really after her.

The crazy DA? The woman obviously resented Amber enough to want to hurt her. When she'd slapped her...

Rus had had to hold him back. Milek had nearly broken through the glass between the interrogation room and the room where he'd stood with the FBI agent watching the former colleagues.

After the interrogation, they'd gone back to Nick's office while Amber had gone to a holding cell. His stomach muscles clenched with dread. He hated the thought of Amber being locked up—the way he'd been locked up. It wasn't right. She didn't belong behind bars.

And it wasn't safe. He couldn't be with her—couldn't protect her. And he didn't trust her safety to anyone but himself.

"What's taking so long?" Milek asked.

"My boss had to wake up a federal judge," Nick said.

"Was he afraid to do that?" Milek asked.

Nick snorted. "Chief Special Agent Lynch is afraid of nobody." His admiration for his boss was understandable.

Milek had met the man when a couple of his agents had gotten married in the wedding chapel Penny Payne owned. Milek had helped with protection duty. Every time he'd been in that little chapel he'd imagined himself standing at the altar, waiting for Amber to walk down the aisle to join him.

But he could never again ask her to marry him. He couldn't ruin her life—if she managed to survive the killer determined to end it.

Nick's cell rang and he grabbed it up. After listening for a moment he let out an exultant "Great!"

"You got the charges dropped?" Milek asked, the tightness in his chest easing slightly.

Nick nodded. Then after listening a few more moments, he hung up and chuckled. "Not only are the charges dropped, but the mayor is going to appoint a new interim DA."

"Amber?" he asked hopefully.

He shook his head. "While no charges are being pressed against her, she's not entirely clear of suspicion."

"Are you still suspicious of her?"

Nick shook his head again. "No."

And that tightness eased a little more. Rus would help clear her name. "Let's go get her," Milek said.

But he'd no more than turned toward the door when it burst open, and a uniformed officer rushed in. "There's a problem in the holding cells, Agent Rus."

Milek's heart lurched in his chest as he realized what the problem was: Amber. He'd known she wouldn't be safe in lockup. Someone could have recognized her. Or Reynolds could have hired someone to take her out while she was in custody. Maybe that was why she'd brought the phony charges against her to begin with—to get her alone and vulnerable.

If that was the case, he'd take care of that bitch. She'd lose more than her job…

* * *

Amber hadn't thought she would ever see her son again, so she couldn't stop staring at him, watching him sleep. The minute she'd stepped into the room Michael had let out a shuddery sigh—as if he'd sensed her presence.

There was no way she wouldn't have come back to him. He was everything to her—he and his father.

As obsessively as she watched Michael, Milek watched her. He stood beside her in the doorway.

"You're really all right?" he asked, his voice a deep whisper.

But Michael must have heard him anyway; he shifted in his bed, burrowing in as his sleep deepened. He felt safe now—with his father.

Amber should, too. Milek had saved her life over and over again. But even though he watched her, something had changed. There was a distance between them.

That distance scared her nearly as much as being locked up had. If not for the woman she'd prosecuted two years ago, Amber might not have survived lockup. But she'd recommended rehab for the young prostitute instead of jail time two years ago. And the woman had been grateful—grateful enough to fight for her when the others had turned on her.

Not wanting to wake their son, she stepped away from the doorway and headed across the living room to the room she shared with Milek. Did he want her sharing it anymore?

He followed her inside and turned on the light. Then he touched her chin, tilting it toward the glow. "You might have a bruise," he said.

"I didn't get hit," she said. The fight had been broken up right away. And then she'd been released.

"Reynolds hit you," he said.

"You saw that?"

He nodded.

And she realized he'd seen the rest of it—the interrogation. "She's wrong," Amber told him.

He nodded again. "She knows that now—since her phony charges cost her the job she wanted."

The job she might have killed to get. Would she have? The blonde lawyer was ambitious and vicious. But a murderer?

"I wasn't talking about that," Amber said. "I was talking about what she said about you…"

He shrugged. "It's true," he said. "I killed a man…"

"In self-defense."

"I wasn't the one he was trying to hurt."

Stacy had been. Their stepfather had nearly raped their sister before Milek and Garek broke into the room where he'd been holding her. Amber knew the story. Not from Milek. He had never talked about it. But Stacy had.

That was all Amber knew, though, because Stacy had been strangled into unconsciousness. She probably would have been strangled to death if her brothers hadn't come to her rescue. She didn't know what had happened next— just that her stepfather had died and both her brothers had been charged with manslaughter.

That had been another travesty of justice.

"You saved your sister's life," Amber said. "Just like you keep saving mine."

She hadn't had a chance to thank him for earlier— for saving her life in the parking garage. If he hadn't pushed her down, some of those bullets might have hit her—or the flying glass would have. She had it in her hair. Remembering the fragments, she reached her hand up toward it.

But Milek caught her fingers the way she'd caught his earlier. "You'll cut yourself," he said. Linking their hands, he pulled her toward the bathroom off the bedroom. He stepped inside the walk-in shower and turned on the faucet.

The shower was huge, the walls and floor and ceiling tiled in slate—which changed into a myriad of colors as the water washed over it. Without even waiting for her to undress, Milek pulled her inside with him. And fully clothed, they stood under all the showerheads.

The glass washed away with the water, running down into the drains. Her clothes molded to her, plastered against her body as her wet hair was plastered against her head.

Milek pushed back her hair as he stared down into her face. She couldn't read his expression—didn't know what he was thinking.

Then his gaze dropped lower, over her body. Her nipples pressed against the wet fabric of her blouse and her lace bra. He reached for the buttons and began to part them. She didn't know what he was thinking. But she knew what he wanted—the same thing she did.

Her fingers moved to the buttons on his shirt, quickly parting them. She pushed the shirt from his broad shoulders. Muscles rippled in his arms and his chest.

And her mouth went dry with desire. He was so damn beautiful—the most handsome man she'd ever seen. And for a little while he'd been hers.

He had loved her.

Hadn't he?

Why else had he asked her to marry him?

He must have loved her once. He'd even used the date he'd proposed as the code to the security panel for his studio. It had meant something to him.

She had meant something to him.

Could he love her again?

She had never stopped loving him. Even when she'd been hurt and bitter over his rejection, she had loved him yet. She lowered his zipper and his pants, and she dropped to her knees on the slate floor to show him that love.

She closed her lips around his erection.

"Amber…"

Finally he said her name, his voice thick with desire. His fingers grabbed her shoulders. But he didn't pull her up—not right away.

She made love to him with her mouth, sliding it up and down the length of him. But before she could push him over the edge, he lifted her. She wrapped her legs around his waist. But he slid her up higher so that he could take one of her nipples into his mouth. He teased it with his tongue and then nipped it lightly with his teeth.

She moaned as tension began to build inside her. She needed him there—driving deep. But instead of his erection, his fingers moved between her legs. He touched intimately, pushing his thumb against the most sensitive part of her.

She whimpered as the tension wound tighter, threatening to snap her. Then he moved again—pulling her down onto his erection. He slid home—that was how it felt when he filled the emptiness inside her.

He was home. His arms. His body.

She had never loved anyone as she loved him, and she never would.

But she didn't hold out hope that he would ever again

ask her to marry him. Because even while he made love to her body, Milek held a part of himself back from her.

There was a distance between them that Amber wasn't certain she could ever bridge. Even as she opened her body and her heart to him…

She skimmed her lips along his tense jaw, over his chiseled cheekbones—to his mouth. She kissed him as she clutched at his broad shoulders, holding on to him as tightly as she could.

He moved inside her, sliding in and out. And his fingers teased her nipples. He kissed her deeply, his tongue sliding in and out of her mouth as he did her body. And finally the tension inside her broke. She screamed as the orgasm overwhelmed her.

He tensed, and a low groan came from his throat, echoing off the slate walls. Despite his orgasm, the tension didn't ease from his body. Maybe that was because there was still a threat out there—someone still intent on killing her and her son.

Or maybe it was because Milek would never be able to completely let himself go with her. He wouldn't ever let her have all of him.

That knowledge hurt more than Evelyn's slap had earlier. Milek could protect her life. But he couldn't protect her heart—because he'd already broken it.

Chapter 22

Nick stared out the windows of his office, studying the detectives and the officers who milled around the department. Had he wasted the past year of his life?

Apparently he hadn't cleaned up as much of River City as he'd thought he had. After digging a little deeper into Evelyn Reynolds and her financial records, he had found bribes. Ones paid to her and ones she had paid.

She was dirty as hell. But was she a killer? He didn't know—even after he'd questioned her. Now she was locked up in the holding cell where she'd had Amber Talsma held. He doubted anyone would come to her rescue as they had Amber's. With her accounts frozen, she wouldn't be able to make bail. He didn't have to worry about her right now.

What about Brad Jipping? He picked up his cell and punched in the number for the best River City detective and asked, "Any leads on Jipping?"

"Since his kid died last year, the guy's gone off the grid," the detective replied.

Nick breathed a slight sigh of relief. Then Nikki wouldn't be able to find the guy, either, and he was sure Milek had her looking. Nick didn't want the Payne Protection Agency finding Jipping before he did. He didn't entirely trust Milek Kozminski—especially not if Jipping proved to be the killer.

The guy might wind up dead before Nick could have the chance to arrest him. Then Nick might be arresting Milek instead. Not that he'd blame him for wanting to take out the guy who'd terrorized his son and the woman he loved.

If Nick ever had a kid and someone put out a hit on him…

But that wasn't likely to ever happen. He pulled open his desk drawer and reached for a gooey cookie. The closest he had come to a relationship since moving to River City was with Penny Payne. But that was a strange bastard-son-of-her-dead-husband relationship that nobody understood.

Especially not him…

But he'd never been good at relationships. He suspected Annalise Huxton would heartily agree with that—since he'd crossed the line and ruined their friendship. Maybe it was good her brother had gone missing on his last deployment or he probably would have tracked Nick down to kick his ass before now.

No. He understood Milek Kozminski wanting to hurt the man who'd threatened his child and the woman he loved. He just couldn't let him do it.

He had him. Jipping was here. Milek knew it. At his nod, Garek kicked open the motel room door, and Milek rushed inside—gun drawn.

Despite his bleeding shoulder the guy had moved quickly enough to grab his gun. He pointed the barrel at Milek.

"Put it down!" Garek yelled at him. "You're not going to be able to hit us both."

He probably wouldn't be able to hit either one of them. If the way he'd shot at the SUV in the parking garage was any indication, he was no marksman. Maybe that was why he had hired Frank Campanelli to kill Gregory Schievink. The district attorney would probably still be alive if Jipping had tried to shoot him himself.

"Who the hell are you?" Jipping demanded to know, his voice a drunken shout.

Milek pointed at the guy's shoulder. Blood oozed through the gauze he'd pressed to it. More blood-soaked bandages littered the bed on which Jipping sat. "I'm the one who shot you."

"You're her bodyguard."

He was much more than her bodyguard. He was the father of her child. Her former fiancé. Her lover...

Why couldn't he control his desire for her? Every time they had made love it was harder for Milek to hide his feelings for her—to hide the fact that he still loved her.

Maybe Jipping would do them both a favor if he shot him. It would probably hurt less than letting her go again.

But Jipping wasn't in a hurry to pull the trigger— probably because he knew Garek was right. He couldn't hit them both and whichever one he didn't shoot would kill him. "How'd you find me?" he asked, and his blood-shot eyes darted nervously around them.

Maybe he was expecting the police, too. But they hadn't called them yet.

Agent Rus would be pissed they hadn't called him

and they had found Jipping first. But he didn't have the resources they had.

They had connections in the darkest parts of the city. And that was where they had found Jipping—just off skid row. A guy Milek had been in juvie with had recognized the picture Milek passed around and told him where they could find the drunk. For a price.

Their old connections didn't give away information for free. Nor would they have talked to police. That was why Rus hadn't been able to find Jipping yet. He hadn't known where to look. But knowing Rus, he would figure it out—eventually.

Along with the bloodied bandages, empty beer cans and liquor bottles littered the filthy motel room. Maybe that was why the guy was a lousy shot. He was too drunk to shoot straight.

"Finding you wasn't that hard," Milek said. Which probably meant the police would find him soon, too. Rus was smart enough to barter for information. He'd struck a helluva bargain with Viktor Chekov.

But it wasn't Agent Rus who burst through the door behind them—it wasn't Nick at whom Jipping swung his gun. It was Amber. How the hell had *she* found them?

"I'm sorry," Candace said as she rushed in behind Amber. "She insisted on coming here…"

"Get out of here," Milek told her.

"No!" Jipping shouted. "That bitch isn't going anywhere."

Milek stepped in front of her. He would gladly take the bullet meant for her—gladly give his life for hers. Their son didn't even really know him. His mother was the parent he needed. The parent who had always been there for him.

Amber's small hand touched his back, pulling on his shirt. "Don't," she told him.

Did she think Milek was going to kill the guy? Was that why she had insisted on Candace bringing her here? To talk Milek out of murder?

Her doubts stung his heart. But Milek had had doubts himself. He hadn't known what he would do when he confronted the man who'd terrorized his family. But if Milek was the killer everyone thought he was, wouldn't he have already pulled the trigger?

For that matter, wouldn't Jipping have? But then Amber was the one Jipping wanted dead—and Milek stood between her and his bullet. He braced himself—waiting for the shot.

Amber knotted her fingers in Milek's shirt and tried pulling him away. She didn't want him giving up his life for hers. "No," she said. "Don't…"

"I won't kill him," Milek said.

She wasn't worried about Jipping. She was worried about him.

"If he puts down the gun," Milek continued. "Put the gun down," he told Jipping.

"You all need to put down the guns," a deep voice said as Agent Rus stepped into the motel room with them.

She glanced back at the agent, whose jaw was clenched so tightly a muscle twitched in his cheek. He was furious—angrier even than Milek was at her for showing up.

But she hadn't wanted him risking his life when she was the one Jipping wanted. Not that she intended to give up her life, either. She didn't want anyone getting killed.

Brad Jipping had already lost enough when his son

had died. He didn't need to lose any more—no matter the hell he had put her and Michael through.

"Jeremy wouldn't want this," she told Jipping.

"Don't say his name!" he shouted. "Don't you dare say his name!"

Amber drew in a sharp breath and tugged harder on Milek's shirt. He was certain to get shot if he kept standing in front of her. And maybe she needed to see Brad Jipping to get through to him.

She had always been able to reach the members of the jury when she'd taken the time to look each one in his or her face—to speak only to them. Gregory used to call her the jury whisperer.

"Jeremy was a good kid," she said.

"Then why'd you send him to prison?" his father asked.

Technically the judge had sent him to prison. She had only gotten him convicted; the judge had sentenced him. Maybe that sentence had been stiff. But the judge was rumored to have lost someone he loved to a drunk driver.

"He killed two people," she said.

Just as Jipping had killed two people. Schievink and the man he'd hired to pull the trigger for him.

"Jeremy didn't mean to do it," Jipping said. "It was an accident."

One that wouldn't have happened, had Jeremy not been drinking and then gotten behind the wheel. She'd used that in her closing argument. But if she repeated that here, with Jipping armed, it might prove a closing argument of another kind—one that got more people killed.

"I tried to get him sentenced to a rehab facility," she reminded Jipping. But the judge had refused her recommendation. And Gregory had concurred with him. "I wanted to get him some help."

Maybe she should have focused on getting his father help, too. Especially after Jeremy had killed himself in jail.

"He didn't need help," Jipping protested. "He just made one mistake—one night. He was a good kid. He deserved a second chance."

And he would have had one—had he served out his sentence. But Jeremy had been too guilt-ridden to give himself that second chance. Because he'd taken those innocent lives, he had taken his own—that was what he'd said in the suicide note he'd left behind.

So why did his father blame her? Why had he blamed Gregory? And what about the judge? Why hadn't his name been in Frank Campanelli's little leather book?

Maybe he'd always intended to take out the judge himself. She hadn't come here to plead his case, though. She was pleading her own.

"My son's a good kid, too," she said. "He's just a little boy—just five years old."

"I remember when Jeremy was five…"

The sadness in his voice struck a chord of sympathy within Amber.

"He was probably like my son," she said. "Sweet and funny and full of promise."

Tears cracked the older man's voice. "He was…"

"So why would you hire someone to kill him?"

"Jeremy?"

"No, why would you hire someone to kill my son?" she asked. Her heart ached with the pain she'd felt when she'd thought he had been hurt in the car accident. "Why would you hire someone to kill me?"

"You sent him to prison!" Jipping shouted.

And she flinched. With Milek standing between her and the barrel of Jipping's gun, she didn't want to incite his temper any more than she already had.

"She didn't send him to prison," Milek defended her. "The judge sentenced him. Amber only did her job. She got justice for the innocent people your son killed."

Amber tightened her grasp on Milek's shirt, trying to pull him aside; he was going to incite Jipping now.

"Jeremy wouldn't want anyone else to die," Amber implored him. Surely he had to know how guilty his son had felt.

"Stop!" Jipping yelled. "Stop talking about him. You have no right to talk about him!"

"And you have no right to try to kill my son," Amber said. "You have no right to hurt anyone else. Enough people have already been hurt."

"No!" Jipping shouted.

She felt Milek tense. It was as if he suddenly got taller and broader—as he tried to shield her from what he was certain would happen. The others tensed, too. Garek and Candace tightened their grips on their weapons.

Agent Rus was behind her, so she couldn't see him—couldn't see what he was doing. But she was certain he was still furious—the way Milek was probably furious with her for interfering.

She'd thought she could talk to Brad Jipping. That she could get him to understand this wasn't what his son would have wanted. Jeremy had been a good kid who'd made one mistake. He should have been given that second chance.

He should have given himself that second chance.

Suddenly an arm wrapped around Amber's waist. But

Milek hadn't even moved. Then she realized what Rus had been doing. He hadn't drawn his weapon, as everyone else had. Instead, he grabbed her, lifted her from her feet and pulled her from the motel room.

The flurry of movement must have startled Jipping. Or he had been so desperate to kill her that he couldn't let her get away. Because a gun went off, the noise exploding inside the small room.

And if Jipping had fired that shot trying to hit her, then Milek would have taken the bullet meant for her.

"No!" The scream tore from her throat as she flailed in Rus's arms, trying to get away from him—trying to get to the man she loved and might have lost again.

This time, forever.

Chapter 23

It was over.

Milek had had his doubts—even after Jipping had killed himself. But Rus had found some crisp hundreds in the motel room. He had also found Jipping's prints in the stolen truck. The teenager Logan had talked to had been wrong—or Jipping hadn't worn gloves every time he'd been in the truck.

He must have been the one who'd tried running Candace off the road. He'd definitely been the one who'd shot at them in the parking garage. And ballistics would probably link the gun he'd used to kill himself to the gun that had killed Frank Campanelli.

It was really over.

Amber had no reason to stay with him anymore. She loved him. He knew it from the way she'd broken away from Agent Rus and run back into the motel room. Her face had been pale with terror; she'd been worried he'd been shot.

She'd clung to him when she'd realized he was all right. And his arms had instinctively closed around her. He hadn't wanted to let her go then.

But he hadn't wanted her to see what Brad Jipping had done to himself, either. So he'd had Candace bring her back to the condo.

He'd spent the rest of the night divided between the crime scene and talking to Rus back at the River City PD—even while he'd ached to be with her, to make love to her one last time in his bed before she left. But Rus had had questions, had wanted to tie up all the loose ends to be certain it was over before he let Milek leave.

He uttered a shaky sigh as he punched in the code for the door of the condo to slide open. The guards were gone from outside; nobody from Payne Protection lurked in the shadows anymore.

He suspected the inside was just as empty. She'd had plenty of time to pack up Michael and their things. His breath caught as he thought of his son—of having to let him go again, just as he had let Amber go five years before.

He should have been relieved to be alone again. Unlike his siblings, he enjoyed solitude; that was why he'd always spent so many hours alone painting. But that had changed when he'd met Amber; he'd always wanted to be with her instead. Until he'd realized what being with him would cost her: everything.

That hadn't changed.

"Daddy's home!" Little arms caught him around the knees as his son hugged him.

Love and pain constricted Milek's heart. He reached

for the child and swung him up into his arms. He was safe now. His son was safe.

Over the little boy's head, he met Amber's gaze, and he saw the same relief in her eyes. There was also a question in them. She wanted to make sure Agent Rus had closed the investigation.

He nodded.

"Me and Mommy are going to the park," Michael said. "Do you want to go, too, Daddy? You can see how high I can get on the swings!"

Now the sense of longing constricted his heart. He wanted to go with them—wanted to be a family outside the walls of the condo. But he loved Amber too much to cost her the future she'd wanted—the one she'd had to put on hold for a year.

Michael's small hand touched his cheek. "Daddy? Do you?"

More than anything. But he shook his head.

Michael's bottom lip stuck out as disappointment darkened his silver eyes.

"Your daddy's been up all night," Amber said. "He needs to get some sleep."

Michael ran his hand over the whiskers on his chin. "You need to shave, too."

Milek laughed. He loved the boy so much. How would he walk away from him? He would have to work something out with Amber—some type of visitation. While he didn't want to ruin her life, he wanted to be a part of his son's life.

He hugged Michael closely, swinging the little boy around before releasing him with a quick kiss to his forehead. "Have fun at the park."

Already over his disappointment that Milek wasn't

going along, Michael ran toward the door. He was probably excited to finally leave the condo. But Amber didn't follow their son right away.

She stopped next to Milek and lifted her hand to his cheek the way their son had. But her touch had his skin tingling, had his pulse quickening.

"You look exhausted," she said. "I hope you finally get some rest." She knew he hadn't slept well since he'd found her. She didn't know about all his sleepless nights when he'd thought she and their son were dead.

He was beyond exhausted. So he just nodded.

Then she rose on her toes and pressed a kiss to his lips. "Thank you..."

He wasn't sure what she was thanking him for. Not going to the park? Saving her life?

He wanted to kiss her back, wanted to close his arms around her. But he held his arms stiffly at his sides. And he forced himself to remain where he was—as she opened the door and left with their son.

He expected to find her bags in the bedroom—already packed and ready to go. But when he walked into the master suite, he found no suitcases. The bed had been made but the blankets were folded back—as if ready for him to crawl between the sheets.

He hadn't slept all night. He should have been exhausted. He should have been relieved enough to sleep. But maybe it was the thought of her and Michael leaving, not just for the afternoon but forever, that kept him tense and unable to relax.

He couldn't sleep. He could only lie there and worry. About her leaving.

About whether she and the boy were really safe...

But of course they were. Brad Jipping was dead. He

couldn't hurt them anymore. Evelyn Reynolds was in jail—unable to make bail. So even if she had a vendetta against Amber, she had no way to act on it now.

They were safe. Maybe it was just because they had been in danger so long that he struggled to accept it—that he felt as if he'd missed something. Was there another threat against them?

Or was the only other threat him?

While it was just early spring, the sun was shining so brightly the temperature felt warmer than it was. Amber breathed in the fresh air, grateful to finally be free to enjoy the park like the joggers and dog walkers who milled about. She didn't have to look at them anymore—with suspicion, with fear—as she had looked at everyone the past year.

Now she could just watch her son as he pumped his legs on the swings. He squealed as he went higher and higher.

"Mommy, look at me! Look at me!"

"I'm looking," she said. But her attention was divided. She kept glancing toward the parking lot. Not for threats but for the person she'd invited to join them.

Would she come?

Amber hoped so. She really needed to clear up the woman's misconceptions—the ones Evelyn Reynolds had shared with her. Her pulse quickened when a Lincoln SUV pulled into the nearby parking lot. The driver sat behind the wheel for a while before finally stepping out.

In her expensive-looking wool overcoat, gloves and designer boots, the middle-aged blonde looked out of place in the neighborhood park. She was no soccer mom—no young nanny. She oozed money and class. She was an heiress, though, to her family fortune. Her money was old and her class ingrained.

Amber had met Mrs. Schievink before, but she hadn't seen her since Gregory's funeral. They had always been cordial with each other. She'd never detected any suspicion in the woman, hadn't been aware she'd not only heard the rumors about Amber and her husband but she'd believed them.

She glanced at Michael—making sure he was happily swinging away before she walked over to meet the woman. "Thank you for coming," she said.

"I was surprised you called," Patricia Schievink said. "I've seen the news and know you've been going through a lot."

"It's over now," Amber said. "The person responsible for Gregory's murder and for the attempts on my life and my son's life has killed himself."

"Did he say anything before he died?" Patricia asked.

"He just talked about his son," Amber said, and she glanced again at hers. She understood Brad Jipping's inconsolable pain. "It was horrible what he did—to Gregory and to me. But I don't know how I would react if something ever happened to my son." She flinched as she remembered those moments she'd worried that something had happened to him—that he'd been injured in the car accident. "I probably wouldn't survive."

Patricia sighed. "I don't know what the bond is like between a mother and her child. Unfortunately, Gregory and I were never able to have children."

Amber heard the woman's yearning and regret. She'd obviously wanted a child. She reached out and touched her shoulder. "I'm sorry."

"Why?"

For so many reasons. "I'm sorry you two were never able to have a child."

"I didn't have one," Patricia said. "But Gregory did..." She had followed Amber's gaze to Michael. She watched the little boy swing.

"No..." Amber said. "He's not Gregory's..."

The woman didn't reply. She said nothing—just continued to stare at Michael.

"Evelyn Reynolds told me what you think," Amber said. "That you believe those awful rumors about your husband and me. But I want you to know the only relationship we had was professional." She'd once been foolish enough to think they'd had a friendship, too. But she realized now that Gregory had never been her friend.

Patricia glanced at her now, and a perfectly arched eyebrow rose in skepticism. "You expect me to believe that? I could tell how he felt about you."

Why hadn't Amber been able to tell? Why hadn't she realized the lengths Gregory had gone in order to break up her and Milek? The things he'd said to him...

Claiming her baby was his.

"He wanted you," Patricia said.

Amber shook her head. "You were his wife."

"I was his meal ticket," Patricia said. "The bank for his campaigns. He never felt about me the way he felt about you. He never wanted *me*..."

Frustration tightened Amber's stomach into knots. "I'm sorry," she said again.

"You should be," Patricia replied. "You should be..."

"But I wasn't involved with Gregory," she continued. "I never had an affair with him."

Despite her class and elegance, Patricia Schievink snorted—derisively. "You expect me to believe that?"

"It's the truth."

She pointed one of her gloved hands at the boy. "That's his son."

"No," she said. "Michael is Milek Kozminski's son. I was going to marry Milek." She still wanted to marry him—wanted to be with him always. "I love him. I have always loved him."

"So you just used Gregory?" Now the woman laughed. "There's something almost poetic about it. You used him like he used me."

Amber shook her head. "I didn't use anyone."

"You expect me to believe you were given all the best assignments because you were that good?"

"I was." And would be again if she was given the chance. But there was something about the woman's cold fury that chilled Amber's blood, making her uneasy.

This had been a bad idea—asking Gregory's wife to meet her.

"That's not what Evelyn Reynolds told me," Patricia said. "She told me all about the two of you."

"Evelyn was lying," Amber said. "She's opportunistic and vindictive. She wanted Gregory's job."

Patricia snorted again. "She could have had it. He had his sights set much higher than the DA's office." She glanced at Amber's face. "But you knew that. He shared all his aspirations with you."

Amber just shrugged. She knew there was nothing she could say—nothing that would make Mrs. Schievink believe her.

"Why was he going to give it up?" Patricia asked.

"Give what up?"

"His job. His career goals."

"I didn't know he was."

"I found the plane ticket," Patricia said. "The one-way ticket. I assumed he'd already given you yours."

Amber shivered as realization dawned. "It was you…" Tears threatened, but she blinked them furiously back so she could see Michael. He had stopped swinging to watch them. He must have noticed she was getting upset. He rose from the seat of the swing and started toward them.

"Run!" she yelled at him.

But instead of running away, he ran toward her—as if he instinctively knew she needed protection. He took after his father in so many ways—the artistic talent, the protectiveness.

"I found this, too," Patricia said as she drew a gun from her designer bag. The sleeves of her coat were so long that it covered the weapon, leaving only the end of the barrel visible. None of the joggers or dog walkers were close enough to see it—to call for help. "You look as surprised as Frank Campanelli was."

"What's wrong, Mommy?" Michael asked as he joined them. "Do you want to play tag?"

Biting her lip to hold back a cry, she shook her head.

He turned toward Mrs. Schievink. "Do you want to play tag?" he asked.

She smiled at him—a strange, sad smile. "We're going to play another kind of game," she said.

Amber reached for her son, trying to step between him and the madwoman—as Milek had stepped between her and Brad Jipping. But Brad Jipping hadn't been the killer. Patricia Schievink was.

The woman grabbed the little boy before Amber could. While she held his hand in her left one, she pointed the gun at the back of his head.

Amber's heart slammed against her ribs with fear and

pain. She held in a cry—not wanting to startle either of them. If Michael moved...

He turned slightly toward Mrs. Schievink. But he must not have seen the gun, because he calmly asked, "What kind of game?"

"Hide-and-seek," she said. "You and I are going to hide, and your mommy will have to find us."

"Patricia," Amber implored her. "Please, don't do this..."

"You should have thought of that before you got involved with my husband," Patricia said.

The little boy's brow furrowed with confusion, and he stared at the woman before turning back toward Amber. He must have seen what she could see now—so clearly. The madness. "Mommy?" he asked nervously.

"It's okay," she said. But she didn't know how.

What could she do? If she grabbed for her son, the woman would shoot him. And with where she was holding the gun, it wasn't possible that she would miss.

But if Patricia left with him...

She would undoubtedly shoot him anyway—once she took him wherever she intended to take him. With her financial resources, she would be able to take him anywhere she wanted.

"Please," Amber said. "Don't..."

The woman shook her head. "Tell him to leave with me. To play nicely and maybe everything will be all right."

Just as Patricia had refused to believe her, Amber couldn't trust her, either. She hadn't gone to the lengths she had to let her and Michael live.

No. Nothing would ever be all right again. She couldn't

let Patricia Schievink leave with her son—because if she did, she would never see him again.

Not alive…

She should have killed Amber—should have pulled the trigger. But there had been witnesses in the park—people who would have been able to testify against her. Nobody but Amber had seen her gun. The little boy hadn't even seen it as Patricia had held it behind his back. She could have shot him there—in front of his mother. Could have had her revenge then.

Finally.

But maybe this was better. Amber would suffer now—worrying whether her son was dead or alive. She wouldn't be able to sleep. To eat.

Just as Patricia hadn't been able to when Gregory had worked late with that slut. She'd imagined the two of them together—laughing at her. Thinking her too stupid to know what was going on between them.

The only reason Gregory hadn't asked her for a divorce was because of her money. He was too ambitious to give that up—knowing she would be able to finance his bid for mayor. For governor.

For president. He'd had such aspirations.

"What do you want to be when you grow up?" she asked the little boy. Not that she would ever give him the chance. She just wondered…

"I want to be a bodyguard," he said, "like my daddy."

Gregory was the boy's father. She'd heard him say it himself.

Why were Amber Talsma and her son claiming that it was another man? Why were they denying Gregory?

"Your daddy is a bodyguard?" Patricia asked the child.

He nodded his blond head. In the photos Frank Campanelli had sent her, the boy's hair had looked darker—more like Gregory's. And she didn't remember ever noticing how light his eyes were, how they were nearly silver...

Gregory's eyes had been dark. And the woman's were green again. Not dark like those photos Frank had sent.

No. She was letting Amber Talsma get to her. And she, of all people, knew better than to trust a lawyer. They were natural liars. Gregory had always been a liar. All those promises he'd made her.

To be faithful.

To love her forever...

Amber had to be lying.

Because why would Gregory have claimed the boy was his if he wasn't...?

Had it just been wishful thinking?

Amber had been sleeping with both men, and Gregory had just assumed her child was his. Had Amber played Gregory?

She laughed at the irony of the ultimate player being fooled. And the boy looked at her nervously.

"When's my mommy coming?" he asked.

"Whenever she figures out where we are," she said. "Is she very good at hide-and-seek?"

The little boy giggled. "No. I always win."

This time Patricia would win. Amber had given her the perfect revenge when she'd told her that she wouldn't survive losing her son.

That was why Patricia hadn't shot her in the park. She had waited too long for her revenge for it to be over so quickly. No. This was better. So much better...

Amber would suffer. She would suffer wondering where her son was—if he was alive. If he was dead...

And when she found him...

She would suffer for the rest of her miserable life.

All Patricia had to do was pull the trigger. Frank Campanelli hadn't thought she could do it, but she'd proved him wrong. She had had no problem taking his life.

And she would have no problem taking another...

Chapter 24

Amber couldn't stop shaking. Her muscles quivered uncontrollably. "I shouldn't have let her take him. I shouldn't have let her…"

She'd prosecuted so many cases where nothing good happened if a suspect got a victim to a second location—to somewhere private. Somewhere horrible things would happen.

What was Patricia doing to her son? Their son…

Milek's face was flushed with fury, his hands fisted at his sides. He was probably angry with her. She didn't blame him; she was angry with herself.

"I shouldn't have…"

"You couldn't risk that she might pull the trigger," Milek said—as if he understood.

Tears overflowed her eyes again and cracked her voice. "She had it right at the back of his head…"

Brad Jipping had shot himself in the head. Milek had caught her in his arms, had tried to stop her from seeing it. But he hadn't been fast enough. She'd seen the horror...

And that was what she had immediately imagined when she'd seen that gun so close to her son's head.

She blinked, trying to clear her vision, so she could focus on Milek. There were others in the condo. Agent Rus was there—along with every member of the Payne Protection Agency and their spouses. But Milek was the only one she needed.

"Will we get him back?" she asked. "Will we ever see our son again?"

He nodded. "Of course we will." He moved closer and slid his arm around her shaking shoulders. She didn't deserve it—not after failing to protect their son, but he was offering her comfort. "If she'd intended to hurt him, she would have shot him in the park. In front of you."

Remembering what she'd told the woman, she shook her head. "No..."

"What?"

"I gave her the perfect revenge," she admitted. "I was talking about Jipping and I said I wouldn't survive losing my son..."

There was no way Patricia had missed that, no way she wouldn't take advantage of the situation. Which meant Amber would never see her son again.

Not alive...

Amber was blaming herself. But it was Milek's fault. He shouldn't have let them go alone to the park. He'd known something wasn't right.

He'd still been on edge. He'd thought it was because

he'd been worried that she was leaving—or already gone. But it hadn't made sense that Brad Jipping had had the money to hire Frank Campanelli. With his drinking problem, the man hadn't been able to hold a job. He'd lost his home. And his vehicle had been repossessed.

Those hundred-dollar bills. The ones he'd given to the kid to drive the battered truck and the ones on his table—those weren't Jipping's. They must have belonged to Patricia Schievink.

She had plenty of money. Enough to have hired Frank Campanelli to kill her husband and Amber and Michael. Enough money to have hired Jipping to finish the job the hired assassin had failed to carry out.

She must have known about the case from her husband. They had talked about his work. About Amber...

Patricia Schievink had enough money to get out of the country and never come back. So why had she brought Michael here?

The house was smaller than the mansion in which she lived now—in front of which the hit man she'd hired had gunned down her husband. The front door of the little brick Cape Cod was locked, but she might as well not have bothered, since Milek picked it so quickly.

As he pushed it open and stepped inside, the hardwood floor creaked beneath his weight. But that was the only sound inside the house. The only movement but for the dust particles dancing in the sunshine pouring through the bare windows. He could see through the windows to where the woman sat in the backyard with a child playing on an old swing set.

He pushed open the sliding door and stepped outside to join them. His quiet movements had been a waste of time.

Michael pumped his legs harder to carry his swing

higher. "Daddy!" he called out as he waved. Then he turned toward the woman sitting on a rusted lawn chair in the middle of a patio overgrown with weeds. "Daddy found me. He's good at hide-and-seek."

She didn't turn around to look; she must have trusted his son. "How did you find me?" she asked.

"You didn't turn off your cell phone."

"It brought you right to this house?"

"This block," Milek admitted. "The property records confirmed you still own this house. Actually, Gregory owns it still."

"He bought it when he asked me to marry him," she said. "Probably to convince me that he wasn't marrying me for my money." She snorted at that—as if embarrassed she hadn't known better. "He said it had a great yard for kids to play in."

Michael had moved to the slide of the old swing set. Milek wanted to reach for the boy, but the woman sat between them, the barrel of the gun she held pointed toward the boy.

"It is a great yard," he said but hoped that agreeing with Gregory didn't upset her. While she once must have loved the man, in the end she'd hated him enough to have him killed.

"But we could never have kids," she continued.

"Is that why you took my son?" he asked.

She sighed. "He is yours, isn't he?"

Milek nodded. "Yes. You heard Schievink tell me that he was the father of Amber's baby?"

Schievink had called him to that mansion he'd bought with his wife's money. Milek had wondered if she'd been home then or if it had been a member of the staff he'd heard moving around in the hall outside Schievink's home office. But she hadn't come to her husband's aid when Milek had struck the smug son of a bitch.

"Yes…"

"He lied," Milek said. She couldn't see, but he pointed at his son. "It's obvious the boy is mine." And Milek never should have believed the man—not even for a moment. He never should have doubted Amber. She loved him.

Did she still? Would she be able to love him if he failed to save their son?

"Why did you stay with him?" he asked. "Why didn't you divorce him then?" Or kill him?

She shrugged. "I still loved him. And he didn't leave me then."

"He was going to leave you last year?"

She nodded. "I found his plane ticket. One way to an island near Bermuda. I figured she was going with him. He was leaving me."

So she had hired Frank Campanelli to kill her husband.

"He was fleeing," Milek said, "the country, not you. He must have known it was only a matter of time before Agent Rus discovered he was corrupt."

"Corrupt?" she repeated. And she laughed now. "That's ridiculous. I gave Gregory everything he wanted—all the money he needed."

"Maybe it wasn't for money that he bent the law," Milek said. "Maybe it was for power—influence. Or just because he was a liar and a cheat."

She released another shaky sigh. "He was a son of a bitch, wasn't he?"

"Yes," Milek heartily agreed. He'd let the man affect his life—affect his relationship with Amber and with his son. "He sure was…"

"He deserved to die," she said, as if rationalizing what she'd done. What she'd had Frank Campanelli do for her. "Even if he wasn't leaving me for her, he was leaving me."

"He wasn't leaving you for her," Milek insisted. "Amber was never involved with him."

"You believe her?"

"Yes."

Patricia's slender shoulders slumped with defeat. But she didn't let go of the gun. She didn't move the gun barrel away from where the boy played.

"Frank Campanelli lied," she said. "He claimed he caused that accident. But he'd known all along she and the little boy were alive. He waited until he needed money to let me know he hadn't completed that job."

"Maybe he couldn't bring himself to hurt an innocent woman and an innocent child." He hoped she couldn't, either.

"He was lazy," she said. "And greedy. He was a horrible man who killed so many people."

"I know. We found a book he kept of all the names of his victims."

She shuddered. "He deserved to die, too."

"Yes," he agreed. He moved closer to her then. And as he feared, she tightened her grasp on the gun. He could kill her; he had his gun out.

But her safety was off. She might fire the gun when he hit her. And her bullet could hit his son. He couldn't risk it. And maybe he didn't need to...

"My son doesn't deserve to die," he told her. As he knelt beside her chair, he holstered his gun.

He should have wanted to kill her—for the terror she had put Amber and Michael through. And because she held a gun, it would have been self-defense. Instead he took that gun from her shaking hand and closed his arms around her as she fell apart.

She clung to him, weeping. "I'm sorry," she said. "I'm sorry. I just couldn't lose him to her. I couldn't lose him. I loved him too much. I loved him too much…"

Milek doubted she had loved her husband at all. Because if you loved someone, you did what was best for them—even if it was letting them go.

He'd done it once. He'd done what was best for Amber. Now he had to do it again. He had to put aside his wants and his needs and let her go.

He couldn't be as selfish as Patricia Schievink had been. He had to do the right thing.

For Amber…

Nick had been behind the glass of that interrogation room with Milek Kozminski. He'd heard the same nonsense Milek had—about his reputation ruining Amber Talsma's chances of ever becoming River City's next district attorney. He couldn't deny the Kozminskis were notorious.

But maybe it was time they were notorious for the right reasons. Maybe it was time they were known as the men they really were. Not the criminals.

But the heroes.

"What the hell is this?" Milek asked as he read the commendation Nick had written up for him and on which the mayor had signed off—thanks to some pressure from Chief Special Agent Woodrow Lynch.

Nick shrugged. "I got sick of everyone giving me the accolades for bringing down Chekov. You did more work than I did on that case. And you solved this latest case completely on your own."

Milek dropped the paper on his kitchen counter and snorted. "If Amber hadn't called Patricia Schievink to meet her at the park, we might never have solved it."

"That crazy bitch would have tried again," Nick said. "It wasn't Amber's fault."

"Tell her that," Milek said.

"Haven't you?"

Milek shrugged. "She moved out of the condo. I haven't talked to her since I brought Michael back to her."

Fool.

Sure, Nick knew Milek thought he was doing the right thing. But for the wrong damn reasons...

The guy was nearly as miserable as he'd been when he'd thought Amber and their son were dead. Nick had interfered then, too.

"You haven't seen your son?"

"I've seen him," Milek said. "I've had Stacy pick him up for me, so we could hang out." His lips curved into a slight smile.

At least he hadn't cut himself off from his son—just from the woman he loved.

Milek glanced down at the commendation again and his smile faded. "You need to retract this press release," he said.

"It's too late."

"It's a lie."

"It's the one thing about you that's actually the truth," Nick said.

Milek shook his head. "No, it's not. I'm nobody's hero."

"You saved Amber and your son," Nick said. "You even saved the woman who tried to kill them."

"She didn't try to kill herself like Brad Jipping," Milek said. "I didn't save him."

"He was already gone," Nick said. That was why he'd grabbed Amber and pulled her from the motel room. He'd known Jipping hadn't intended to leave that room alive. "I was there when you found Mrs. Schievink holding a weapon on your son." He'd entered the house right behind Milek. And he'd seen and heard everything through the sliding door Milek had left open. "You could have pulled the trigger and nobody would have questioned you doing it."

Nick would have backed him up. He'd nearly taken the shot himself when he'd seen that barrel pointing toward the little boy. He couldn't imagine how Milek had managed such control.

"She wasn't going to shoot him," Milek said.

"She'd terrorized him and his mother," Nick said. "Another kind of man might have killed her and considered it justice."

Milek sighed. "I'm not that kind of man."

Finally he'd said what Nick wanted to hear. "No, you're not."

Milek glanced up from the commendation and met Nick's gaze. His voice full of realization and wonder, he murmured, "I'm not…"

"No, you're a hero," Nick said. "Just like that commendation says." It wouldn't have mattered if the press release convinced the rest of River City Milek Kozminski was a hero if the man didn't believe it himself.

If he wasn't able to believe in himself…

"Not everybody will believe what that says," Milek said. He was still worried about Amber's career.

"Your record speaks for itself," Nick said.

"I killed a man."

"You saved your sister's and brother's lives," Nick reminded him. "You're a hero. Your stepfather was twice your size. It was a miracle he hadn't killed you."

"I lost it," Milek said. And all the guilt he'd been carrying for all those years was laid bare in his silver-gray gaze.

"You were scared," Nick said. He had been there himself—as a marine and on the job. But he had never been as scared for his life as he'd been for his heart.

He suspected that was what was really holding Milek back. He was scared Amber was going to hurt him. "Don't let fear rule your life," he advised his friend.

Those words echoed in Nick's head as he drove to his place. So he was distracted when he unlocked his door—so distracted he hadn't noticed someone else had already unlocked it.

And that person waited inside for him—in the dark. He snapped on the light and cursed. Frank Campanelli was dead. But there was a ghost in his apartment.

"I thought I'd never see you again," he admitted. "You've been missing for months…"

So many months that nobody had thought it possible the man had survived his last mission with the marines.

Gage Huxton leaned back in Nick's recliner and groaned. "The rumors of my demise were greatly exaggerated."

"Son of a bitch…"

"I didn't come here for you to call me names."

No. He'd probably come here to call Nick names—if he knew what Nick had done with Annalise, how he'd crossed the line that never should have been crossed. Gage had been like his brother, so Annalise should have been like his little sister.

But she wasn't his sister.

"Why are you here?" Nick asked. "Shouldn't you be with Annalise?" She'd been so worried about Gage—so distraught.

Gage shook his head and flinched.

Whatever hell he'd been through had come back home with him; the man wasn't healed yet. Physically or emotionally. "I can't see her like this."

"You can't let her think you're dead."

"I told her I'm alive. She just doesn't know I'm here." Which was probably good—for Nick.

"You can stay as long as you like," he said, figuring that was what his friend wanted.

Gage lifted his chin. No matter what he had been through—it hadn't hurt his pride any. "I don't want a handout, man. I want a job."

"With the FBI? You need to talk to Lynch—not me."

Gage snorted. "Not talking to Lynch. I don't want to be an agent anymore. I want to be a bodyguard."

Maybe Nick was just getting disillusioned with the politics of cleaning up River City, but the job sounded good to him, too. "I'll talk to Payne Protection."

Chapter 25

Fury gripped Amber as she reread the article about Milek Kozminski. He'd been awarded a commendation from the mayor and hailed a hero.

"Bullshit!" she said as she pushed her way through the door to his studio in the back of the warehouse.

He glanced up from the canvas he was painting. But he didn't look at her; he looked past her.

"I'm alone," she said.

Obviously he'd wanted to see their son—not her. He'd been seeing Michael, while he kept avoiding her. Stacy apologized every time she picked up her nephew for a playdate with his father.

He hadn't tried to see her since the day she'd let a crazy woman kidnap their son. Knowing he probably blamed her, she'd moved out of his condo immediately. She was staying in an apartment now—until she could find a house for her and her son.

She hadn't really been looking, though. Maybe because she'd been hoping Milek would come for them again—that he would bring them home with him as he had the day he'd rescued them from that overturned van. From the hotel...

He had saved her life and Michael's so many times. Just as the article claimed. But it hadn't told the entire truth.

He returned his attention to the canvas. She could see only the back of it leaning against a giant easel. She couldn't see what he was painting as he moved the brush. More spatters dotted the concrete floor like brightly colored raindrops.

She slapped the newspaper against the back of the easel. "This is a lie," she said.

"I agree." His voice calm, he didn't even glance up again.

"You're not a hero at all." Now she was the one lying—not the paper. But she was so mad. So hurt he'd let her leave...

"I told Nick that," he said. "But he insisted on the commendation and the press release."

She knew Milek had had nothing to do with it. He wouldn't have sought out accolades. Because if that was what he wanted, he never would have stopped painting.

But he was painting again.

Or maybe he'd never stopped.

She didn't know. He'd shared so little of himself with her. And she'd come to a conclusion about why he hadn't. "You're a coward!"

He chuckled. "I've never been called that."

"You are," she said. But he wasn't the only one. She had been a coward, too, or she would have asked her next question five years ago. "Why else did you break our engagement?"

"It wasn't because I'm a coward," he said.

"Is it because you don't love me?" She braced herself for his reply. Because if that was the reason, she had no argument. She had nothing.

"It's because I love you too much."

Her breath caught in her lungs, as hope burgeoned in her heart. He loved her?

Was it possible?

She shook her head, refusing to believe him. "You don't love me," she insisted. "Or you wouldn't have hurt me like you did."

Losing him had nearly destroyed her. It might have if she hadn't had Michael—who was a little piece of his father. The best piece.

"If you loved me," she said, "you wouldn't have broken our engagement."

"It would have hurt you more if I'd married you," Milek said. "It would have ruined your chance of ever furthering your career. You'd never be elected district attorney."

"What are you talking about? Five years ago I was lucky to be an assistant district attorney."

"You had higher goals than that, and the brains and talent to take you wherever you wanted to go," Milek said.

She should have been flattered. But she was confused. "What makes you think I wouldn't have achieved those goals as your wife?"

He pointed toward the paper she still held. "That's the first good press I, or anyone in my family, have ever had. My reputation would have brought you down. Evelyn Reynolds just told you that."

She waited, knowing there was more.

And he continued, "Gregory Schievink told me the same thing five years ago."

"When he claimed to be Michael's father?" How had she never realized her boss had been obsessed with her? Because he'd been careful to never cross the line far enough that she would have been able to press charges for harassment. Just as he'd been careful to never get caught for corruption.

"He told me before I found out you were pregnant," he said. "And I knew he was right."

"He was a creep."

"Just like Evelyn Reynolds, he was right," Milek insisted. "If you'd married me, my reputation would have ruined yours. That's why I broke our engagement. I didn't want to be the reason you never reached those goals of yours. You would have resented me."

He wasn't the man she resented. But she was angry at him for listening to other people—for making the decision for both of them instead of discussing it with her.

She held up the paper and the article she'd called bullshit only moments ago. "This tells the real story. You're a hero."

"Nobody believes what they read."

She remembered what else she'd found in this room—besides the heartbreakingly beautiful portrait of their child. "If that's true, why did you keep the review of your last art show?" she asked.

His broad shoulders rippled as he shrugged. But his body had tensed, his square jaw clenched.

"That was over five years old," she said. Right around the time he'd broken their engagement. "Why would you have kept it if you didn't believe it?"

"A person's art reveals a lot about them…"

The rage. That was what he'd worried about—the rage the reviewer had worried about him unleashing someday.

"It wasn't just my *reputation* you were worried about hurting, was it?" she asked.

"Counselor, you're badgering the witness," he said with a faint smile, as if he was only joking. But the seriousness was in his voice and the darkening of his silver eyes.

"You believe that garbage one reviewer wrote?" she asked. "Some bullshit about you having all this rage? Everyone says you're the easiest going of the Kozminskis."

A muscle twitched in his cheek. "Ever since that day I killed a man, I've had to work hard," he said. "So I would never lose control like that again."

"You had every reason to lose control that day," she said. Her friend had had nightmares for years over what her stepfather had nearly done to her—what he would have done had Milek not stopped him. "You were protecting your sister—your brother. If you hadn't done what you had, he would have hurt you all more than he did. He might have killed you."

He shuddered as if he was remembering the awful day. That was why she'd never really asked him about it. She'd known how traumatic it had been for Stacy; she hadn't wanted to bring up the nightmare for the man she loved. And she'd thought he'd made peace with it. He had seemed at peace. But maybe it had just been that control for which he'd fought so hard.

"Is that why you broke our engagement?" she asked. "Why you refused to acknowledge your son until now? You're afraid you're going to hurt us?"

The answer flashed in his eyes—the fear.

"Oh, Milek…"

Something in her voice must have affected him, because he finally moved around the easel that had separated them. He finally stepped close to her—close enough that she could touch him.

She stroked her fingers along his tightly clenched jaw. "You are the sweetest, gentlest man I know. You would never hurt us."

He caught her hand in his and held her fingers tightly. "I force myself to be gentle with you," he said. "I fight to stay in control…"

She shuddered now—imagining how hard that must have been for him. And suddenly she understood his artwork. "It wasn't rage that reviewer saw," she said. "It was passion—passion you've been holding back from me."

"I don't want to hurt you."

"You won't…" Not now that she knew it all. And she believed he hadn't broken their engagement because he didn't love her but because he did.

He shook his head. "I wish I knew…"

She knew.

"Find out," she said.

He stared at her intently, his gaze questioning. "How?"

"Lose control," she said. And she reached for him. She skimmed her hands down his chest to his belt and lower. She rubbed her palm over the erection already straining against his fly. And she dared him, "Lose control!"

"Amber…" The hesitation was in his voice and in the tension in his body. He didn't trust himself.

But she trusted him. She stepped back.

And disappointment flickered in his gaze. He thought she was changing her mind. But she had no doubts about him. She lifted her sweater and pulled it over her head.

She dropped it onto the paint-spattered floor. Then she undid her jeans and kicked them down her legs, pushing her panties down with them. She unclasped her bra next and let it fall, too.

Milek's breath hissed out between his teeth. "Amber…" His voice had gone gruff with desire.

"Milek…" She stood before him totally naked, totally vulnerable. But then she made herself more vulnerable. She touched herself—with him watching. She touched her breasts.

He groaned. "You're killing me…"

Then she moved her hand lower.

Instead of reaching for her, he reached for his shirt. He tore the T-shirt from the hem to the collar so it fell off. His chest heaved with his deep pants for breath.

His jeans went next, shucked down his legs along with his boxers. And he stood before her as naked as she was. When she touched herself—where he had touched her so many times—his control snapped.

He dragged her up against him. And he lowered his head. He didn't just kiss her. His mouth marauded hers, his tongue driving deep.

She gasped.

And he tensed.

But she wrapped her arms around his neck, holding his head down—holding him against her. "Don't stop," she implored him. "Please don't stop."

He kissed her again—passionately. Then he touched her where she'd touched herself. His hands moved over her breasts, his fingertips teasing the already taut nipples.

And Amber felt her own control snap. She dug her nails into his shoulders as she arched against him, rubbing her belly against his erection. She wanted more. She skimmed her nails down his chest, making his muscles ripple. Then she closed her hand around him.

As her fingers wrapped around his erection, his fingers slid inside her—as his thumb teased the most sensitive part of her. She came apart at his touch, screaming his name.

Then he lifted her. But he didn't carry her far—just until her back came up against a wall—up against a canvas. Before she could protest that he might ruin his art, he was inside her.

And she forgot everything. She forgot her own damn name until he called it. He thrust inside her—in and out, his hands holding her hips—driving her up and down.

Pressure built inside her—winding tightly from the tips of her nipples to the core of her—the core he stroked with his erection. She arched, taking him deeper. She met each of his thrusts.

His fingers dug into her hips and then her ass cheeks. He lowered his head and kissed her again. Her mouth. Her shoulder. Then he bent lower and pulled a nipple into his mouth. He nipped it lightly with his teeth.

And she screamed.

He tensed, as if worried he'd hurt her. But she was coming—her body shuddering with the powerful orgasm he'd given her.

"Milek!"

His grip on her butt tightened. He drove deeper and deeper. Chords stood out in his neck and his arms. His body tensed—then pulsed—as he came, filling her. He shouted her name, his voice cracking with emotion.

He'd lost control. And it had never felt so wonderful. Not just that first time they'd stood up and made love, but again, rolling around on drop cloths he always forgot to lay on the floor when he painted.

The cloths had wrinkled and curled beneath them. He had a bruise from the concrete. And they were both spattered with the paint he'd been using.

"Did I hurt you?" he asked—concern filling him as she lay limply on top of him, her back slick with sweat and paint. "Are you okay?"

"I think I passed out for a moment," she murmured.

He wound his fingers through her tangled hair, gently feeling for lumps on her skull. His guts tightened with dread over the thought that he had hurt her. "Did you hit your head?"

She giggled. "No. I blacked out from pleasure overload." Then her hand slapped his shoulder. "You've been holding back on me."

"Not anymore," he promised. He'd been such a fool. "I'm sorry…"

She lifted her head from where she'd burrowed into his neck. "You didn't hurt me," she assured him. "You made me feel incredible. Loved…"

And she hadn't felt as though he'd loved her before— because he'd broken her heart.

"I didn't hurt you now," he said. "But I hurt you five years ago."

And he would never forgive himself for the pain he'd caused her. Needlessly. He'd let the opinion of others affect his judgment. He'd let them judge him as harshly as he'd judged himself.

Too harshly.

"I understand," she said. "And I'm sorry…"

His arms tightened around her. "Why? You did nothing wrong."

"I should have figured out what was wrong," she said. "I shouldn't have doubted your love or your feelings for me. I should have known something else was going on."

"Amber…" He hated that she was blaming herself now. "I should have told you what was going on. But I was worried you'd talk me out of breaking up. And I didn't want to ruin your life."

Her breasts pushed against his chest as she uttered a heavy sigh. "For a while I thought you had… It hurt so much…"

Guilt twisted his stomach into knots. "I'm sorry. I really thought I was doing the right thing for you. That I was protecting you."

"You would have never physically hurt me or our son," she said.

"But I hurt you emotionally."

Tears glistened in her green eyes. "I loved you so much."

"Loved?" he asked. "Are you over me?"

She shifted against him, rubbing her naked body against his. "Technically I'm on top of you," she teased. "But I've never been over you."

If she still loved him, maybe she would be able to forgive him. He stroked his hand down her back and asked, "Do you want to see what I was painting?"

She smiled brightly. "I'd love to. I'm so glad you're still painting."

"I stopped showing and selling my art," he said.

"Because of that stupid review," she surmised.

Correct.

"But I never stopped painting," he said. "It started as therapy—when I was in juvie." And he'd needed therapy even more after he'd broken their engagement.

"You're so good," she said. "I can't believe you've never had lessons." She wriggled out of his arms and jumped up. Wrapping one of the drop cloths around herself, she headed toward the canvas he'd been working on.

He knew what it looked like, so he focused on her face—her beautiful face as she stared in awe at the canvas. Tears glistened in her eyes again before brimming over to trail down her cheeks.

He read what he'd painted for her. *Will you marry me?*

Despite her tears of emotion, she laughed. "I came tearing in here with that newspaper as my first exhibit. And you'd already changed your mind before you ever heard my argument."

He wasn't certain whether she was happy or disappointed. But she laughed again—at herself—and his breath caught at the beauty of her happiness.

She was relieved. If she hadn't seen the painting, she might have always worried he wouldn't have changed his mind on his own—that he wouldn't have trusted their love more than his fears.

"You won your case before your opening remarks, counselor," he told her. "But I wasn't sure you would say yes." He'd worried she would laugh at the painting—but with derision, not happiness.

"What makes you think that I will now?" she asked.

He wouldn't blame her if she said no. He'd hurt her—even more than he'd realized.

"I'm sorry," he said. He stepped behind her and wrapped his arms around her curvy body. Instead of stiffening in his embrace, she leaned back against him.

"I can't make up these past five years to you." But he wished like hell that he could—that he could take back every minute they'd spent apart. He'd wasted so much time. If she had really died...

He shuddered to think of what he would have lost—of how he would never have had the chance to plead his case for her to trust him again.

"I will spend the rest of my life trying to make it up to you," he promised. "If you'll let me..."

"Oh, I'll let you," she said. And she turned in his arms so she could loop hers around his neck. She pulled his head down for her kiss. Her lips moved over his, pushing his apart so her tongue could slip inside—over his. Panting for breath she pulled back and said, "Especially if you keep making up for it like you just did."

"I'll make it up whichever way you'd like," he said, "as long as you give me the chance, as long as you'll become my wife."

"I still have my ring," she said.

He was surprised. She'd tried to give it back to him. But he had refused. Since she hadn't broken the engagement, she'd been entitled to keep the ring. But he hadn't actually thought she would. He figured she would have tossed it out years ago.

"I will have Stacy make you a new one," he said. He didn't want the ring she wore to be tainted by what he'd done—by how stupid he'd been.

"Stacy made that ring," she said. "And I love it."

"But..."

She pressed her finger over his lips. "It's perfect. And from now on our lives will be perfect, too. And we'll appreciate more how wonderful it is because of the years we spent apart."

He kissed her finger and closed his hand around hers.

"I hope you're really not planning on perfection," he said. "I am still a Kozminski."

"Milek—"

"I think Nick gave me that commendation and issued that press release to try to repair my reputation," he said, "because he heard what Evelyn Reynolds told you, too." The FBI agent's last name wasn't Payne, so he wasn't related by marriage or blood to Milek. But he was family now.

Amber sighed. "I feel bad for ever doubting him. I was right to trust him."

"You were," Milek agreed. She might not have survived the past year if she hadn't trusted someone. He tightened his arms around her, holding her closely. He couldn't let her go again. But he was still worried.

"There's no guarantee it'll work," he warned her. "There's no guarantee my reputation can ever be repaired. Marrying me could hurt your chances of becoming district attorney."

She shrugged as if she didn't care.

He hooked his finger under her chin and tipped up her face to his. "I know you want that job."

She nodded. "I do. And I'll get it," she assured him. "And your love and support will help me accomplish more than I ever could have on my own."

"Amber…" He loved her more every moment he spent with her. "I don't want to wait to get married."

She shook her head. "Me, either. We already waited five years."

"Let's start our life together as soon as we can."

Penny Payne hung up the telephone and clapped her hands together in triumph. The little boy playing on the floor near her desk looked up at her, his silver gaze inquisitive.

She couldn't tell him why she was so happy and ruin his parents' surprise for him. She was finally able to plan their long-overdue wedding.

She clapped again and praised the little boy's artwork. "That's a wonderful picture!"

He picked it up from the floor and brought it to her desk. Then he wriggled onto her lap. "That's me and Mommy and Daddy," he said.

They weren't the crude stick figures most children—heck, Penny herself—were capable of drawing. These images were fully fleshed out.

Penny glanced up at the canvas on the wall of her office. Milek had painted the portrait years ago. His son had obviously inherited his artistic talent.

Milek's portrait was of family, too. Penny's family. He'd painted her three sons and her daughter for her. And there was such longing in every brushstroke. He'd wanted to be part of a family like hers.

Did he realize he was now?

She would have to have him paint her a new portrait—of the entire family. All her daughters-in-law and all the Kozminskis, Garek and Candace, and Milek and his bride and their son.

Nick had to be in the portrait, too. He would protest. So would Nikki. But she wanted him included. Nick had spent too much of his life on the outside looking in; she wanted him to know he was part of her family.

She smiled down at her new grandson. Little Michael would be so happy to have his parents together. She suspected Nick had had quite a bit to do with their reunion.

He was not related to her by blood but somehow he took after her more than her own children did.

He knew how others felt—what they wanted and needed. But she suspected he was like her in another way. She suspected Nick didn't really know what he needed. Or maybe he was so worried about everyone else that he didn't acknowledge he had needs, too.

Wants…

What, or whom, did Nicholas Rus want?

* * * * *

Look for the next thrilling installment in the
BACHELOR BODYGUARDS *series, coming soon!*

And if you love Lisa Childs, be sure to pick up her other stories:

THE AGENT'S REDEMPTION
AGENT TO THE RESCUE
AGENT UNDERCOVER
THE PREGNANT WITNESS

Available now from Harlequin!

REQUEST YOUR FREE BOOKS!
2 FREE NOVELS PLUS 2 FREE GIFTS!

ROMANTIC suspense

Sparked by danger, fueled by passion

YES! Please send me 2 FREE Harlequin® Romantic Suspense novels and my 2 FREE gifts (gifts are worth about $10). After receiving them, if I don't wish to receive any more books, I can return the shipping statement marked "cancel." If I don't cancel, I will receive 4 brand-new novels every month and be billed just $4.74 per book in the U.S. or $5.49 per book in Canada. That's a savings of at least 12% off the cover price! It's quite a bargain! Shipping and handling is just 50¢ per book in the U.S. and 75¢ per book in Canada.* I understand that accepting the 2 free books and gifts places me under no obligation to buy anything. I can always return a shipment and cancel at any time. Even if I never buy another book, the two free books and gifts are mine to keep forever.

240/340 HDN GH3P

Name	(PLEASE PRINT)	
Address		Apt. #
City	State/Prov.	Zip/Postal Code

Signature (if under 18, a parent or guardian must sign)

Mail to the **Reader Service:**
IN U.S.A.: P.O. Box 1867, Buffalo, NY 14240-1867
IN CANADA: P.O. Box 609, Fort Erie, Ontario L2A 5X3

Want to try two free books from another line?
Call 1-800-873-8635 or visit www.ReaderService.com.

* Terms and prices subject to change without notice. Prices do not include applicable taxes. Sales tax applicable in N.Y. Canadian residents will be charged applicable taxes. Offer not valid in Quebec. This offer is limited to one order per household. Not valid for current subscribers to Harlequin Romantic Suspense books. All orders subject to credit approval. Credit or debit balances in a customer's account(s) may be offset by any other outstanding balance owed by or to the customer. Please allow 4 to 6 weeks for delivery. Offer available while quantities last.

Your Privacy—The Reader Service is committed to protecting your privacy. Our Privacy Policy is available online at www.ReaderService.com or upon request from the Reader Service.

We make a portion of our mailing list available to reputable third parties that offer products we believe may interest you. If you prefer that we not exchange your name with third parties, or if you wish to clarify or modify your communication preferences, please visit us at www.ReaderService.com/consumerschoice or write to us at Reader Service Preference Service, P.O. Box 9062, Buffalo, NY 14240-9062. Include your complete name and address.

SPECIAL EXCERPT FROM

 **HARLEQUIN**

ROMANTIC suspense

*When search-and-rescue worker Ridge Colton comes
across his most unexpected find yet—an abandoned
baby—he's surprised by his sudden paternal feelings!
With a serial killer plaguing their Texas town,
can Ridge and his ex, Dr. Darcy Marrow,
guard themselves, their charge...and their hearts?*

Read on for a sneak preview of
COLTON BABY HOMECOMING
by ***Lara Lacombe***,
the third volume of the 2016
COLTONS OF TEXAS *series.*

Her breath ghosted across his lips as she moved up onto
her toes to get closer. His body tightened in anticipation
of her touch, all too eager to resume where they'd left
off last night. She placed her palm against his chest, the
contact arcing through him like lightning. Did she feel
the sparks, too, or was it all in his head?

He lifted his hand to trace the angle of her jaw with
his fingertip and was rewarded with a small shudder. He
smiled at her reaction. So she wasn't immune to him.
That was good to know.

"Ridge," she murmured, her eyelids drifting down in
preparation for his kiss.

I should stop this, he thought. *It's a mistake*. But
no matter how many times he thought it, he still found
himself leaning down, getting ever closer to Darcy's
waiting mouth.

HRSEXP0216

He had just brushed his lips across hers when Penny started to bark, a deep, frantic sound that made his blood run cold.

Darcy drew back, frowning. "What—?" she started, but Ridge took off for the house before she could get the rest of the question out.

Penny only made that sound when something was terribly wrong, which meant either she or the baby was in danger. He snagged a branch to use as a club, then ran as fast as he could in the mud, slipping and sliding as he moved. The dog kept barking, but now there was a new note in her voice: fear.

Oh God, he's back. The realization slammed into him, and Ridge kicked himself for having left the baby in the house. He'd never forgive himself if something happened to her. He took the porch steps two at a time and lunged for the back door, his heart in his throat.

Please, don't let me be too late.

Don't miss
COLTON BABY HOMECOMING by Lara Lacombe,
available March 2016 wherever
Harlequin® Romantic Suspense
books and ebooks are sold.

www.Harlequin.com